# THE RIVER MURDERS

## THRILLERS

# JAMES PATTERSON
## & JAMES O. BORN

**GRAND CENTRAL**
PUBLISHING

NEW YORK    BOSTON

Grand Central Publishing
Hachette Book Group
1290 Avenue of the Americas, New York, NY 10104
grandcentralpublishing.com
twitter.com/grandcentralpub

First Edition: January 2020

*Hidden* was first published by Little, Brown in January 2017.
*Malicious* was first published by Little, Brown in February 2017.

Grand Central Publishing is a division of Hachette Book Group, Inc. The Grand Central Publishing name and logo are trademarks of Hachette Book Group, Inc.

The publisher is not responsible for websites (or their content) that are not owned by the publisher.

The Hachette Speakers Bureau provides a wide range of authors for speaking events. To find out more, go to hachettespeakersbureau.com or call (866) 376-6591.

ISBN 978-1-5387-4997-5 (trade paperback) / 978-1-5387-3404-9 (large-print paperback) / 978-1-5387-5001-8 (ebook)

Library of Congress Control Number 2019953290

Printed in the United States of America

LSC-H

10 9 8 7 6 5 4 3 2 1

# CONTENTS

# HIDDEN

**JAMES PATTERSON
& JAMES O. BORN**

# CHAPTER 1

**MY MOODY MONGREL,** Bart Simpson, kept watch from the warm backseat. He rarely found my job interesting. At least not this job.

I was next to the loading dock, folding newspapers for delivery. A surly driver named Nick dropped them off for me every morning at 5:50 sharp. What he lacked in personality he made up for in silence. I always said hello and never got an answer. Not even a "Hey, Mitchum." It was a good working relationship.

Even with the wind off the Hudson, I could crack a sweat moving the heavy bundles of papers. I used the knife I had gotten in the Navy to cut the straps holding them. My station wagon sagged under the weight of a full load. My two-day-a-week afternoon gig in Milton didn't strain the shocks nearly as bad. I usually dropped Bart off at my mom's then. My dog was as close to a grandchild as she had, and they could both complain about me.

In the early morning gloom, I caught a movement out of the corner of my eye and reacted quickly, turning with the knife still in my right hand. It was an instinct I couldn't explain. I was raised in upstate New York, not Bosnia. But I relaxed as soon as I saw Albany Al, one of the few homeless people in Marlboro, standing near the loading dock, a dozen feet away.

The older man's whiskers spread as he grinned and rubbed his hand across his white beard. "Hello, Mitchum. They say you can never sneak up on a Navy SEAL. I guess that's true."

I was past the point of explaining to people that I was never an actual SEAL.

When I took a closer look at the old man, I realized he wasn't ready for the burst of arctic air that had descended on us. "Al, grab my extra coat from the car. It's too cold to be wandering around dressed like that."

"I couldn't."

"Go ahead. My cousin usually wears it, but she didn't show today. She's a wuss for avoiding the cold."

"I wondered where Bailey Mae was. I was hoping she had some of her coffee cake."

Then I realized the older man hadn't come to keep me company. He'd wandered over to snag some of Bailey Mae's famous coffee cake, which she handed out like business cards.

I said, "I miss her cake, too."

The old man said, "I can tell." He cackled as he rubbed his belly, but he was looking at me.

I patted my own belly and said, "It's my portable insulation." Maybe I hadn't been working out as hard as usual. A few warm days and some running would solve that.

The old man continued to cackle as he walked away with my coat.

# CHAPTER 2

**WHEN I'D FINISHED** my route, I headed over to my office off Route 9. At least, my unofficial office. I always hit Tina's Plentiful at about 8:15, right between the early breakfast crowd and late risers. The old diner sat in an empty strip mall that hadn't been updated since 1988. A couple of framed posters of the California coast hung on the walls. No one had ever explained their significance, and none of the customers seemed to care. The place had the best Reubens and tuna melts in upstate New York, and they treated me like family. Maybe it was because one of my cousins worked in the kitchen.

The lone waitress, Mabel, named by a mean-spirited mother, lit up when I walked in. Usually I sat in the rear booth to eat and see if I had any pressing business. There was never much pressing in Marlboro. Today I headed toward the counter since there wasn't much going on and it would make it easier on Mabel.

Mabel was a town favorite for her easy smile and the way

she took time to chat with everyone who came into the diner. As soon as I sat down she said, "Finally, a friendly face."

I gave her a wink and said, "Is the world not treating Miss Teenage New York well today?"

"Funny. You should cheer me up by taking me to the movies in Newburgh one night."

"Only if my cousin Bailey Mae comes with us."

"Why?"

"So you understand it's as friends and not a date."

"Am I so terrible? You've had some tough breaks and I'm a lot of fun."

I couldn't help a smile. "Of course you're not so terrible. You're also so *young*. And I'm not going to be the guy who holds you back from all the suitable young men in the area." That was as much as I wanted to say today.

Before she could answer, I glanced out the wide front window and saw my cousin Alice, Bailey Mae's mom, hustling across the street toward the diner. She is a year older than me and was only twenty when Bailey Mae was born. She is a good mom, and the rest of us help. Her usual smile was nowhere to be seen as her long brown hair flapped in the wind behind her. She yanked open the door and rushed right to me.

"Mitchum, Bailey Mae is missing."

Suddenly, the day got colder.

# CHAPTER 3

**I SPENT A** few minutes trying to calm Alice down as we started to check some of the places Bailey Mae liked to hang out. Bailey Mae hadn't been to school that day or to the library or to the sad little arcade where she sometimes played out-of-date games. Alice had gone to sleep early the night before, after her shift at the bottling factory in Gardnertown. Bailey Mae usually came home about eight o'clock. She's a smart fourteen-year-old, and a quarter of the town is related to her.

We wandered around town, asking a few questions. No one thought it was unusual, because I am the unofficial private investigator for the whole area.

Mrs. Hoffman on Dubois Street hadn't seen Bailey Mae but took the time to thank me for finding her son, who had been on a bender in Albany and didn't have the cash to get home.

After nearly an hour, I tracked down Timmy Jones, a

buddy of mine from high school who now worked for the Ulster sheriff's office.

Timmy raised his hands, showing his thick fingers, and said, "I spoke with your cousin Alice already. We're making a few checks, but Bailey Mae has wandered off before."

I knew she sometimes got frustrated and left the house, but she usually ended up at my house or my mom's house. I said, "She's a good girl."

"No one's saying she's not. But we can't just call out the troops every time a teenager is out past curfew or mad at their parents."

"Bailey Mae is more responsible. She wouldn't do something like that."

Finally Timmy said, "Okay, we'll get everyone out looking for her. But get your family involved, too. There's more of them than there are cops in the area."

# CHAPTER 4

**BAILEY MAE HAS** always been my favorite relative, and I have plenty to choose from in Marlboro. After I rounded a few up and explained the situation, the look on my cousin Todd's face said it all: they were worried. Bailey Mae is the family's shining light. Todd is a self-centered dick, and even he was concerned enough for our little cousin that he closed his precious auto repair shop to help search.

I pulled Alice aside and hit her with some simple questions about what was going on around the house, what the last thing she said to Bailey Mae was, and whether they'd been fighting. The usual.

She said, "I told you everything. There were no problems. I haven't been drinking and she hasn't been angry. The only thing that's new is that she's been hanging out with Natty a little bit."

That caught me by surprise. I blurted out, "Natty, as in my brother, Nathaniel?"

Alice nodded. "No real reason for it. He's nice to her and she likes his car. That's all I ever hear about. You know teenagers and cars. Just another crazy dream of hers."

"Natty shouldn't be anywhere near Bailey Mae."

Alice said, "He did his time."

"He always does. But he's still a drug dealer."

"He's family."

"Maybe by New York State law, but not the way I see it."

# CHAPTER 5

**I PURPOSELY LEFT** Alice in Marlboro when I made my way down to Newburgh. My old station wagon sputtered a couple of times but got me there in about twenty minutes. Route 9 was open this time of day and I parked directly in front of the State of Mind Tavern, just past the I-84 underpass, the dive bar where Natty, my older brother, does business. I immediately spotted his leased sports car on the side of the dingy building. Natty had gotten tired of having cars seized every time some industrious cop stopped him and found dope inside. All it took was enough weight to be charged for trafficking and the car became part of the crime—and also part of police inventory up for auction. So now he switched out cars every year. The hot little convertible was near the end of its term.

As I opened the door, the bartender looked up through the haze. They aren't as strict in upstate as they are in the city, so cigarette smoke hung in the air. The smell of toaster pizza was permanently stuck in the discolored wallpaper. The bartender, who looked like he dined on steroids every day, gave me a cursory look and deemed me unworthy of an acknowledgment.

My brother, Nathaniel, or "Natty" as he's been called his whole life, is two inches shorter than me, at six feet even, and thin as a rail from a life of drugs, coffee, and cigarettes. I had no clue why he got called Natty while I've been called by my last name, Mitchum, since childhood. Only our mom calls me by my first name.

His head jerked up instantly. Instinct from his line of work. We have the same blue eyes and prominent jawline, but not much else in common.

I headed directly toward him when the bartender, who doubled as Natty's bodyguard, stepped from behind the bar to grab my left arm. Now he wanted to dance; a second ago he was too good to speak to me. A quick twist and thumb lock with my right hand dropped the ox to one knee in pain until the man understood how stupid his idea had been. Thank you, SEAL basic training class 406.

Natty stood up quickly and said, "Tony, no need for that. This is my little brother." He moved around the table to greet me, rushing past Angel, his semi-regular girlfriend, who once posed for *Penthouse* or one of those magazines.

I held up my hand and said, "Save it."

That brought Natty up short. "Why? What's wrong? Is it Mom?"

"Where's Bailey Mae?"

"Bailey Mae? I haven't seen her in a couple of days. Why?"

"She's missing and I heard she's been hanging out around you. You're a shithead so I came here first."

"How could you suspect me of doing anything to our own cousin? I love that girl. She's got dreams."

"We all do."

Natty stepped closer and said, "Look, Mitchum, I know you don't like what I do, but it's only a little pot and I don't force anyone into anything." He put his arm around my shoulder and started to lead me back toward the front door.

I stopped short and grabbed his arm. The bartender saw his chance at some payback, stepped forward, and took a swing at my head with his ham fist. It might as well have happened in slow motion, given all my years of preparation and the months of Navy training. It was almost an insult. I bobbed back a few inches and the big man's fist passed me. Then I swung Natty into him like a bag of potatoes, and they fell back into the barstools and got hopelessly tangled together on the grimy floor.

Another guy who'd been sitting at Natty's table grabbed a pool cue and stepped forward. In an instant I had my Navy knife out of my pocket and flipped open. I needed to blow off some steam and had just now realized it. As I'd expected, the jerk focused all of his attention on the knife, so I landed a perfect front kick in his gut, knocking him off his feet. To give the guy credit, he was upright and holding the pool cue again in a flash, his face beet red from the shock of being kicked and the momentary lack of oxygen.

Natty scrambled off the floor, his hands up, and jumped between me and the guy with the pool cue. Natty yelled, "Wait, wait!" He turned toward the other man and said, "Chuck, chill out!" He changed tone and attitude as he turned toward me. "Mitchum, just calm down and put the knife away. I want to help."

I had never heard my brother say that to anyone. Ever.

# CHAPTER 6

**I HAD TO** fight the lunch crowd at Tina's Plentiful but somehow managed to grab my regular booth in the back. I needed to calm down and get some perspective before I even tried to get Mabel's attention. Contemplating fratricide is exhausting. At least it looked like I had one more relative in on the search. Natty had jumped in his hot convertible with his dullard girlfriend and raced back here to help our cousin Alice look for her daughter.

I needed thirty minutes to get my bearings, and the most efficient way to do it was to eat. I would need calories to help me during what could be a long day, so I gave Mabel my hand signal for one of their famous tuna melts. Her little wink let me know she understood.

The diner was busy and made a kind of relaxing noise. At least it was familiar and natural to me. After a few deep breaths, I looked up and saw an elderly woman from my route marching down the narrow space between the counter and booths, headed right for me. She lives on

Robyn Drive and her name is Lois Moscowitz. I know most people's addresses and whether they get the local paper, the *New York Times,* or the *Wall Street Journal.* This one is the local-only variety. She never broke stride until she plopped down in the booth across from me.

"Hello, Mrs. Moscowitz."

"Mitchum, I need help." She had that cute, friendly local accent that made it clear she had never lived in the city.

I said, "I'm kind of booked up right now."

"But you're the only one who can help me."

"What's wrong?" I looked up at the pass-through to the kitchen and stared lovingly at my tuna melt, which had just landed.

"My husband is missing."

There were a lot of excuses I could make, but once I looked into those lonely brown eyes, all I could say was, "I'll take the case." I had to. I was the town's unofficial PI. It was part of the job description. I knew enough people were looking for Bailey Mae at the moment that I wouldn't make much difference, and this woman needed me right now.

Like a mind reader, Mabel had already wrapped my sandwich to go, tossed it across the counter to me, and blew me a kiss as I followed Mrs. Moscowitz out of the diner.

She sat straight and dignified in the passenger seat of my station wagon as Bart minded his manners and didn't try to force his way to the front. I didn't trust the little bugger enough to leave the sandwich back there, but it was good to know I had my buddy close by.

Mrs. Moscowitz didn't say a word as we drove north on

Route 9 toward Milton. She didn't have to say anything; I knew where we were going.

I turned off the road and back toward a small private drive with a view of the Hudson. She glanced around but still didn't say anything as I brought the station wagon to a stop. I scurried around the front of the car to open her door. The private cemetery covered about two acres and had a lovely picket fence around the border, with a narrow, winding road that cut through the property in a seemingly random route.

The gravestone closest to the asphalt road had a simple inscription: *Herman Moscowitz. Devoted Husband.*

I stood close by in case I needed to grab her, but all Lois Moscowitz did was stare at the inscription. It could've gone either way.

Then Mrs. Moscowitz turned to me and started to laugh. Loudly. She wrapped her arms around my shoulders and gave me a hug, laughing the whole time. I needed the hug as much as she did. She was suddenly a different person. Younger, animated. As I drove her home, she chatted about her hobbies of knitting and skeet shooting and asked about my mom.

When we got to her tidy two-bedroom house, I pulled in the driveway and ran around to open the door for her again. She tried to give me a five-dollar bill and some change from her purse.

I kept refusing until she said, "How's an investigator going to stay in business if he doesn't charge people for his time?"

I finally took the cash, then waited until she was safely inside.

# CHAPTER 7

**I HADN'T EVEN** gotten back into my car when Timmy Jones, my buddy from the sheriff's office, pulled up in his marked unit. The cold wind blew his thinning blond hair in a swirl around his wide head. The look on his face told me he had news. It didn't look like good news.

My mind raced with all the possibilities: Bailey Mae had just been found dead at the foot of a cliff, or her body had washed up on the shores of the Hudson. I'd done a good job of tamping down the darker visions of what might have happened to her. Pretty much the whole day had been spent either looking for her or avoiding thinking about what might have happened to her. That was one of the reasons I'd helped Mrs. Moscowitz. I was good at avoiding tough issues. The private investigation business was my main means of not dealing with my own emotions. If I was distracted by something else, I couldn't dwell on the past. On dead fiancées. On missed opportunities. On my screwed-up family.

My stomach did a flip-flop as Timmy slowly walked around the front of his patrol car and then up the short driveway to face me. The frustration of his silence made me bark out, "What is it?" My voice couldn't hide the dread I felt.

Timmy started slowly, looking for the words. "My partner and I were knocking on doors, asking about Bailey Mae near her house." He paused and ran his hand through his hair.

"Timmy, get to the point," I almost snapped.

"Sorry. The old couple down the street from your cousin Alice's house, the Wilkses, were found dead inside their own house."

"Dead? From what?"

"They'd been shot."

This made my head spin. I even had to put my hand on the hood of my car to steady myself. "Shot? Bob and Francine Wilks have been shot?"

Timmy just nodded and mumbled, "In the head."

This was just too bizarre. I spoke to the elderly couple every day. If I didn't see them while I delivered the paper, I'd run into them at the diner or Luten's grocery store. Something didn't add up. All I could do was look at my friend and say, "Let's go."

# CHAPTER 8

**MY MIND WAS** still racing as I followed Timmy, driving at his normal, conservative pace. Shit like this just doesn't happen in Marlboro. Maybe in Poughkeepsie or even Newburgh. But not here. What the hell was going on?

I was anxious to get to the crime scene but realized I needed to be with Timmy to get past any of the other cops, so I chugged along behind him. I figured I might be of some help. I'd been through a number of forensic and crime scene schools in the Navy. Since then I had been through more than a few similar classes at Dutchess Community College. I probably understood these things better than the local cops, who never had to deal with them. At least when I was a master-at-arms in the Navy, I'd seen a few crime scenes on base. And I knew the local cops' weakness: They didn't want to call in the state police unless it was absolutely necessary.

Timmy knew my background and got me past the yellow crime-scene tape and the disturbingly young patrolman who was standing guard. I got a few odd looks from the other cops, and the only detective on the scene completely ignored me as she silently made notes in the corner.

The bodies were still in place as someone from the coroner's office took photographs. They were sitting right next to each other, as if watching TV from the ancient plaid couch they probably bought in the seventies. Single gunshots, probably from a 9mm, had left holes near the center of each of their foreheads and had caused just a trickle of blood to run down each pale face. It was neat and probably quick and professional.

I glanced out the window and saw that the sun was starting to set. Where had the day gone? Then I noticed it. I moved toward the kitchen, careful not to disturb anything, and stared for a moment until Timmy eased up beside me.

He said, "What is it, Mitchum?"

I nodded toward the counter. "That's one of Bailey Mae's coffee cakes." I leaned over and touched it, then broke off a corner and popped it in my mouth. "It's fresh. She was here."

# CHAPTER 9

**IT WAS AFTER** midnight when I finally left the Wilkses' house. The sheriff's office was still there collecting evidence and taking photographs. In fairness, I didn't have to prepare and document a criminal case. All I wanted to find out was who shot the friendly older couple and where Bailey Mae fit into all of it. That was what kept me there so long: I had been looking for other clues that pointed to where Bailey Mae was and what had happened to her.

Who says nothing ever happens in Marlboro? It had been a long, hard day.

After I snatched a few hours' sleep, I was preparing to deliver my papers early again. It gave me some normalcy and allowed me to be out in the town in case I saw something that could help.

Even Nick, the guy who dropped off the bundled papers, was interested in our sleepy little town for a change.

The husky teamster said, "I heard about your cousin. I'll keep an eye out."

I was stunned. I had been starting to think he didn't even speak English.

Then he pointed at the front page of the first paper strapped in the bundle and said, "Shame about the old couple, too. You guys need to get your shit together." Then he was gone.

He was also right. One of the reasons I stayed in Marlboro was because of the atmosphere. It is a nice place to live with nice people around. Even if I am related to a bunch of them.

By the time Bart and I were rolling in the loaded station wagon, a sleet storm had made the roads a crapshoot and visibility shitty. I had never seen the weather turn so cold and ugly this early in the year. It matched my mood about Bailey Mae's disappearance.

No one was out this morning as I cruised the streets slowly, tossing papers to some houses and walking them up to the front door at the homes of really old or infirm people. It hurt to drive past the Wilkses' house and not throw a paper. The yellow tape was still up, but the house was dark and no one was around.

Even the diner was nearly empty because of the weather as I hustled in through the driving sleet. Bart, as usual, elected to sleep in the back of the car.

I slipped onto a stool at the sparsely populated counter as Mabel walked up with a plate already in her hands.

"What's this?"

She gave me one of her dazzling smiles and said, "I knew you'd be in and knew you'd feel like scrambled eggs."

"How'd you know that?"

She just shrugged as she slid the plate in front of me. The smell was intoxicating and it really was just what I wanted.

Mabel lingered, and I could tell she was troubled by something. I didn't push it, since I noticed her checking to be sure no one was close enough to hear our conversation. She leaned on the counter and put her face close to mine. She still had that goofy look in her eyes that tends to make me uncomfortable.

She said, "Listen, Mitchum, I need to tell you something."

I didn't answer, just waited for it to come out.

"I'm worried. I've seen the same strangers here for the past few days. I didn't think it meant anything, but with Bailey Mae missing and now the Wilkses dead, I feel like I need to tell someone."

She had my attention. "I'm listening."

"Two men and a woman came in right as we opened at about 5:30 yesterday and this morning. It reminded me that I'd seen them before, a few weeks ago. They're not from around here."

"What makes them suspicious?"

"Who in their right mind would hang around this town if they didn't have to?"

"Me, for one. But tell me more about these strangers. What did they look like?"

That's when she surprised me. Instead of describing the strangers, she pulled out her phone and showed me a photograph she'd snapped of them leaving the diner. Two guys in their thirties with good builds and short hair and a tall woman about the same age who wore her dark hair in a neat braid down her back. Nothing unusual about them except they were all in good shape.

I had Mabel text me the photo, and then I gave her a stern look.

She said, "What? What's wrong?"

"I don't want you risking yourself snapping photos of who-knows-what. You can tell me anything, but don't do anything stupid. Let's figure out what's going on first. Don't stick your neck out."

That was *my* job.

# CHAPTER 10

**I CONTINUED MY** search for Bailey Mae by looking around Marlboro and the surrounding area, and I showed the photo from Mabel to the people I came across. No one seemed to recognize the three strangers from the diner.

My family had blanketed the area well. There were now flyers up on virtually every telephone pole, and most people that I visited had already talked to one of my cousins or my mother.

I decided to try a new tack and headed down to Newburgh to talk to the cops there. Newburgh was a much larger city and had seen better times. It had a crime rate that bucked the national trend by rising every year, and it was now considered one of the most dangerous small towns in the country. The city had a dingy look to it that I was afraid would never clear up.

The Newburgh cops knew me. Partly as a local and partly, unfortunately, as the brother of one of the town's drug dealers. My status as a veteran overcame some of that, but the cops still weren't thrilled with my brother's profession. Fortunately, most of the cops knew I wasn't on that level. What kind of an idiot would bust his ass on a paper route every day if he was really a drug kingpin?

The police station house was located on Route 300, not far from the State of Mind Tavern. The station was quiet when I stepped inside and walked toward a heavyset desk sergeant. I knew the big guy was from Buffalo, and I appreciated that he listened to me, paid attention, and even looked at the photo of the three strangers in Marlboro.

"I've already been keeping an eye out for your cousin and asking a few questions, but no one has seen her down here in a few days. I guess you already knew she would hang out over at the tavern with your brother sometimes."

I nodded my head, making sure I didn't add my approval to it.

A tall, muscular patrolman who had already been on the force when I'd gotten back from the service stopped to see what we were talking about. The cop was named Tharpe and I recognized him from high school. He wore his brown hair in a crew cut like he just got out of the Marines. He took a look at the photograph on my phone and said, "Sorry, dropout, don't recognize any of them." Then he turned and pushed through the swinging double doors into the control room off the lobby.

I'd heard it before. Sometimes "dropout," sometimes "washout." I got it. I didn't make it to the end of the SEAL course. It was just something I had to deal with.

A few minutes later, as I was headed out of town, I

turned a few blocks out of my way to go past the State of Mind Tavern. The parking lot was packed and music pulsed from inside. There aren't a lot of nightspot options in Newburgh.

I immediately spotted Natty standing at the edge of the parking lot, speaking on his cell phone. As I pulled the station wagon to the curb, he looked up and immediately walked toward me, ending his call.

Natty said, "Hey, Mitchum." As he stepped up to the car and leaned down, he looked into the backseat.

I knew what he was looking for. I said, "Bart's at home."

"Why? Thought he went everywhere with you."

"Who can tell? Maybe he liked the warmth of the house and knew I'd be in and out of the car." When we were kids, Natty and I loved *The Simpsons*. I would pretend to be Bart and Natty played Homer. It was a blast. I have no idea when we split. Probably in high school when he found an easy way to make a buck.

Natty made a quick scan of the area, then looked back at me and said, "What brings you down here?"

"Bailey Mae." Then I held up my phone and asked, "You ever seen these three before?"

Natty studied the photograph and said, "There've been a few more strangers around lately, and maybe I saw these three around somewhere. Let me think about it some more."

As I nodded and started to pull away, my brother reached in through the window and put his hand on my shoulder. "Be careful, little brother. This isn't the Navy.

There's no telling who's nuts. I'll get back on Bailey Mae's trail tomorrow. I have all of my associates out looking. We'll find her."

Maybe my brother had changed. At least that's what I kept thinking as I spent another hour stopping at a couple places on the way back to Marlboro. Bailey Mae had vanished, and she had seen the Wilkses sometime before they were murdered. That didn't leave me with a good feeling.

Once I was in Marlboro, I saw my cousin Todd and his wife out knocking on doors. It made me realize how grim things had turned in our little town. *Everyone loved Bailey Mae.* I had to stop the car at that thought and correct myself out loud. "Everyone *loves* Bailey Mae."

# CHAPTER 11

**IT WAS AFTER** nine when I rolled up to the diner for a shot of coffee and a snack before going out again on the only case that mattered to me.

Before I even sat down, Walter, a middle-aged man from town, approached me.

He was nervous and always spoke fast. "Mitchum, Mitchum, got a second?"

I was too tired to answer. He took it as a yes. I rubbed my eyes as he blurted out, "I've got a job for you."

All I could do was stare and let him finish his thought.

"My wife is gone. Missing. I think she's in the city with her personal trainer. I can pay. Double your normal rate."

I shook my head.

"Triple."

In my head I thought, *Triple of nothing is still nothing*, but I said, "I'm sorry, I can't."

He turned and left the diner in a huff.

Now Mabel and I were alone. She actually sat in the booth with me, something she never did.

I said, "What are you still doing here?"

"Worked a double. I need money for college. I've been taking classes over at Dutchess Community College, and I just got my GED at the end of the summer."

That was one of the first things to cheer me up all day. I said, "That's great. Any idea what you want to study?"

She just shrugged her shoulders, and we stared at each other for a few seconds. Finally Mabel said, "It's not easy, is it?"

"What?"

"Life."

"Not always."

She put her chin on her hands and it made her cute face seem even younger. "You really wanted to be a SEAL, huh?"

"I dreamed about it as a kid. I practiced for it. I did it all. Ran, studied karate, pull-ups, push-ups, anything I thought would get me ready. I even became a history buff because I read that all great soldiers were students of history."

"What happened?"

"I underestimated my ability to do a basic and simple skill."

"What's that?"

"I couldn't swim well enough."

"You didn't know that before you applied?"

"I thought I just needed more practice. And I did get

better, but not good enough. I was right at the top of the class, that's why they cut me a break about my swimming ability at first. Ultimately it wasn't meant to be. And I nearly drowned in the Pacific. It's deeper than you think."

Mabel laughed at that and her smile changed the whole room. It made me smile for the first time in two days.

She said, "So you could shoot and fight, but not swim."

"Basically. Now I just try to do my part in other ways."

"Like the PI stuff?"

"Sometimes."

"You don't ever feel bitter about the SEALs?"

I forced a smile. "I don't think the Navy would want that. Life's too short to waste it on regret."

She reached across and placed her hand on my forearm. "You're a good egg, Mitchum."

I put my hand over hers and said, "So are you. Now let's both go and get some rest."

I gave her a ride to the double-wide trailer that used to belong to her mother and refused an invitation inside. Right now all I needed was to lie down with Bart for a few hours and sleep as best I could.

# CHAPTER 12

**I WAS AS** tired as I could ever remember being as I pulled the station wagon up the narrow driveway and came to a stop twenty-five feet from my front door. I liked my simple house with two bedrooms and an attic a hobbit couldn't fit in. My front porch light was on a timer and illuminated the pathway, but the inside was pitch-black. That wasn't good. I always left one light on in my kitchen. Normally, I could see it through the front window, and it cast a little light across the whole house. I didn't want Bart walking into a wall in the dark. Someone had turned it off.

The only defense I had was my Navy knife, which I dug out of my front pocket and flipped open. I use it as a tool, but its original purpose was as a weapon. The door was still locked, and I wondered if the light had just burned out. Still, I entered carefully, slightly crouched with the knife in front of me. Clouds had obscured the moon, and the inside of my house could have been a cave.

I was relieved to hear Bart's nails click along the tile

as he came to me. But he whimpered slightly, something I rarely heard. I felt my way to the wall and flipped the switch that turned on the single light. Instantly my house seemed more natural. It was a light I was used to. Then I walked around and turned on several more lights, taking some time to lean down and comfort Bart. The dog was spooked. His wide little body, a cross between a boxer and a bulldog, was shaking.

The place looked in order. I checked the back door and the windows, and everything was secure. But there were a few little things out of place. The magazines on my coffee table were too straight. I wasn't that neat. They were usually plopped in an uneven pile. The drawers in my kitchen were not quite how I had left them. I remembered grabbing a pen and paper to make a grocery list and leaving my main junk drawer a mess. It was still chaos, but not the same chaos that I left it in.

My house had been searched. By professionals. Probably in the late afternoon, so they thought they were leaving everything in order when they shut down all the lights. I took a quick glance through the bedrooms and single bathroom, but nothing obvious was missing.

I immediately went to the high cabinet in my kitchen, to a stack of dish towels and extra pot holders. I stood on my toes to find the blue oven mitt I was looking for. I pulled it down, reached inside, and slid out the Beretta 9mm that fit inside the mitt like it was made for it. An old trick I learned from a chief petty officer in San Diego. No one ever wants to look through your kitchen linen.

As soon as my head hit the pillow, Bart was up on the bed, nuzzling in close to me. I wrapped my left arm around him and kept the pistol in my right hand. I was nearly unconscious in seconds.

It felt like I had only dozed off for a minute when my alarm went off, blaring Led Zeppelin's "Dazed and Confused." Habit pushed me up out of bed, and I led Bart to the front door so he could race outside and do his business.

Bart opted to stay in the house while I headed off to work and went through the motions of delivering papers. Maybe that's why I kept this job: on the days I needed it, I didn't have to think about it at all.

I was hungry and looking forward to chatting with Mabel, so I got to the diner a few minutes earlier than usual. Now every time I walked into a public place I automatically looked for the three strangers. This morning it was just locals. But there was one surprise. Instead of Mabel behind the counter, it was the lovely Tina herself. She rarely stepped in as a waitress anymore, preferring to run the kitchen and do all the restaurant managing.

Tina had been a year ahead of me in school, and she still looked great, if a little stern. She'd always been businesslike, but this morning she acted like a Marine drill sergeant, barking orders back to my cousin in the kitchen and telling her nephew to be quicker busing the tables.

My booth was taken, so I sat at the counter directly in front of the door. Tina managed to flash me one quick smile and got right to the point. "Make it fast, Mitchum. What do you want?"

"Where's Mabel?"

"She didn't show this morning and she's not answering her damn cell."

I could tell it wasn't a good time to pursue any more questions about the tardy waitress. Not if I didn't want to risk her job.

Instead, I just said, "It's not like her. She never misses a shift. She needs the money."

But Tina's glare told me Mabel might not get a second chance.

# CHAPTER 13

**I MAY HAVE** been overreacting, but with all the crazy shit going on around town I needed to go check on Mabel. She had seemed fine the night before. Maybe the double shift had caught up with her and she had just missed her alarm.

The double-wide trailer she had lived in with her mother, before her mother died of a brain aneurysm two years ago, was only a few blocks from the diner, at the end of a gravel drive behind the post office on Orange Street.

Every one of the fourteen trailers in the tiny park was well kept, and Mabel's had a few pieces of flair that told you a younger person lived inside. A little hand-painted street sign pointing south that said KEY WEST 2230 MILES, the doormat that read BRING JOY OR BEER INTO THIS HOUSE. I knocked on the door and got no answer. I thought about walking back to my car and grabbing my pistol. Instead, I slipped my hand into my pocket and felt my knife for security.

I tried the knob and found the door unlocked, then called out in a loud voice, "Mabel, it's Mitchum." Nothing. I eased into the front room, quickly scanning in all directions, then called out again. The heat was on, and Mabel's beat-up Chevy was in the carport.

I crept down the cramped hallway toward the bedroom, calling her name again. I paused to knock gently on the bedroom door, then pushed the door open.

I froze. Sprawled on the floor next to her bed was Mabel's pale body. Dressed in shorts and a T-shirt, she had a hypodermic needle stuck in her ankle. I knew she'd overdosed. I knew she was dead and, most important, I knew she didn't normally use drugs.

My brother would've told me if she'd had this kind of problem. After all, he was the local drug dealer.

# CHAPTER 14

**I WAS LOST.** At least for a while. I still had hope of finding Bailey Mae, but Mabel was gone. Gone forever. I just sat in my car, shocked, while the cops and the coroner examined the trailer. I wanted to leave. To be productive. But I couldn't. It was as if I'd been hit in the stomach. I was shattered.

I didn't have time to grieve. People were counting on me. Alice and Bailey Mae needed me. Through some deep sixth sense, I felt like Bailey Mae's disappearance and Mabel's death were somehow connected. I had to swallow my grief and find Bailey Mae. I had to get some goddamn answers.

I headed straight to my brother's house, north of Milton. He always said he liked some distance between work and home. A different set of cops got to harass him. The house and detached garage sat off a long gravel driveway that entered directly onto Route 9. The place was rented, of course, with no neighbors close by.

I didn't see any cars but went to the front door anyway and pounded like I was the lead member of a SWAT team. No answer. He didn't pick up his cell when I called, either. Was he avoiding me? If he was, it was the most common sense he'd shown in a long time.

I came back down to Marlboro and started thinking how crazy it was that my quiet little town had gone off the rails in the last few days. I had to find out why. I would go on the offensive and nothing could stop me.

The search for Bailey Mae started again with a vengeance. I was asking questions about her at the businesses up and down Route 9, showing them the photo of the three strangers that Mabel had taken.

I worked my way all the way down to Newburgh before I found a barber who didn't know anything about Bailey Mae but thought he had trimmed the hair of one of the men in the photo. He said it was just a touch-up on a crew cut. Similar to a military style. The older man had never seen the customer before or since, and the man was alone when he came in to get the trim. That was three days ago.

I stopped at a gas station on North Plank Road, just before it met Route 9, to fill up. I knew the doofus working at the station was one of my brother's regular pot customers. I almost didn't say anything to the gangly twenty-year-old with greasy hair that hung down into his face.

He came out of the station and walked up to me at the pump. "Hey, Mitchum. Where's your brother?"

"Why?" I knew the reason.

"I'm low on weed and someone said he had a new shipment this morning."

I shook my head and couldn't believe how open people were about doing something illegal. I didn't care about pot use; it just annoyed me how much money my brother made doing something that was against the law.

"You heard about my cousin, Bailey Mae?"

He nodded his head. "Natty was by here asking about her yesterday. I haven't seen her."

I held up my phone. "What about any of these three?"

He took a second to study the photo then surprised me by saying, "Yeah, I've seen them a couple times. All three of them were in a dark SUV."

"When was the last time you saw them?"

"Yesterday afternoon."

# CHAPTER 15

**I WENT BY** a couple diners in Newburgh. They were bigger, impersonal places, and the people there didn't know my cousin. They didn't recognize the strangers on my phone. At the second diner, the waitress made me a turkey sandwich because she thought I looked tired and underfed. While I wolfed it down, she refocused her attention on the other tables, leaving me all alone.

As frustrated as I was, it was kinda nice being in Newburgh. It was bigger than our town, and it would be easier to go unnoticed there. That's where I'd stay if I came to the area from somewhere else.

I got nothing from a couple of hotels on the main drag, so I stopped at one tucked off Windsor Highway, called the Red Letter Inn, an obvious nod to *The Scarlet Letter* and adultery. What a nice place.

The clerk barely looked up when I walked through the front door. He was about my age, but much heavier and not particularly chatty. He didn't even grunt as I stepped up and stood by the counter. Behind him, a small TV played *Family Feud*.

Even after I cleared my throat, he didn't acknowledge me. Then I held up a photo of Bailey Mae and said, "I was just wondering if you've seen this girl. She's missing."

The man looked up, scratched the three-day-old growth on his chin, and gave the photograph a cursory examination. His eyes shot up to meet mine briefly, and all he said was "Nope."

I stood there, thinking of different ways to approach this idiot. I dug in my pocket and pulled out my phone, calling up the photograph of the strangers. As I held it up, the man said, "If you're not checking in, you need to be on your way."

I essentially ignored him as I held up the phone and said, "What about these three? Have you seen any of them?"

Now he lifted his head and gave me his full attention. "What do I look like to you? Lost and Found?"

He was big. An inch or two taller than me and at least eighty-five pounds heavier. But I was at the end of my rope. I had to dig deep to be polite as I kept the phone in position and said, "It's really important. Have you seen any of these three people?"

But now he wouldn't even look up.

I pulled a pizza flyer from the edge of the counter, flipped it over, and took a moment to write on it in tiny letters. I slid the flyer across the counter and said, "I guess you know this already."

The big man glanced at the paper, then took a second

to try and read it. The letters were so small he had to lean in close and put his head near the counter.

That's when I grabbed his hair and slammed his face into the counter as hard as I could. "It says, 'You're an ass-hole.'" Then I pulled him right over the counter into the lobby. It was a lot more work than I thought it would be.

I jerked his face up so he was looking at the photo on my phone. I tried to keep my tone even when I said, "Like I was asking, have you seen any of them?"

The big man, who had a trickle of blood running down his face from a broken nose, focused on the photograph, then turned and looked at me sheepishly, saying, "The guy on the left is in room 16. He's driving an older Ford pickup with a snowplow on the front of it. Looks like he's in the military. A little strange, maybe even scary." Then he took a moment, wiped the blood with his bare hand, and said, "But not as scary as you."

# CHAPTER 16

**I HELPED THE** clerk clean up and get settled in his chair. He understood that he wasn't supposed to tell anyone I'd been asking questions. The look on his face told me he'd keep that promise.

It was time to use some of my private investigation skills. This was the one area I was a little weak in, but it was time to try it: surveillance. I was going to conduct my own stakeout at the motel. I parked my car across the highway, at an empty strip mall. No one coming down the road would give a beat-up station wagon a second look.

There was a pickup truck with a professional-looking snowplow attached to the chassis parked directly in front of room 16, which was the last one on the left side of the motel. The truck had been backed into a spot, so I couldn't read the license plate. It didn't matter; I just wanted to see where he'd go.

The whole experience made me feel like a legitimate private investigator. It didn't have anything to do with my knowing the background of someone who needed help and understanding what they were looking for. Often my private investigation business was more about comforting elderly people than actually solving some kind of crime. I never took divorce or cheating cases, and I slept pretty well most nights. Now, in my station wagon, I was waiting for someone who might be dangerous to leave the hotel. Shit was getting real.

# CHAPTER 17

**I FELT THE** weather move in before the snow started to fall. In a few minutes the road was completely blanketed, and more was coming. I looked at my watch and realized it was getting late. I sat, staring at a motel that no one had come out of or gone into in more than three hours. Maybe that's why I don't do much surveillance. It's definitely frustrating.

I couldn't wait any longer. I grabbed my pistol from under the seat, tucked it into my belt, and crossed the road quickly on foot. The motel office was dark, and no one moved anywhere on the property. I checked out the snowplow before I stepped to the door. It was bolted to the truck's chassis and about four feet wide. It looked like it was used to clear small roads or trails. I was trying to think: What kind of trails needed to be cleared around here? The roads were all handled by commercial snowplows, and even though I'd seen a few of these around over the years, none were as expensive and elaborate as this. Usually they were homemade jobs on the front of beat-up pickup trucks that would clear driveways for ten bucks. This was something else.

I moved to the room. There were no lights, and I felt no movement inside when I placed my hand on the door. The moist air made me shiver. At least I think it was the air. I was in uncharted territory professionally. This was nothing like finding out who'd hacked a Facebook account or looking for a husband who had had a few too many drinks.

I couldn't waste any more time. I rapped on the door. In a reasonable fashion at first, then a bit louder. My right hand rested on the butt of the pistol underneath my untucked shirt.

There was no answer, and none of the other customers opened their doors, either.

I looked down at my watch and realized time had gotten away from me. I had to race back to Marlboro to get my papers ready to deliver. But I'd be back to have a talk with the guy at the Red Letter Inn.

# CHAPTER 18

**IT WAS ONE** of the worst mornings I could ever remember. I've seen heavier snowfall, but not this early, when no one was ready for it. Bart had no interest in leaving the comfortable confines of our little house. His flat face looked out the window as I trudged through the snow that had accumulated on my front walk in just a few hours. And the snow was still falling.

As soon as I got to the loading dock and grabbed the papers Nick dropped off, I realized I was just going through the motions. I could do this job with my eyes shut. Almost literally. If it wasn't for the fear of hitting a pedestrian, I might even try it one day. Some days I was in a hurry, and I could be efficient and fast. Today it was just a duty. It was my responsibility to deliver papers, and I was going to do it. I recognized that some of the elderly people on my route depended on the papers for their window to the world. But today it was more about killing time and giving my mind a rest.

As I pulled away from the loading dock in my sagging station wagon, my head was somewhere else. It wasn't somewhere pleasant, but at least it wasn't dwelling on the fact that Mabel was dead and Bailey Mae was still missing.

Just a block from the loading dock, as I pulled up to the closest intersection, I felt a sudden impact. Wham! My whole world started to spin. It was as if I felt the collision before I even heard the deafening crash. My giant old station wagon spun across the icy road, and nothing I did with the steering wheel or brakes seemed to make any difference at all.

As the car started to slow its wild spin, I felt a second impact as the station wagon drove into thick trees on the side of the road. The abrupt stop threw me from the driver's seat into the passenger seat, and my papers spilled from the crates in the rear all over the car.

Somehow I managed to open the passenger door and tumble out onto the cold, hard ground. For the first time, I wondered if the people in the other car were hurt. I struggled to my feet and took a moment to catch my breath and get my bearings. When I looked up, I recognized the vehicle wedged against mine. It was the Ford pickup truck with the snowplow, and it had done a number on my front quarter panel.

As I processed this image, I saw a figure slide out of the driver's side of the pickup. I didn't even know if it was a man or a woman. All I saw was the gun.

I quickly patted my waistline. Damn it. I'd left the pistol

in the car. That was a mistake, and now I had to make sure it wouldn't be a fatal one.

I took three quick steps and jumped behind a snow-bank, hoping to put some distance between me and my attacker just as he fired two quick shots.

My head jerked as I felt the impact of the second shot. I was hit.

# CHAPTER 19

**EVEN THOUGH I'D** been shot, I somehow managed to low crawl through the brush until I was behind a thicker stand of trees about fifty feet from my disabled car. I leaned up against a tree, taking shallow breaths, and ran my fingers up my forehead and over my scalp. There was some blood, but the bullet must've only grazed me, because my brain was still functioning. I was alive and able to see, and I still understood what it meant to be scared.

Suddenly I realized all that training I got in the Navy hadn't been wasted. It was kicking in. I automatically took in my full surroundings, figured out my best chance of escape, and identified exactly where the danger was coming from. The guy with the gun was now standing at the foot of my car, peering into the dark woods.

I weighed my options. I could turn and run down the path away from the road, but that would give him a clear view and opportunity to shoot me. If I waited, he might walk into the woods searching for me and I'd have a chance to strike if he got close enough. But this guy seemed too professional for that. He was weighing his own options and knew time was on his side.

I needed something, some distraction to make him look away or run toward me. Without conscious thought, my right hand was in a fist and ready for action. But the last thing I wanted to do was get in a fistfight with a guy who had a gun.

Then I heard a noise on the other side of me. It was a low rustle in the brush. I jumped when a figure appeared out of nowhere. My fist almost struck out on its own. Luckily, my brain was able to register who it was.

"Jesus, Al. What are you doing here?" It was a hoarse, harsh whisper, but this was not the time for the older homeless guy to be hanging out.

"It looked like you could use a hand, Mitchum." He slipped off the fleece coat I'd given him a few days earlier and said, "Put this on. You're not used to the cold like I am, and if you lose too much blood the coat will help." Then he peeked at the spot where the man with the gun had stepped farther into the woods. Then Al said, "Be ready to take this guy out."

Before I could even ask him what he was talking about, Al stood up and sprinted, though not all that fast, on the path where the man could see him.

The man took one wild shot then fell into pursuit, immediately running hard right down the middle of the path. He had no idea I was behind a tree that was coming up quickly.

I could hear his footsteps as he raced down the path and was able to time the swing of my arm to clothesline him perfectly. His whole body rose in the air as my arm caught his chest and slid up to his chin. He landed on the ground with a thud.

The gun flew from his hand and landed somewhere in the brush, out of sight. In the few seconds I spent looking for the gun, the man was on his feet and facing me.

He was about my size, with close-cropped brown hair and a tattoo of a teardrop next to his left eye. That meant either he had never been in the military or had been out long enough to get the facial tattoo. Right now that kind of deduction wouldn't help me. He was tough. Too tough for his own good.

He also knew how to fight. His stance gave away nothing, with his fists up to protect his face.

I stepped in and his right leg swung up, blasting me on the right side of my body with a round kick. I deflected some of it with my arm but it still sent a shiver of pain and shock through me. So now I knew he was as fast as lightning, too. I leaned in again and drew a swing of his right fist, which was what I wanted. I dipped slightly and connected with a big punch into his side and was rewarded with the sound of a rib cracking. It might not stop him, but it would make him think every time he moved.

The man backed off slightly but gave no acknowledgment of the blow. We were both breathing hard already and starting to sweat. Most people have no idea how hard it is to actually fight. Adrenaline and physical exertion together can be a bitch.

The man moved forward and threw two front kicks, which I blocked, but they were still powerful. I managed a glancing elbow to his chin, which drove him back and also convinced him he wasn't going to beat me hand to hand.

He kept his distance as he reached into his rear pocket and yanked out a knife. It was the Army Ranger version of mine.

I matched him by jerking my knife from my front pocket and flicking it open, then holding it steady a little in front of me.

The man had a loose grasp on his knife and swung it from side to side as he circled me, looking for an opening.

A trickle of sweat slipped into my eye, but I couldn't wipe it.

The man's lip was bleeding from my elbow strike.

He still said nothing. I had no real idea who had told him to make me the target of this attack. But I wasn't the one who'd regret it. The last thing I wanted to do was stab anyone. Well, second to last. The last thing I wanted to do was die. That meant I had to take serious action.

He swung at me once, with his blade landing on the back of my left hand and cutting me. The next backhand swipe missed me. When he stepped forward again, I knew what he was going to do. As he started his strike again, I raised my bloody left hand and blocked him, and at the same time, I drove my knife straight up into his solar plexus. I heard the sickening sound of the blade piercing the flesh and then driving up.

The man froze mid-strike and just stared at me. Then he took a few staggering steps away as he tried to form a word. Then he collapsed onto the path, holding his wound.

I leaned down and could already feel his pulse had stopped. I must have nicked his heart.

A quick search found no identification on the man. Not that I really needed any. I knew why he had attacked me: I was looking for Bailey Mae and whoever killed the Wilkses—and maybe even poor Mabel.

And I didn't have any real regret for killing this guy unless it kept me from finding Bailey Mae.

# CHAPTER 20

**I SAT ON** the frozen ground, leaning against a tree, trying to catch my breath. I'd used the snow to clean my knife and pack the cut on my left hand. I can't say why. I seemed to be operating on instinct now. It didn't particularly bother me that a few feet away there was a body that I had killed. It had clearly been in self-defense.

A noise to my right made me jump. Then I realized it was Albany Al coming back.

He said, "When this asshole didn't follow me, I figured you'd cleaned his clock." The older man inspected the body more closely. "You don't do anything halfway, do you? Nice job." Now he looked at me and stepped closer, then ran his index finger across my forehead. "Jeez, you're bleeding like a stuck pig. The bullet must have nicked your scalp good." He showed me the blood on his finger. "You are one lucky son of a gun."

All I could do was shrug my shoulders and say, "Yeah,

lucky." I didn't feel so lucky. The older man shivered, so I gave him the coat back. I struggled to my feet. My vision was a little blurry.

Al said, "What about him?" He pointed at the body a few feet away.

"I'll worry about explaining him later."

Al held up both hands and said, "I didn't see a thing."

Once on my feet, I really felt the blood. It was a warm sensation in the bracing wind. I nodded good-bye to Al and stumbled back to my car. No one had even driven past the accident yet. It was too early and too nasty out. I had to yank the fender away from my front tire, but the good old station wagon would run. A minute later I was on the highway, headed to the one place I knew I'd be safe. I loved that car. At least for the moment.

My mom's house was a few blocks from mine. I don't care how old you are or what you do in life, your mom's place is always a safe haven. It was the house I grew up in. I stayed there alone with my brother when my mom worked a late shift as a nurse at the emergency room in Newburgh. It was the one place in the world where my troubles never caught up with me.

She was home, and Bart was sitting next to her on the sofa as they both watched a talk show.

She said, "I went to walk Bart and he wanted to come here after." She always made up an excuse to spend a little extra time with my dog. Then she took a closer look and sprang to her feet. "What happened to you? Are you okay?" She was a typical mom at heart.

My mom sent me into the bathroom as she gathered her supplies and made a quick phone call. When she came in, I was already sitting on the stool we'd used for medical treatment since I was a kid. Both Natty and I had most of our injuries tended to here.

Mom had me lean over the sink as she washed my scalp, first with warm water, then peroxide. She parted my thick hair carefully with her fingers and then doused the wound with more peroxide.

I flinched.

My mom said, "Relax—it's not that bad."

"You could be a little more gentle."

"I could be, but this way is faster. I've had too much practice with you. Always pretending to be a SEAL and then all those crazy training courses you invented. You got nicked up all the time." She continued to check my head, then finally said, "This isn't like any of your crazy cuts or bruises. This was a bullet, wasn't it? You going to tell me what happened?"

"I was hoping to avoid that."

"The cut on your hand could be anything, but now I'll assume it was part of a fight." She inspected my left hand, cleaned it easily, and used three butterfly bandages to close it. "You're lucky it's superficial. A deeper cut could have damaged the tendons and affected your grip."

She refocused on my head wound, dumping more peroxide on it and moving my hair again, making me jump. It was like a needle in my head. "I can patch you up a number of different ways."

"But I still won't tell you what happened. I don't want to get you involved."

"Okay then, go bleed to death somewhere else."

"I'm sorry, Mom. But there's something weird going on around town, and it may be related to Bailey Mae. I'm okay—that's why I came here."

"And you didn't want anyone at a hospital asking questions, did you?"

"Yeah, that, too."

She worked miracles with a couple of fancy bandages and some dissolving glue. When it was all done, the bleeding had stopped, and she even combed my hair the way I like it. As she dabbed the dried blood from my forehead, I heard the front door open. I sprang from the stool and reached for my knife. My first thought was that someone had followed me to her house. Exactly what I didn't want to happen.

I stood in the hallway that led to the living room and listened for a moment. I wanted to have an idea of how many people had entered the house. It didn't matter—at this point I was going to deal with all of them at the same time.

Then I heard a male voice that froze me in place.

It was my brother, Natty. That explained the phone call my mom had made.

Crap.

# CHAPTER 21

**MY MOM WALKED** casually past me into the living room, saying, "I called Natty so you could work together to find Bailey Mae. You each have your own strengths and complement each other very well."

I said, "I'm looking for three strangers." I faced my brother and said, "You sell any of your nasty poison to any strangers passing through town?"

Natty said, "I told you I didn't recognize the three people in the photo. I only sell to regular customers."

"You're lying, Natty. Don't be an asshole. Those strangers are tied to Bailey Mae somehow. Bailey Mae and the Wilkses. I know it."

"You don't know shit. You're just a pretend private investigator in a shitty little town. Bailey Mae probably ran away, so we'll find her. I don't have time for any of this shit. At least *I* have a business to run."

"Selling crap to people who can't help themselves? Like the heroin that killed poor Mabel."

Suddenly Natty was indignant. "I never sell heroin and never sold *anything* to Mabel. If she had asked for anything, I would've told you."

I couldn't stand it anymore. My brother's self-righteous excuses for how he made a living caused something to snap inside of me. I punched him right in the face. Hard. The punch was so solid it made *my* head hurt.

To Natty's credit, he wasn't on the floor long. He sprang to his feet and hurled his whole body into me with a vengeance. I stumbled back and we both crashed onto my mother's coffee table, breaking it into a thousand pieces. Magazines flew in every direction.

We ignored our mother's shouts for us to calm down. She even threw in a few curse words, which was rare for her. We tore up her living room, knocking books off the mantel, bending her floor lamp, and flipping her recliner end over end, with my brother's scrawny body lost in the heap. It might've been the loss of blood or the fact that I underestimated my brother's fighting abilities, but going up against him was harder than I would have thought. I guess he had to be in a few fights before he could afford a bodyguard.

We took a moment and backed away from each other when we were both on our feet. I moved to the mantel and caught my breath. He backed toward the kitchen door.

Then I heard an odd sound, like the chime of an old grandfather clock. My brother fell onto the floor, holding his head, as my mom stepped out from behind him with a heavy cast-iron skillet in her hand.

She looked at me with those cool, brown eyes and said, "You want some of this, Bobby?"

I glanced down at my brother, on all fours and shaking his head. "No, ma'am." I didn't want to have anything to do with that skillet.

# CHAPTER 22

**I TRIED TO** be a good brother and helped Natty off the floor and onto the couch. My mom took charge quickly and said, "Bobby, go get the ice bag out of the cupboard and fill it."

That's right. My name is Robert Mitchum. Just like the actor. Named for my grandfather, who was a long-distance trucker, born a few years after the famous Robert Mitchum.

Bart hopped onto the couch just as I came back with the ice bag. He licked Natty's face as my brother slowly regained his senses. His eyes were dilated, which made him look like a cartoon character. My mom, who was acting like she had nothing to do with his present condition, sat on the edge of the couch and gently placed the ice bag on his head.

She said, "You two shake hands and make up."

Way to make your adult sons feel like eight-year-olds, Mom.

Then my mom said, "Are you idiots ready to talk?" She

looked at Natty. "I don't care what you do for a living. I'm your mother and I love you. But we need to find Bailey Mae. I'm her great-aunt. So you're going to tell Bobby anything he wants to know, and you're going to do it right now."

Natty mumbled, "Yes, ma'am."

Apparently moms work as well as enhanced interrogation because Natty turned to me and said, "What do you want to know, Mitchum?"

"Have you sold to any strangers?"

"I don't sell to anyone but regular customers."

"Have you seen anything unusual?"

Natty thought about that for a few seconds and said, "The Clagetts have been buying some 'medicinal' pot over the last few weeks. A lot more than usual."

The name didn't spring to mind, so I knew they weren't on my paper route. Then I remembered. "You mean the people who bought those old cabins up in the hills off new Unionville Road?"

"Yeah. But they seem like a nice enough couple."

"Let's head out there and pay them a visit." The fact that we were working together seemed to make my mom happy, even if she was a little worried about what we were doing. She kissed us each on the cheek as I called for Bart to join us. He happily hopped off the couch and trotted toward the door.

# CHAPTER 23

**WE TOOK MY** brother's sports car because it was a little more dependable than my beat-up station wagon. He was clearly uncomfortable with a dog riding unattended in the backseat. It brought a small smile to my face.

We'd been in enough fights with each other since childhood that there was nothing awkward in the aftermath of our last dustup. But as always, Natty was hesitant to talk about his business.

I said, "All I'm asking is to know how you met the Clagetts. No one in town has seen them, except for when they do a grocery run once a week or so."

"I just met them one day and it all worked out."

"Is that how you describe business transactions? They work out?"

"What do you want me to say, Mitchum? We can't all know what we want to do from childhood."

"You noticed my dream didn't work out too well for me."

"At least everyone looks up to you around here. I'm just the drug-dealing brother."

"You can't change that?"

"Not now. Not after all these years. I am what I am, and you're the guy in town everyone counts on. No one cares if you were a SEAL or not. You're still the Man in Marlboro."

I had never considered how my brother felt or knew that he might resent me. It was disconcerting to have to reevaluate my relationship with him, which was based on mutual contempt. He wasn't the shallow narcissist I assumed he was.

We didn't say much more as we turned off Unionville Road up the winding, unnamed gravel path that rose in the foothills and then the steeper inclines of the mountains.

I'd never been back here, just heard about the three cabins that had been part of a resort back in the sixties. The front cabin was clearly the main residence. It had been remodeled, and an asphalt driveway ran up to it. The carport connected the detached garage to what appeared to be a three-bedroom building. Behind it on each side were smaller cabins that were more run-down and had no carports.

A Ford sedan was parked in the driveway. As we approached the front door, I touched the hood of the car to feel if it had been driven recently. It was ice-cold.

I let Bart out of the car to get some exercise and do his business. There were a few patches of grass around the house, but the snow got thicker heading up the hills.

The front porch creaked as we carefully stepped up to

the door. This time I'd thought ahead and had my pistol tucked in my pants. My knife was safely in my pocket. I was tired of getting surprised and abused by strangers.

Natty tapped on the door like we were visiting a relative. There was no immediate answer so I pounded on it with my left fist. When we got no answer for a second time, I tried the handle. It was locked.

The deadbolt hadn't been turned, so I pulled out my Navy knife and flicked it open with my thumb. The sound of it clicking into place caught Natty's attention, and when I wedged it into the door to jimmy the lock, he started protesting.

Once the door was open, I stepped inside.

From the porch, Natty said, "Are you crazy? We could get arrested for this."

"That's funny coming from a drug dealer."

"With two convictions. I can't risk a simple breaking and entering. They'd send me upstate for five years."

I walked farther into the house, looking for any clues about the people who lived there.

Reluctantly, Natty followed me inside. "We could both be killed. Is that what you want?"

I didn't turn to face him when I said, "All I want is to find Bailey Mae."

When I got to the rear of the cabin I noticed Bart in the backyard. He was sniffing something and interested in it.

I went out the back door and Natty followed. When I got to Bart, I kneeled down to pat his back and said, "What did you find, boy?" That's when I realized there were several sets of tracks in the snow from the rear of the cabin heading up into the hills. It was a well-used path and the latest set of tracks was fairly fresh.

Without a word I started the trek up the hill, following the tracks. Natty started to protest, but then just followed me.

# CHAPTER 24

**THE TRAIL WAS** firm, with the snow piled on either side. I was surprised how steep the incline was and felt my heart rate start to climb as I kept a steady march up the path. After a few hundred yards I was glad we'd left Bart on the porch of the cabin. He seemed happy to let us go on our way, and I knew he'd be safe there.

Natty started to complain as the path entered the thick woods and continued to go higher. Every once in a while I could see remnants of the old resort and where a road off to the side followed the path. The road would be tough to navigate in winter, but in summer it seemed wide enough for any kind of vehicle. Unless you had a snowplow— then it could be open year-round.

The cold wind whipped down off the mountaintop and made me shiver even though I was working pretty hard. Natty's breath became more ragged as his lifestyle started to catch up with him.

Natty said, "What are we doing out here in this frozen tundra?"

"You know exactly what we're doing: looking for Bailey Mae."

"You don't think this is a little crazy? We go from asking people if they've seen a missing teenager to trekking through the woods behind someone's cabin? This seems pretty thin and a waste of time."

"You don't have to be here."

"Mom said I did. Besides, I can't leave you out here alone. I just think our time could be spent more efficiently. There's nothing out here. We're following some kind of old hunting trail."

We cleared a rise in the trail and stopped, amazed by what we saw.

In front of us, about a hundred yards away, was a small cabin with the lights on and smoke coming from the chimney. I had never seen it or heard anyone mention a cabin all the way back here. It was more like a shack, hastily constructed to protect people from the weather.

I had to look at Natty and say, "What were you saying about nothing being back here?"

Then Natty mumbled, "Maybe you *are* a good investigator."

# CHAPTER 25

**WE CAREFULLY MOVED** around to the front of the shack, which had a window on each side of the only door. As we got closer, we could see one guy inside, sprawled out on the couch with a computer on his lap. He was in his thirties and kind of pudgy but looked like he'd been in pretty good shape at one time. Now he just looked like a couch potato. The fireplace made the room look cozy, and for some reason it pissed me off.

Natty eased up beside me and took a peek.

Then I realized what was on a plate next to him on the couch: a piece of Bailey Mae's coffee cake.

I pulled Natty away from the window and said in a low voice, "Ever see him before?"

Natty was sheepish and finally stammered, "No, well, I mean, maybe. I think."

"Natty," I growled.

"Yeah. I guess I sold him some weed once."

I glared at him.

"Maybe a few times. And a little coke. And some pills. That ADHD shit." He paused and cocked his head like a puppy. "What's the look for? Any good businessman needs to diversify."

"I thought you only sold pot to regular customers."

Natty shrugged. "After the first time he *was* a regular customer. And just how am I supposed to remember everything and everyone?"

I looked back at the cabin and crept toward it with Natty close behind. I pulled my pistol from under my shirt.

Then he grabbed my arm and said, "Wait, what are we doing? Do you have any idea what kind of trouble we could be in for using a gun in a home invasion?"

"Yeah, I do. But this guy might lead us to Bailey Mae." I jerked my arm away from Natty and stepped up to the door.

# CHAPTER 26

**THE DOOR WAS** unlocked. I was disappointed I didn't get to kick in anything in a dramatic fashion. We rushed inside just the same. The effect was perfect. Couch Potato Man stared in stunned silence for a moment then tried to get to his feet, knocking the plate with Bailey Mae's coffee cake onto the floor.

The sight of my gun pointed at him slowed the man down. Now he eased back onto the couch and said, "You scared the shit out of me." He looked at Natty and said, "I'm all paid up with you. What's the problem?"

I said, "Where's the girl? Where's Bailey Mae, you son of a bitch?"

Couch Potato Man said, "I have no idea what you assholes are talking about. Who the hell is Bailey Mae?"

Then he stood up. That was his mistake. I was pissed off and he was in range, so I popped him in the face with my left fist, keeping the gun pointed at him with my right hand. Although I felt it in the cut on the back of my hand,

I was glad to get off a good, solid punch that knocked him back. He tumbled across the couch and landed on the hard floor. He immediately covered himself with his hands like there was a gang about to pummel him.

I was breathing hard as I stood over the man with the pistol still in my hand. "Don't make me ask you again. Where is she?"

Couch Potato Man kept his head down with his hands shielding his face. "Please don't hit me," he whined as he scooted away from me, toward the couch. He sat up with his back against the couch but kept his hands up like he was terrified. Was this some kind of act? Was he buying time? I didn't care. I needed answers.

Couch Potato Man said, "I didn't do anything to anyone. I don't know anyone named Bailey Mae. I'm basically camping here. Squatting."

I noticed his eyes shift to the right, looking past me. About the same time I caught a movement outside the window. Before I could turn, the door burst open.

Natty squawked like a bird.

I spun and found a gun in my face. My eyes ran up the barrel to the owner. It was the woman from Mabel's photo.

# CHAPTER 27

**THE MAN STANDING** next to her said, "Put the gun on the ground. Do it now."

That was a command from someone who had either military or police experience. I slowly bent down to place the gun on the floor, but I kept my eyes on the couple who'd stepped inside the shack. The man was also from the photo. He was lean and in good shape, with close-cropped hair. The woman was about five foot ten and had straight black hair that hung to her neck, with very little styling. She had sharp lines to her face and didn't look like she took much shit.

I didn't make any sudden movements and did nothing to cause alarm or force them to shoot. But as I stood back up, I felt a strong emotion—and it wasn't fear. It was anger. These people thought they could do whatever they wanted in my town. They probably took Bailey Mae, and now they were pointing guns at my brother and me.

Natty could never keep his mouth shut. As a kid he was

fearless, even though he didn't have the muscle to back it up. Sure enough, he said, "Just who the hell are you guys?"

Now Couch Potato Man was standing up behind us, no doubt looking forward to some payback. But like the other two, Couch Potato Man was now focused on Natty.

Natty continued. "I sold this slacker some weed. He didn't seem so bad. What the hell is your problem?" He jabbed his finger at the couple.

While the armed couple focused their attention on my idiot brother, I eased my right hand into my front pocket. No one even noticed. My brother could hold people's attention.

He said, "If you assholes think you can move in on my territory, I got news for you."

I made my move. My Navy knife was out and flicked open in a heartbeat, while they all stared at my brother like he was some kind of evangelist who had gone insane on the pulpit. I was close, but not quite close enough. That forced me to try something crazy, but this whole situation was crazy. I leaned into it and threw the knife. Hard. It hit the woman in the upper chest, knocking her back, and she staggered from shock.

Her male companion fired as I moved. The round went wide and I was on him before he could pull the trigger again. I was bigger and had momentum. He went down and his pistol flew across the floor. I put him in an arm lock, making him gasp in pain.

When Couch Potato Man moved toward the pistol, Natty took action. He threw a solid elbow into the man's chin. Nice. Then he shoved the man back onto the couch. Right where a couch potato belonged.

We had no time to waste. I twisted my body and broke the other man's arm.

The woman was on the floor in shock.

Natty picked up the loose pistol. "Now this is what I'm talking about." He pointed the gun at Couch Potato Man.

I rolled away and onto my feet. My anger came out in a scream. "Where's Bailey Mae?!"

# CHAPTER 28

**NATTY LOOKED LIKE** he enjoyed holding the gun on Couch Potato Man. I had other things to do. The man on the floor, closest to me, was moaning and holding his arm. The woman by the door was barely conscious. Now I had both her pistol and mine.

I looked at Natty and said, "Pull off a couple lamp cords and grab some rags from the kitchen. Let's tie these jerks up."

Natty hesitated at first, then tucked the gun in his belt and ripped the cord from a floor lamp, then the cords from some old blinds. The cords and a couple of longer dishrags made for decent restraints as we tied the men's hands behind their backs. The man with the broken arm whimpered. Then, for good measure, I tied each man's ankles together with a lamp cord. That would keep them from having any ideas about running.

I carefully examined the woman on the floor, then eased my knife out of her chest and used a dish towel and duct tape over her wound to stem the bleeding. She moaned and seemed to be in and out of consciousness. Then her eyes focused.

"Get me to a hospital." Even in this state she was scary.

I gave her a smile and said, "No problem. Just tell me where Bailey Mae is."

She looked puzzled.

"My cousin, fourteen, cute, brown hair." I took time to look at each of the other assholes. Couch Potato Man wouldn't meet my eyes. The other man said, "I don't know what you're talking about, but she needs help. Now."

"So do I."

Then I thought of a way to make them talk.

# CHAPTER 29

**I KNEW NATTY** would never look at me the same way again, but we had to get some answers. I got his attention and said, "Come on, let's drag them all outside."

"Outside? Are you crazy? It's freezing out there."

"Exactly."

The snow was still coming down hard and the wind had picked up. None of them had coats on. They weren't ready to be stuck outside. That made me realize the couple with the guns had come to the shack from somewhere close.

Natty was silent as we dragged them out the front door. I pulled the two men about twenty feet from the shack, then tightened the cord tied around their ankles so they couldn't get loose or walk. Natty was careful with the woman as he eased her onto the snow a few feet from the men.

Couch Potato Man rolled so he could face me. He had a hitch in his voice when he said, "You can't do this."

"Apparently I can." I calmly took Natty by the arm

and led him back into the shack. The door was open so they could clearly see inside. A little psyops, just like the military would use.

Once inside I stoked the fire, found a turkey sub in the refrigerator, and gave half to Natty, then had him plop down on the couch within view of our hosts.

I said in a low voice, "Let them see you eating."

I poked around the shack. Aside from Bailey Mae's coffee cake, there was nothing of any interest. The laptop Couch Potato Man was working on was a high-end model with a tough outer body, and the screen was secured by a password.

When I was done, I grabbed my half of the sub and sat down next to Natty. Both of the men stared at me from outside. I toasted their discomfort with my sub and gave them a smile.

# CHAPTER 30

**NATTY SURPRISED ME** with his compassion. I didn't realize drug dealers were so concerned with other people's needs.

He said, "We can't let that woman die out there."

"She knows how to save herself."

Things were quiet outside. It looked like the woman had passed out. Even though I wouldn't admit it out loud, I was worried, too. After another minute I stood up and casually strolled outside. Even in my coat I felt the bite of the wind. The guy who seemed to be in charge, the one who surprised us with the woman, spoke directly to me.

"You're in way over your head, Mr. Mitchum."

That got my attention.

I said, "Look who's talking. The guy I have in custody. But I'm honored you know my name."

The man kept calm. "Don't wash out here like you did in San Diego with the SEALs. Just walk away from the whole thing. You'll thank me later."

"I'll thank you right now. I'll even let you go when you tell me where my cousin is. I'm impressed you know about my military record. You must have some decent connections."

The man wasn't falling for any of my banter and gave nothing away, but Couch Potato Man was looking increasingly scared and was now shivering uncontrollably.

I stood up and stretched. "Think I might be ready for a nap." I turned toward the shack. That was all Couch Potato Man needed to break.

I took one step and he shouted, "Wait, wait. Get us inside and I'll tell you what you need to know."

# CHAPTER 31

**THE FREEZING WIND** had hurt my exposed face so I knew it had done a number on these three thugs. By the time Couch Potato Man made his plea, I was concerned about leaving the trio out there much longer. I was tempted to take him up on his offer and drag him back inside before he talked, but I knew it could be a ploy. These guys had already proven to be shifty and more cunning than me. Now I had to turn ruthless just to get answers. I needed to hear what he had to say, and I needed to hear it outside. Now.

I looked at Natty and finally said, "Carry the woman inside and cover her with a blanket on the couch."

For a change, Natty did exactly what I asked. He even lifted the woman off the ground completely, instead of dragging her. I had to trust him and not take my eyes off the other two as he secured her inside.

The guy tied to Couch Potato Man gave me a hard stare and said, "You're making a mistake. It's not too late to just walk away."

"If that was true, you wouldn't be trying so hard to

convince me. You know we're about to blow whatever you're up to and the couch potato here is gonna tell me all about it unless he wants to freeze into a statue."

The guy looked at Couch Potato Man and said, "Don't say a goddamn word, Becker."

*Becker,* one more piece of information to file away. But I liked the name Couch Potato Man better. It was more descriptive.

I leaned down and used my knife to cut the cord around the men's legs. When Natty popped his head out, I motioned for him to bring the other man inside as well. It had the right psychological effect on Couch Potato Man.

He was now shivering uncontrollably as ice formed in his eyebrows and his face changed to a dark shade of blue.

"You better start talking," I said.

He hesitated as his eyes drifted past me to the path that disappeared into the woods on the hills.

I rose to my feet, like I was out of patience. Actually, I really was done with this whining fake tough guy. The woman was safe, and I had no more time to waste. I turned and took one step before I heard him say, "Okay, okay."

He had the manic speech of a guy who was not only scared but maybe on too much speed or meth. No wonder I found these guys through a drug dealer. What else was there to do up here so isolated?

"Was there a girl here? Fourteen, cute, brown hair?"

Couch Potato Man shrugged and said, "I guess."

This time I grabbed him by the throat. It felt like I was holding a block of ice. But it got his attention.

He nodded his head. "She was here, she was here, but I'm not sure where she went. She wasn't supposed to see anything. No one was. It was just a misunderstanding."

I looked at the cabin in the wilderness and said, "Why *are* you here? What the hell are you asswipes doing?"

"Look, I answered your question. Do you want to find the girl or not?"

I was tired of being jerked around. I had a lot of questions that needed to be answered. I lost it. I pulled my pistol from my belt and shoved it in the creep's face. The barrel pushed against his nose, making him look like a terrified Porky Pig.

Couch Potato Man knew I was serious and called out, "Try the trail, try the trail." He turned his head and I followed his eyes along the trail that led into the woods. "Straight up the path a ways. She might be up there."

I realized this guy was like the devil. He could tell you what you wanted to hear, but it could also be a lie. The whole setup gave me a bad feeling.

I left the man on the ground as I released my grip and stood up. I said, "Tell me what you're doing here. I don't care what happens to you or the others, I need answers."

Couch Potato Man looked up at me and said, "Who the hell are you anyway?"

"Just a guy worried about his family. Now talk."

"I told you, mister, follow the path and you'll find out everything you need to know."

Then he told me a little about what I might find in the hills. And it didn't sound inviting.

# CHAPTER 32

**WHEN I ENTERED** the cabin, shoving Couch Potato Man in front of me, the other guy who had shown up with the woman said, "You better not have said anything, Becker."

Couch Potato Man just shrugged, still shivering.

Natty and I spent a few minutes securing the men into chairs. The duct tape came in handy, and I couldn't resist using a small square on each man's mouth. They looked like cartoon characters with so much tape and the cords holding them in place. The man who'd come in with the woman was silently furious. I knew he was a guy to watch out for. Hopefully this would go the way I planned. Otherwise he would be an issue later. Men like that never forget and never forgive. Not only had I screwed up his little operation, I had embarrassed him in front of his comrades. He watched me and calculated what he could do to me later.

The woman was unconscious on the couch, and there

was no way she was faking it, so we left the shack and hustled up the trail that Couch Potato Man had told me about.

The walk gave me a few minutes to think. Couch Potato Man had said to follow the trail, but he wasn't clear about exactly what we'd find. That was never a good plan to follow in a situation like this, but I had no choice. I hated the idea of losing Bailey Mae more than anything.

After almost four hundred yards and a steeper than expected incline, I started to understand more of what Couch Potato Man was talking about. I almost ran right past it, hidden in the side of the hill. Instead, I skidded to a stop on the icy path and stared as Natty moved in beside me.

He mumbled, "What the . . . ?"

"Exactly," was all I could say as I stood mesmerized.

An entrance to a subterranean complex sat before us. I couldn't take my eyes off it. I stepped forward and touched the black steel frame around the matching door. It was built solidly into the side of the hill. A bunker, just like Couch Potato Man had told me about. Freezing temperatures are helpful like that.

I paused, considering what could lie beyond the door. More important, I wondered who could be waiting beyond the door. That was a question I should have asked the freezing Couch Potato Man, but I was learning as I went. I had to admit my mistakes.

The door was ajar just a crack. This was where the armed couple had come from. I shoved it open and stood back with the gun in my hand. There was a strong odor of unwashed flesh coming from the dimly lit corridor carved directly from the rock.

Natty said, "I guess he was telling the truth." He reached up and ran his finger across the rough walls.

The corridor was more of a tunnel with a ceiling that hung just above my head, giving me a jolt of claustrophobia. Sounds carried in a place like this, but that was a two-way street. I didn't want to alert anyone who might be down here, so I signaled Natty to keep quiet.

A low yellow light came from the end of the corridor. I took each step like I was walking on rice paper. I was nervous, but knew the answers I needed were somewhere ahead of me.

I marveled at the construction and realized it was extraordinarily well built. What the hell was a bunker doing here? How did they build it without the town talking about it? Unless it was already here and someone just spruced it up. Maybe it had something to do with the resort or even a bomb shelter from the fifties.

As soon as we stepped inside, I could feel nominal heat. Low-level lighting cast shadows on the walls. I found myself swallowing hard. As I moved forward, Natty was right behind me. He didn't care if he showed his fear. I could see a small room up ahead with a cot and some stacked supplies.

My heart pounded in my chest.

As we approached the room, Natty bumped an electrical box built into the wall of the bunker. That's when we heard a man's voice. He was somewhere lost in the shadows of the supply room. In the stillness his words startled me like an air horn. He said, "What was Becker worried about? Nothing, as usual?"

Then I saw him. Sitting on a stool, writing in a ledger. A man in his mid-forties, as bald as the old Mr. Clean from the commercials. He was built like him, too.

Natty and I just stared at him until he looked up. I started to bring my gun up as the man burst off the stool and barreled into us, knocking us onto the ground. Poor Natty acted as a cushion and was trapped beneath the man and me.

The man punched me in the side of the head. I returned an elbow, but at this close range, it had little effect. Natty yelped beneath us.

This was going to be a real fight.

# CHAPTER 33

**THE BALD MAN** was incredibly strong and moved like a cat. He had shoved two full-grown armed men off their feet without using a weapon. The impact and punch had knocked me senseless for a moment, and I'd lost track of my gun, which was somewhere on the hard, roughly finished rock floor.

I had a grip on both of the man's wrists and was trying to slide off Natty so he could breathe and maybe help me in the fight. As we struggled, the powerful man jerked his right hand free, and I felt him reach toward his leg. I figured he had a gun secured somewhere on his ankle. I had already felt the bite of his combat boot as it ripped down my shin.

I tried to stop him from reaching for what I thought was a gun. Then I learned I was wrong. It was worse.

He had a knife—and not a commemorative folding one like mine. This was a full-length, straight-edged combat knife like one a Marine would carry. He got it free of its scabbard and brought it up with his right hand to drive it into my throat.

I blocked the blade and parried it to the side. I could feel the steel edge as it grazed my ear and made a click against the hard floor.

The man twisted on top of me, bringing the knife back up. A knife is a weapon of terror and it was working. I couldn't take my eyes off it. I had almost nothing left.

Then he slid up higher to get his weight into his next thrust. That's when instinct kicked in. My left hand was trapped between us. I shoved it lower, then squeezed. Squeezed with all the power in my hand around his testicles. His face registered surprise, then pain. He rolled to get away, but I held on. Then it was Natty's turn to surprise me.

As soon as we were off him and lying on the hard rock floor, Natty swung his pistol and struck the man square in the face with the butt of the gun. The blow was phenomenal and shattered the man's nose. The fight went out of him at once, and he dropped the knife.

I had to lie on my back and stare at the low ceiling while taking in a few breaths. Between the closed-in space and the knife, I was a little freaked-out. I sat up and scanned the room to make sure he was the only sentinel. I also noticed that there was almost no noise. Our struggle had brought a stillness to the bunker.

The man was laid out, with a broken nose and split upper lip, but he was breathing.

Natty whispered, "What do we do with him?"

"For now we leave him right here. We've gotta search this place for Bailey Mae."

# CHAPTER 34

**WE LEFT THE** man right where he was on the floor of the small supply room and kept moving carefully through the dark hallway, which felt like it was closing in around us and suffocating me.

Across from the supply room there was a long panel of heavy metal grating. It took a moment to realize why the grating enclosed the separate rooms: they were cells, each about the size of a large walk-in closet. The tight pattern of the metal obscured our view, but I could make out the outline of a person in each damp cell.

What the hell?

One cell was open and empty. Inside was a table with straps on it and a water hose connected to a faucet. The sight made my skin crawl and sent a wave of panic through me. Bailey Mae shouldn't be anywhere near a place like this. Whatever this place was.

The people inside the cells started to move forward when they realized Natty and I weren't their regular jailers.

They rattled the doors, and a few said, "Please, out" or
"Open."

I had a bad feeling about the whole situation and realized
we'd stumbled onto something way out of our experience.
It was like we had stepped into hell. We were under-
ground and these people were clearly being tormented.
Natty was so close he bumped against me with every step.
Even though it was cold, I was sweating, and the sweat
stung my eyes and blurred my vision. The odor of human
waste hit me. I ran my fingers over the ceiling to make sure
it wasn't getting lower or narrowing as we walked.

I called out Bailey Mae's name several times but got no
response.

As we moved, I inspected the doors to the cells and saw
that they didn't need a key. Instead, at the top and the
bottom of each door there was a latch that could only be
opened from the outside.

As I started to open the first door, Natty tried to stop
me and said, "We don't know why they're locked up. They
could be dangerous."

"More dangerous than the asshole that just tried to stab
me? Don't be an idiot, Natty. Help me."

"But what if they're criminals?"

"Who locks up criminals in a cave? This isn't Pakistan.
It's upstate New York, for God's sake."

The latches took some effort, but we managed to muscle the doors open. None of the captives jumped up to
get out of the cells immediately. They just stared at us like
they didn't understand what we were doing.

As we worked our way down the hall, I kept asking, "Is there a young girl here?" I noticed all of the prisoners were men and seemed to have trouble with English.

There were no clear answers, and we continued to move forward as we picked up our pace. I screamed, "Bailey Mae!" and looked into each cell.

My hope was fading. What nightmare had we wandered into?

# CHAPTER 35

**AT ABOUT THE** sixth cell, a man in his mid-fifties stepped into the hallway. He was short and frail with streaks of gray in his unwashed hair.

The man said in accented English, "My name is Hassan. I believe the girl is down there." He pointed toward the end of the corridor.

I broke into a run and came to the last cell. It was darker this far down the hall, and when I looked in the cell no one was inside. My heart sank. Then I caught just a hint of movement in the shadows and heard a tiny voice.

"Mitchum? Is that you?"

I stared into the dark cell.

Bailey Mae sat up and a beam of weak light caught her brown hair.

Frantically, I pulled the top latch down, then jerked hard on the lower one and felt the door give. As soon as I had the cell open, Bailey Mae rose from a metal cot and fell into my arms as I stepped inside. I couldn't stop the sob of relief that came out.

She was weak, but alive.

Natty finished releasing everyone from the cells. There were about fifteen, all men. I noticed they were all dark-skinned and probably Middle Eastern. They all turned and started to gather in the supply room. As I hustled down there with Bailey Mae still in my arms, I realized they were surrounding the bald man Natty had hit in the face. The man was conscious now and in a low crouch.

It was clear as they crowded around the hunched jailer that these men were not happy with how they'd been treated. One of them picked up the combat knife that was on the ground nearby.

Although I didn't give a shit about this guy, something inside me made me speak up. "Hold on. We need to let the authorities deal with this jerk-off."

The man who had told me where Bailey Mae was, Hassan, turned and said, "There is nothing they could do to this man that would give us vengeance."

"Just the same, we're gonna lock him in one of the cells until we figure out what's going on." I handed Bailey Mae to Natty so I could face the crowd. I hadn't bothered to find my gun, and although I was the biggest guy there, I realized the numbers were not in my favor.

I said, "He'll be secure in a cell until the police can come."

A man in his forties with a scar on his left cheek and a

beard that meandered down his neck stepped forward and spoke with a heavy accent. "I deal with him." His smile gave away his intentions.

"No, I said we'll let the authorities deal with him."

But that did not sit well with the crowd.

# CHAPTER 36

**ONCE WE SECURED** the bald man in a cell, I faced the former captives. Natty leaned in and said, "We gotta get out of here."

Bailey Mae said, "As long as we take everyone with us."

Natty looked surprised and said, "We can't be responsible for all of these men."

Even in her weakened state, Bailey Mae was resolute. "They're my friends. Hassan helped me and kept talking to me. I'm not leaving without them."

Not only did I not want to argue, but she made sense. If something went wrong and the people in the cabin took control again, these poor men wouldn't have a chance. My only concern was the weather and their weakened condition. I considered the hike back and decided the downward slope to the cabin would help them.

Bailey Mae just gave me a look and I knew that, no matter what, we were bringing these men with us.

I said in a loud voice, "All right, everyone. We have to hike down the hill and it's cold outside. Find whatever you can to wrap yourself up in. Does anyone feel like they can't make it?" I scanned the little crowd and realized there was no way anyone would speak up. They would make it down the hill if their legs were broken.

Natty and I carried Bailey Mae from the bunker and headed back to the cabin, leading the slow-moving group of former captives. I wanted to make the trip as quickly as possible because the men weren't dressed for the weather, but not so fast that they couldn't keep up.

Bailey Mae felt like a feather in my arms but somehow found the strength to hold me around the neck as if she were a rodeo rider. When we reached the cabin, I could tell by Bailey Mae's reaction she knew all three of the people we had tied up. Depending on what she told me, there was a chance I was going to kill one or more of them.

The men crowded into the living room and most of them immediately sat down, exhausted from the hike down from the bunker. They clearly recognized all three of our captives.

Bailey Mae sat next to me at the kitchen counter as I fumbled with my phone to call 911. I told the operator we needed police and fire rescue and that we had multiple injuries. I figured that would get them moving fast. Explaining our exact location was a little more difficult. She wasn't sure who I was, but after I told them to check with Timmy Jones, the dispatcher didn't ask any more questions. I wasn't about to try to explain who my fifteen new friends were. I still didn't know.

It was clear both of the thugs we'd secured in the chairs had struggled and failed to get out of the binds that held them. All I could do was look at them and say, "Nice try, assholes." I had a million questions, but I didn't think these guys were ready to talk, short of me dragging them outside again.

I stepped over to the couch and checked the woman, who was now conscious and staring in disbelief at the men who had been her captives. It looked like she would live, and that was good enough for me.

I took a man's heavy coat from a hanger near the door and slipped it around Bailey Mae. As I leaned in, I said, "Don't worry, kid. Help is on the way."

Natty and I dragged the two chairs with the men tied to them all the way into the kitchen, away from the freed men. I ripped the tape off their mouths, but neither spoke immediately. The man in charge just shook his head and mumbled, "I won't forget you, Mitchum."

"Wish I could forget you and this whole nightmare."

"But you won't be able to. No matter what happens. No matter how this all plays out, I'll still be thinking of how you screwed things up and what I'll do to you the first chance I get."

"What, exactly, did I screw up?"

"A chance to make a difference. A chance to really protect the country. Instead, we're no better off than we were before September 11."

"You really believe that, don't you?"

"Someone has to."

"How does torturing a few scared men protect anything?"

"You don't get it, do you, Mitchum? It's all connected. The Middle East, Europe, the US; every action has a consequence. From supporting Hamas to supplying electrical parts that could be used to bring down a jet. It's all connected and you're gonna have to live with the guilt when shit happens because of what you did here."

I was tired of this guy. "How does kidnapping a little girl protect anything?"

"I didn't say we were perfect. Accidents happen, people make mistakes. One day I hope you're collateral damage to an accident."

I just stared at him as I fantasized about shooting this creep in the head, but I wasn't like him. Thank God I wasn't like him and I had to know there was a difference between us. I gave him a smirk, then turned my back on him. I hoped for good.

When I stepped out of the kitchen, Bailey Mae reached out to take my hand.

She pulled me closer and whispered in my ear, "I knew you'd find me."

That one sentence, those few words, made all this worthwhile. But I was still confused, and confusion doesn't sit well with a guy like me. I like to see a problem and tackle it. Head-on. This was a puzzle, and I didn't see a clear answer. I straightened up. The freed men were all looking at me to see what my next move would be.

I looked over at Couch Potato Man, who had remained unusually quiet. I said, "You guys feel tough locking up a little girl?"

He didn't say a word.

Bailey Mae tugged on my arm and waited for me to lean down so her mouth was close to my ear. She said, "I saw it, Mitchum."

"Saw what?"

She nodded at Couch Potato Man. "I was delivering my coffee cakes to the Wilkses and I saw that man shoot them. They worked with these people. Mr. Wilks found this place for them. I heard them argue about money, and Mr. Wilks said he'd tell the media about it. That's when that guy shot them. Bang, bang, without any hesitation. I was so scared I couldn't move. He turned around with the pistol in his hand, and the only thing I did was put down my coffee cakes and freeze."

Now I definitely didn't regret anything I had done to the man tied in the chair.

# CHAPTER 37

**ON THE OTHER** side of the cabin, the former captives sat in a group as the realization that they had been rescued sank in. Each man accepted it in his own way. One younger man, maybe only twenty, leaned against the wall, sobbing quietly. Several others were smiling or laughing with the joy of being free and out of that hellhole. Two middle-aged men eyed Couch Potato Man and my other two prisoners with palpable malice. I worried that I might have to step over there just to keep the peace, but I had no doubt that these thugs had earned the hatred of the captives.

I tried to imagine being caged in that smelly hole and wondering if I'd ever get out. The idea gave me the willies. It made me realize everything I'd miss. My family, even my brother, was important to me, but so was the whole town. It made me angry to think that someone tried to take that from these men. I almost considered letting them take their revenge. Instead, I plopped silently onto a stool by the kitchen.

Neither of the men we'd subdued looked scared. They didn't even look worried. I didn't like it. The man who had threatened me took in the whole room, listening to what was being said, and seemed to be calculating something. What he was calculating I couldn't say, but the gears were turning in his head.

None of us spoke as we waited for the cavalry to arrive. Bailey Mae stayed close to me, sitting on a stool next to the breakfast bar in the kitchen. I noticed she wanted Hassan near her as well. Despite all the mind-blowing shit going on, my main concern was Bailey Mae. She was a strong girl and had done a phenomenal job just staying alive. She was also the key to justice for these men. At least one of the men in custody was guilty of a double homicide. Could they have somehow murdered Mabel as well?

Timmy Jones was the first to come jogging up the path, calling his exact location into his radio. He skidded to a stop at the front door and took in the scene before looking at me and saying, "Are you guys all right?" Then he looked farther inside the cabin and said, "Who are all these people? Is this some kind of immigrant smuggling ring?"

I stepped outside the cabin and gave him a very quick rundown, only hitting the high points. I told him about the bunker complex, the man locked up in the cell, how we'd released the prisoners, the fight in the cabin. Other than that, I had no real answers yet. But I intended to get them. I wondered if the blank stare he was giving me was similar to the one that had been on my face an hour earlier.

I said, "I know it sounds unbelievable, but you'll see the bunker and the cells soon enough. And Bailey Mae positively identified a man inside as the one who shot the Wilkses. She was an eyewitness."

Timmy tried to hide his shock by looking up the path, then back at me, saying, "I never even knew this was back here."

Within minutes, more patrol cars arrived and someone figured out how to access the path so a rescue vehicle with four-wheel drive could make it up from the lower cabins.

I grabbed Timmy by the arm and said, "There's a bald guy locked in one of the cells. He attacked me with a knife. Natty was a witness. The guy is strong and knows how to fight, so be careful when you or your people deal with him."

A few minutes later, two deputies brought the bald man down in handcuffs. One of the deputies had a bloody lip, and his shirt was pulled out of his pants. The bald man had a red mark across his face where someone had used an expandable baton to get his attention. They tied him up with the others in the kitchen.

Bailey Mae was still sitting next to Hassan. The man was weak and had started shivering. I wasn't sure what else to do, so I draped a blanket over him. The cabin was getting busier as more blankets were brought in for the other men. No one had been transported yet, and there was a great deal of confusion about what to do with everyone.

I leaned in close to Hassan and said in a low voice, "What the hell is going on?"

He shook his head. "I live in Marblehead, just outside of Boston. About a month ago, two men questioned me at my convenience store. They said I was aiding terrorists by donating money to a relief fund. That same night I found myself here, being interrogated." He looked around the room and said, "The man over there"—he pointed to a figure on the floor with a blanket over him—"lives in Yonkers and was brought here just last week. We were all questioned over and over."

Natty had crept up behind us and said, "By Americans?"

The man nodded solemnly.

Natty said, "The FBI?"

The man shrugged. "The bald man on the kitchen floor is in charge. He used the table and water hose to scare us. It felt like I was drowning. He would ask the same questions over and over. He's the one all of my friends want to kill right now."

Right then I realized the people doing this were private contractors. Most of them had been in the military and were hired by some firm contracted by the US government to handle the interrogation and housing of potential threats to national security.

This was bullshit.

# CHAPTER 38

**EVEN THOUGH IT** was the middle of the night, more emergency vehicles had come up the path. There was no doubt the truck with the snowplow had kept this path clear.

I stood at the cabin's front door and watched as a string of vehicles rolled into the open space by the narrow road. They were all black SUVs, and I knew something was up.

A tall woman slid out of the rear seat of the second SUV and I heard her say to a deputy, "Who's in charge here?" She was directed to Timmy, who was standing near me, helping figure out how badly each prisoner needed medical attention.

The woman marched directly to Timmy and flipped open her ID case, showing that she worked for Homeland Security. As if to emphasize her position of power, six men and two women climbed out of the other vehicles, each armed with a different type of automatic weapon. I immediately recognized the unique silhouettes of M16s and saw some more exotic weapons, like a Heckler & Koch, as well as a tricked-out Winchester sniper rifle. None of the agents wore fatigues. Instead, they had on mismatched ski vests and jeans, creating the illusion that they were just like everyone else. But they weren't. They were all in their mid-thirties and in good shape, and each knew to keep watch on a different area. It was clear they'd had military training.

Timmy was shaken by the show of force and waved the fire rescue people back to their jobs. He even called out, "Let's make sure we have all of these men transported in the next twenty minutes." He turned his attention back to the woman and said, "How can I help you Ms.—?"

"Kravitz, Cheryl Kravitz. I'm here to take charge of this scene."

Timmy Jones showed no sign of backing down. He said, "This is our scene. We have it in hand. Thank you."

I was impressed with Timmy's spine. He was a good friend, but not someone you'd usually think of as standing up to the US government.

Agent Kravitz said, "I misspoke. I'm here to take charge of several of the people you have in custody. This is a matter of national security and I *do* have the authority." This was a woman who was used to getting what she wanted.

Timmy said, "Who do you want to take?"

Agent Kravitz leaned in the door and surveyed the room. Then she faced him again. "The three men in the kitchen and the injured woman for now." She looked back inside and added, "We'll decide how to handle the others after we take the ones in the kitchen."

"We're about to transport the woman to the hospital."

"We'll take care of any medical needs." The woman turned and signaled to a man in the closest SUV, who started to walk toward the cabin.

Timmy raised his hands, and I stepped closer to back him up. He said, "One of the men you want to take right now is suspected in a double homicide. The bald guy in the kitchen will be charged with assault. We can take care of both of those matters."

Agent Kravitz said, "Who did he assault?"

Now I spoke up. "Me." I reached up and touched my ear, which was still leaking a little blood.

"You call that an assault?"

"He did it with a KA-BAR knife. Maybe that's attempted murder."

She gave me a cold stare and said, "And you are . . . ?"

"Mitchum. I came for Bailey Mae."

The woman said, "Who's Bailey Mae?"

"The little girl your friends held in a cell up in that bunker. She's coming with me, and I don't care how many agents with guns try to stop me." I gave her the stink eye, although I think it had little impact.

Agent Kravitz looked at my ear and said, "So, Mr. Mitchum, you were trespassing when someone tried to stop you. Dress it up any way you want, but you got what you deserved."

"Dress it up any way you want, but this is bullshit. Those men in there had no due process. Your people ran amok."

"I never said they were 'my people.' I just said we were taking them. And that is exactly what is going to happen."

My blood was rising, and I felt the flash of heat in my face. "The other men have to stay. They need medical attention. There's no way we're gonna let you take those men with you." I had to look over at Timmy to make sure we were in agreement. I was going to need help if I took on the federal government in the form of Cheryl Kravitz.

Agent Kravitz considered my comments, then glanced back in the cabin at the men huddled in the living room. I could see her working through the scenarios in her head. All these witnesses could cause a lot of trouble. She couldn't take us. Could she?

Finally the federal agent said, "Be my guest, but the three men and the woman are coming with me right now."

"You don't care that one of the men is a murderer?"

"On the contrary, Mr. Mitchum, I do care and we will deal with that issue. But due to national security, that's not going to happen here in front of a bunch of locals like you."

Two of the men from the SUVs stepped past us into the cabin to gather up the people they intended to take. As long as Bailey Mae was safe and they didn't try to recapture any of these dispirited men, I didn't intend to engage in a shoot-out.

I stepped inside and herded Bailey Mae, Natty, and Hassan toward the group of men we had liberated. I stood between them and the Homeland Security agents as Agent Kravitz stepped inside and motioned for the former jailers to follow her.

No one said a word. At this point I didn't want Timmy and his people to risk getting hurt, either. Agent Kravitz paused by the door and took one last look around the cabin.

I glared at her.

The federal agent chose not to even acknowledge me and turned back to Timmy. "I'll need your people to get their vehicles out of the way so we can leave."

I stepped to the door and heard Agent Kravitz say to Timmy, "We will look into the need for filing any charges for assault on any of the men or women working here."

I couldn't help the snort that came out as I said, "Good luck with that." The truth was this woman did scare me a little bit. The whole situation was scary. No one would judge this as normal.

She looked at me and said, "I think you would do well to remain silent, Mr. Mitchum."

She used the phrase "remain silent" instead of "be quiet." She knew her shit, and she knew how to intimidate.

Watching the assholes I had tangled with walk freely toward the SUVs, I just couldn't keep my mouth shut. I leaned out the door, shaking off Natty and Bailey Mae, who tried to stop me. "This is bullshit! He's a murderer and people are not going to stand for it. We won't forget this."

Agent Kravitz didn't even turn around. She just called over her shoulder, "Neither will we."

When I turned, Bailey Mae darted into my arms. I squeezed her just to make sure it wasn't a dream. This was real. She was why I was here. But now I had other responsibilities.

Turning, I looked at the group of men we had rescued. I wasn't about to leave until I was certain they were safe. Timmy looked completely flummoxed but was starting to organize the stunned emergency workers again after everything had come to a halt when the feds showed up.

Three ambulances had pulled in. The injured woman had already been taken away by Homeland Security.

"Timmy," I said, "let's get three men into each ambulance and then a couple with each paramedic. We need to get them checked out."

"Yeah, good idea, Mitchum."

I didn't want to make it look like I was giving orders, but we had to get moving.

Hassan paused before he followed a paramedic out the door. He held out his hand, and when I took it, he said, "We will not forget this, my friend. What you did took great courage. Bailey Mae is lucky to have a cousin like you."

I gave him a smile and nod as I shook his hand.

Some of the others waved and shouted their thanks until it was just Timmy, Natty, Bailey Mae, and me.

"What do you think will happen to the people the feds took?"

Timmy shrugged. "I never saw anything like that. The sheriff told me they were legit and I had to let them take the prisoners. I hope they take action."

I slapped Timmy on the back as we walked toward our

cars down at the front of the property. "You're a good man, Timmy." I thought he was naive, but his heart was in the right place and that was important to me.

I realized there was a big bad world out there and I'd spent most of my life in Marlboro, New York, trying to avoid it. The world worked in mysterious and unethical ways, but it was time I took my head out of the sand and stood up to it.

The one thing I wasn't going to let drop was Mabel's death. I knew in my heart it was connected to this mess, probably because she showed me photos of the three strangers. No matter what happened, I intended to find some answers, but that could wait for another day.

I wrapped my arm around Bailey Mae as we walked. I was thankful that at least I got what I had come for and couldn't wait to see Bailey Mae and her mother reunited. We had also managed to free the men held in those terrible conditions. Now, that was a victory I'd accept.

Life here in Marlboro had its moments.

# MALICIOUS

JAMES PATTERSON
& JAMES O. BORN

# CHAPTER 1

**I HAD RACED** through my paper route this morning, chucking papers onto the frozen front yards of Marlboro, New York, in January. Normally, I'd stop and chat with the customers who happened to be up around dawn, but today I just waved. It's a shame, because that's my favorite part of the job.

Now I was in my unofficial office for my unofficial second job. For the past few years I had made my office in a little diner off Route 9 named Tina's Plentiful. Tina didn't mind, because I occasionally brought in a little extra traffic. I have to admit that lately there hadn't been much extra traffic. But right now, Edith Ledbetter sat across from me with a pleasant look on her aging face. No one under seventy is ever named Edith. She'd approached me about three months ago to see if I could locate her estranged daughter. They hadn't spoken in twenty-six years, since the daughter turned twenty-one and thought that Syracuse University had turned her into the smartest human on earth.

But years have a way of making people lonely and feel their regrets more acutely. Even after I explained that I wasn't a licensed private investigator, Edith said that she didn't care and hired me on the spot. Word-of-mouth recommendations in the community had helped me. I was honest and generally let my clients decide how much they wanted to pay.

We'd been waiting together almost forty-five minutes and there was no sign of the daughter. She had told me she would be at the diner at eight o'clock. I didn't like the looks of this at all.

Edith said, "It's some kind of miracle that you found Linda after all these years."

"All I really did was use the internet. It wasn't that big a deal."

"And you drove all the way down to Philadelphia." Edith looked up at the clock on the wall between the two framed posters of the California coastline. "Are you sure she really wanted to see me?"

I hoped Edith wasn't keeping track of the time.

"Of course she wants to see you." It was a shade of the truth. The daughter had been hesitant, but when I told her about the sweet eighty-year-old woman who missed her, she had agreed to meet at the diner when she was on a trip to Albany with her husband.

The new waitress, Alicia, flashed me a wide smile from the counter. She was the only one here I had let in on the plan. Her intelligent eyes darted to the front door. She sensed my apprehension. I just shrugged.

Edith said, "Maybe she changed her mind. She's waited this long. I bet it was too much for her."

Alicia came by with some coffee for us and chatted with Edith about her homemade sweater and how nice her new glasses looked.

Alicia, God bless her, knew to keep Edith's mind off the time.

I said, "Edith, there could have been a mix-up. Although the roads are clear, it's awfully cold and it might've changed Linda's plans. Should we wait at your house where you might be more comfortable?"

"But what if Linda shows up and we're not here?"

I looked at Alicia, who was still standing right next to our booth, and said, "I bet I could talk Alicia into calling us if Linda comes later."

Alicia nodded. She had replaced Mabel, a young woman whose death was still a mystery and haunted me. I respected the fact that Alicia had moved back to Marlboro to care for her father while he recovered from a stroke.

Just as I got Edith to her feet and we turned toward the front, I noticed a woman in an expensive leather coat standing silently just inside the door. It took me a moment to realize it was the same woman I'd spoken to in Pennsylvania three weeks earlier. She just stared at us. That's when my anger melted away. This woman was scared.

As I held Edith by the arm, I felt her tense and knew that she had recognized her daughter even after two and a half decades. Edith took a tentative step forward. The few people in the diner didn't even realize what was happening, but Alicia did. She wrapped my hand in hers and squeezed it.

I watched in excited silence as Edith moved closer to her daughter. Suddenly Linda burst forward and hugged her mother. They both started to cry. So did Alicia. Damn it, so did I, but I was able to cover it well.

They both plopped down in the booth closest to where they'd been standing, holding each other's hands across the table.

Then my phone rang and I saw it was my brother, Natty.

I thought about ignoring the call. Now wasn't the time and Natty wasn't the person I wanted to talk to. I hate to confess it, but the scene made me really want to call my mom.

But guilt got the better of me and I answered the phone, "Hey, what's up?"

"I never thought I'd say this, but I need your help. I need your private investigator skills."

My brother wasn't much for compliments. I was skeptical and knew my brother could be a jackass. I always had to be on the lookout for pranks.

I said, "What kind of case?"

"A homicide. I'm not kidding, Mitchum, I need your help right now."

I looked up at Edith and her daughter, who were chatting like family should, and told Natty, "I'm on my way."

If there was one thing I knew about my brother, it was that he had a knack for making mistakes. And it seemed like this one was deadly.

# CHAPTER 2

**I DIDN'T GENERALLY** look forward to seeing my brother at his place of business in Newburgh, about twenty-five minutes south of Marlboro. He worked out of a bar called the State of Mind Tavern that didn't seem to ever close. It was a dingy, one-story building that spanned a full block, with the parking lot on one side and a busy, industrial street on the other.

As I pulled my beat-up station wagon into the lot, I saw my brother standing by the back door talking to two other men. My brother is two years older than me and thin as a rail, mostly from a life of cigarettes, skipped meals, and little sleep. Despite resembling a sickly marathon runner, he's surprisingly tough. My theory is it has something to do with being a minor-league dope dealer in a tough town like Newburgh.

At the moment, though, he looked like he might be overmatched as he exchanged angry words with two guys. One was built like him and the other was a Hispanic guy who obviously spent way too much time in the gym; he had arms like legs.

I walked up casually, not wanting to give away my intentions. But I knew it might annoy my brother that I didn't look worried.

The big man turned and saw me and waved me toward the back door of the bar, saying, "Move on. This has nothing to do with you."

I noticed my brother had a bloody lip and a red splotch across his left cheek. That pissed me off. Generally, I was the only one allowed to pound on my brother once in a while.

I said, "Everything all right, Natty?"

"Does it look like everything's all right?"

I admired my brother's bravado in the face of adversity.

I said, "You guys think you could step away from my brother for a minute? Maybe we can talk about the issue." I was serious, even though I probably was coming across as a smart-ass.

The smaller guy, wiry like my brother, who I'd already determined was in charge, said, "Ain't nothing to discuss. Got nothing to do with you."

"Except, like I said, he's my brother. Mom expects to see him in one piece."

The wiry guy looked over his shoulder and said, "Manny, deal with this."

Everyone talks about how big guys are scary, but if you've been in a couple of fights, you learned a few things about dealing with giant, angry people. I let this behemoth turn toward me and square off just so I could get an idea of his abilities. Usually, when you're that big, you don't bother to learn the subtleties of martial arts or boxing. This guy was no exception. He balled up both fists and took a wide stance in front of me. I could've played with him and made it look like I had real skills, but instead I used an old, simple trick. I lifted my left hand high in the air and watched his eyes follow it like a puppy watching a ball. Then I used my right leg like a punter and brought it up right between his legs. The big man crumpled onto the ground while he tried to suck in some air.

The wiry guy spun away from my brother and started to reach under his shirt. My brother shoved him hard toward me, and I lifted my elbow to catch him square in the chin. When he stumbled back onto the ground, I stepped over and found the small, cheap .380 automatic pistol he was reaching for. I dropped the magazine and ejected the round in the chamber. Then I threw the thing down hard on the street and was shocked to see it skip along the asphalt and drop into a drain. It was like I had scored a goal in hockey. Without thinking about it, I reached up and my brother gave me a high five. Just like when we were kids.

I helped the giant man with the sore crotch stand and then grabbed the wiry guy by the arm.

"You guys need to be on your way. You can talk to Natty some other time." Somehow, I knew the nice, rented Cadillac parked right next to us was theirs, and I opened the door and stuffed the big guy behind the wheel.

After a minute, when they slowly pulled out of the parking lot, my brother said, "Thanks, little brother."

"Friends of yours?"

"He's the guy I think committed that homicide I called you about."

# CHAPTER 3

**I WAITED UNTIL** the two men had pulled away in the rented Cadillac, then turned to my brother and said, "Is that what you called me about?"

"No, something else."

"You aren't gonna tell me?"

"It's nothing. Business dispute. No big deal."

"Who in the hell were they?"

Natty was rubbing his face where the big man had slapped him. "One of 'em is Alton Beatty, my competition and the main suspect in the homicide I called you about."

"Who's dead? I mean, aside from the usual homicide victims that pile up here in Newburgh."

The way Natty hesitated made me realize the case really did mean something to him. Maybe it'd mean something to me as well.

Natty said, "Pete Stahl was shot and killed on Friday."

I cocked my head. "Petey Stahl from Highland Middle School?"

"The same."

I felt my legs go a little weak and leaned on the hood of an old Dodge. "I haven't talked to him in a few months, but seriously? I really like that guy. Even though he became a..."

"Drug dealer?"

"I'm sorry, Natty, I didn't mean it like that."

Natty said, "I know." Then he surprised me by putting his arm around my shoulder.

Petey was a year older than my brother and three years ahead of me, but I remembered him as a decent football player and one of my brother's few friends who didn't pick on me too much. When I got out of the Navy, we would play basketball and complain about my brother.

"Does Mom know?"

"Yeah, she's the one who suggested I call you. She and Pete's mom talk all the time and his mom is heartbroken. Not just because he was killed, but because no one seems to care. The police aren't even doing anything about it."

I thought about the boy I knew and the man who still seemed like a decent guy, no matter what he did for a living. Now he was dead.

Natty said, "He was a good friend and a good business associate."

I shook my head and said, "You mean dope dealer? At least call it by its name. I understand what you do, but I don't like it."

"Jeez, Mitchum, this isn't the 1970s. No one calls it dope anymore. That's insulting to our customers. We *enhance recreational activities.* Or, if you have to label us, you can say 'drug dealer,' but the word *dope* is offensive."

"So why is Alton Beatty a 'competitor' and Pete Stahl an 'associate'?"

"Because Alton is overly ambitious. That's why I think he killed Pete. They both focus more on meth and some of the more synthetic stuff, and the rumor was they made a big score in the city about a month ago."

"What kind of score?"

"Money and maybe something else. Sounded like some kind of recipe for a variation of meth. I know there's some Canadian dudes who're really interested in it and would pay big money to have it."

I was still wrapping my head around the fact that a kid I used to play football with was dead. This was tough to swallow and started me thinking about how it could've been Natty. I saw Pete's mom every once in a while and knew I wouldn't be able to face her if I didn't get involved. More than that, I had to give her some closure.

Natty said, "There's one other thing I should tell you."

"What's that?"

"You know how Pete was married?"

"Yeah, but I never met her."

"She's a beautiful girl named Katie. She wasn't involved in his business and still doesn't know exactly what he did for a living."

"Yeah, so?"

Natty said, "I think I'm in love with her."

# CHAPTER 4

**THE FIRST THING** I wanted to do was get a look at the scene of the murder. That also got me away from the bar where my brother did business. His life depressed me.

I knew the streets of Newburgh pretty well because I'd lived in Marlboro most of my life. Newburgh is a bigger town that is visually interesting, with grand brick buildings and a downtown that could've been a background for movies about small-town America.

Now the city has seen some rough times and the only neighborhoods that are livable, at least if you have kids, are in the suburbs. The three-story brownstones have blue tarps on the roofs and duct tape patching cracks in the windows.

Route 9 or, as we call it in the city, South Robinson Avenue, weaves through a mixture of industrial, commercial, and residential areas that no longer give the impression of a prosperous city.

Natty told me Pete had been shot Friday night in front

of a well-known drug house on North Miller Street near Farrington Street. It was just a block east of Downing Park, which covered a little bit of the inner city in a blanket of green peppered with some baseball fields. I guess you could call it their version of Central Park.

My ten-year-old station wagon, with its shocks that'd been worn out from carrying bundles of newspapers in the back all the time, sounded like an old diesel trawler as I puttered through the city. I parked more than a block away so I wouldn't attract attention.

Two boys, around six, with a small black dog stared at me as I stepped out of the car. I smiled and said, "Hey, boys."

As I stepped onto the sidewalk, their dog trotted over to me and started sniffing my leg. "He smells my dog on me."

"Where's your dog?"

I thought about Bart Simpson, my mutt, who preferred the heat of my house to the winter wind, and said, "My house."

"Why do you have a dog if you don't bring him with you?"

"That is a good point and I'll remember it."

As I walked along the uneven sidewalk, I noticed several sets of eyes on me and reached in my pocket to feel the familiar weight of my commemorative Navy knife with a combat blade. Generally, I only use it to open boxes and cut the straps on bundles of papers, but I *had* used it to defend myself. I briefly thought about my Beretta back at the house, but I was never one of those guys who felt like he needed to carry a gun all the time. That's how a place like this city got to be a place like this city.

The spot where Pete died was on the steps of a three-story brick brownstone that looked abandoned. The vacant lot next to it had been used as a dumping ground for God knew how long. Plastic bags were stuck on the sagging chain-link fence and piles of trash blew all over the lot. An old pickup truck rusted near the back fence.

A line of young men on the porch of the house next door watched me. Despite the cold, a couple of them sat on a sagging couch wearing nothing but wifebeater undershirts. They were showing off how tough they were.

I had to shake my head and mutter, "Idiots."

There was still evidence of the crime scene right on the steps leading up to the front door of the house. I saw pieces of police tape, and the dark stain on two of the steps had to be blood. No one bothered to clean places like this very thoroughly after a murder. It was the same everywhere. Only this was a place where someone I knew had died.

I crouched down to examine the stain and looked up to see if I could figure out what had happened. The little I had learned on the internet about the shooting said that Pete was unarmed and stumbled onto the stairs with two gunshot wounds to his abdomen. At the time, people had been renting the house, but they had all fled the night of the shooting. It had been nothing but a drug house for the past decade, and no one seemed to be able to do anything about it. The whole situation made me ashamed of my brother and how he made a living.

As I crouched there, drawing the attention of the neighbors, a dark-blue Ford Crown Victoria pulled to the curb directly in front of the house. All it needed was lights on the top to advertise it was a police car. I stood slowly and turned as the car door opened.

A big man, an inch taller than me with more meat on his shoulders, emerged from the car, looked at me, and said, "Hey, dropout, what do you think you're doing in the big city?"

# CHAPTER 5

**I STARED AT** the Newburgh detective, who wore a heavy coat over a cheap shirt and tie, and remembered his name was Mike Tharpe. Last time I'd seen him, a few months ago, he'd also thought it was funny to call me "dropout." I guess it was true, I *had* dropped out of Navy SEAL training during my final week. But it wasn't exactly a decision on my part. Either way, I accepted my past. Now I needed some questions answered and I didn't need to antagonize a cop, especially if he was trying to jostle me.

As the detective stepped toward me, one of the men on the porch made a pretty good pig grunt. It carried across the open space. The men on the porch all started to laugh.

Tharpe looked up at the man who had made the noise and said, "You must've heard that last night from your mom when I was visiting. Sometimes she likes to make a sound like an elephant, too, ya know?" That sent an uncomfortable silence through the group. The man who had made the sound was clearly furious. It made no impact on the veteran Newburgh detective.

Tharpe looked at me and said, "If you're looking for your brother, he usually hangs out at a bar on South Robinson Street."

"You mean the State of Mind Tavern? I know. I talked to him a little while ago."

"What brings you here? I mean to this neighborhood."

"My brother said a friend of ours was killed here."

"You knew Peter Stahl?"

"He grew up in Marlboro." For some reason I didn't want this guy to know how much Pete meant to me. It was like he hadn't earned the right to know my pain. I said, "My brother told me what happened and I was curious about his murder."

"Murder! He died of natural causes."

I stared at the detective and said, "I read that he was shot to death."

"That *is* natural causes for a dope dealer."

"Drug dealer."

"What?"

"No one calls it dope anymore. They call themselves *drug* dealers." I usually didn't split hairs but did when it annoyed someone in a position of authority.

# CHAPTER 6

**THARPE SIGHED, THEN** took a few minutes to explain what had happened. He led me toward the house, pointing through the open door into the hallway.

"Near as I can figure, one of the local dopers"—he paused and looked at me—"sorry, *drug dealers,* thought Stahl was moving in on his territory and made a business decision."

We climbed the five stone steps to the landing in front of the door. The men from next door were acting like we didn't exist, which was fine with me.

Once we were in the hallway, Tharpe looked at me and said, "Did you know Stahl well?"

I calculated my answer carefully. I shrugged my shoulders and said, "My brother says you guys aren't doing everything you could to solve the shooting."

Tharpe stiffened at that. "If I did everything I could on every shooting in this screwed-up town, I wouldn't have time to sleep." His face turned a little red. "Peter Stahl sold dope and got shot. It's the natural order of things. Happens all the time. That's what we call the 'price of doing business.'"

We stood in the door and looked out onto the street. Tharpe explained to me how Pete had stumbled out of the vacant lot next door before he fell onto the steps. He said, "Stahl had been shot twice at close range. No one heard the shots and only a couple of locals acknowledged the body. By the time the crime scene was secured and police arrived, the only evidence was a body on the steps and a pistol that was found in the lot. It's being examined, but there's no telling what they'll find, or when. Our backlog would blow your mind. One of our narcotics guys thinks it might have been Stahl's own gun." He looked out over the neighborhood. "I don't know why we try so hard. There were no casings recovered, no witness who claimed to have seen anything or heard the shots, and all we got was an anonymous call to 911."

I thought about the facts: gunshot death of a known drug dealer. No witnesses. There wasn't much I could do. The police had declared the death a homicide and the listed potential motive as drug-related activity. That was about as much work as the Newburgh police intended to put into the case. I knew I had to at least do something. I wasn't sure I could face Pete's mom or sisters otherwise. They needed to know that someone had looked at the case.

I listened as Tharpe explained what he thought happened and how the police responded. This time I asked him, "Did *you* know Pete?"

"Knew his name from my days in narcotics. Just another lowlife." He held up his hand and said, "No offense. I mean, about your brother."

"None taken. He *is* a lowlife. But he's also my brother, and Pete was my friend, so I'm going to help."

Tharpe turned and focused his full attention on me. He said, "Look, I'm a fellow vet. Did four years in the Marines. I'm telling you, you need to give up being everyone's unpaid private investigator. The Newburgh police are looking for veterans right now. We got some kind of grant to hire them. It's a decent job with a good retirement. No one will hold anything your brother has done against you. You'd like the feeling of camaraderie again."

I was surprised by the offer, and I'd be lying if I said I didn't consider it for a minute. My main career as a paperboy wasn't everything I'd hoped it would be. And with this new job, I'd still be able to live in Marlboro in my little house surrounded by all my family. But I knew this wasn't the time to give an answer.

As we started to walk back outside, Tharpe said, "Sure, there are some headaches on the job. You have to put up with punks and shits, but you also get to knock heads once in a while and do some good. You should think about it."

It was a charming offer, but I was never much for

"knocking heads." And my experience told me that "punks" often matured into decent human beings. Of course, that experience mainly came from being in the Navy, which had a tendency to straighten people out.

Right now I wasn't interested in anything other than the person who killed my friend.

# CHAPTER 7

**I DIDN'T TELL** Natty about my chat with Detective Tharpe as we drove in his new, leased Chevy Camaro to a nice area outside Newburgh close to Firthcliffe, in an upscale development. I wondered if any of Pete's neighbors had known what he did for a living. My bet was that he was smart enough to do business away from his home, especially since he'd been keeping his job from his wife, Katie. Apparently, she didn't even know what business Pete was involved in. Not all drug dealers show that kind of common sense.

As we pulled into the cul-de-sac where Pete Stahl had lived with Katie in a small, single-story house, Natty started acting weird, even weirder than usual. I had no idea what was going on inside that foggy brain of his, but I felt like he was holding something back from me. He clearly didn't feel like talking just yet. I suspected it had something to do with his feelings for Pete's widow.

We parked in the driveway behind a new BMW and I noticed a woman standing at the front door. As I climbed out of Natty's low Camaro, I realized the woman was much younger than I thought she'd be, probably not yet twenty-five. Her loose blond hair, blowing in the breeze, made her look like the girl next door. The beautiful one. Her face lit up as soon as she saw Natty. She wore jeans and a bulky sweater and those crazy boots younger women tended to wear, the ones with the name like "Neanderthal."

Natty introduced us and she had good manners, smiling as she shook my hand and looked me in the eye. She said, "Thank you for helping us. The Newburgh police have been polite, but they showed no real interest in Pete's murder."

I hadn't realized that Natty had told her I was taking the case. I liked her direct approach.

She served us iced tea as we sat on the couch. I couldn't help but glance around at her collection of the Peanuts characters in all shapes and forms, from ceramic to stuffed. The place had a certain childlike warmth to it that I was sure came from her. Even though they didn't have any kids, there were stuffed animals lying around on chairs and her beagle lay quietly in the corner, wearing a homemade knitted sweater.

Katie noticed my interest in the surroundings and said, "I use the toys for my job. I work with kids and they like to play with stuffed animals."

She sat down on a plush chair across from me, and for

the first time I noticed her bloodshot eyes. She had been crying. Maybe it was a cumulative effect from the last few days. I felt her sense of loss.

It made me think how easy it is to write off shootings reported on the news. No matter who was killed—a drug dealer, a gang member, or some poor guy walking down the street who was hit by a stray bullet—they were someone's husband or child.

Katie said, "A detective talked to me on Saturday, but I could tell he was just going through the motions. I'm not stupid, I knew Pete was involved in some shady business, but we had an understanding. I didn't ask as long as he was careful. He also promised me he never hurt anyone. I know that our relationship wasn't perfect, but anything you could do to help find out who killed Pete would mean the world to me."

I said, "I'll do what I can, but right now there are absolutely no leads. I was hoping you might be able to tell me something about the night he was shot."

"No one could ever say Pete wasn't a hard worker. He was ambitious. He worked every Friday and Saturday night. It was one of the things that had driven us apart. I don't know what he was doing the night he was killed, but he usually wandered home around two or three in the morning. The Newburgh police came by and told me what had happened somewhere around one."

"Can you think of any reason someone would want to kill your husband?"

She just stared at me with those wide blue eyes and

shook her head. "Pete was a great guy. No one wanted to hurt him."

She stood up and took our glasses into the kitchen. A few moments later, she was back and sat on the arm of the chair that Natty was sitting in. She draped her hand across his shoulder and gave him a hug and a kiss on the top of his head. It was a show of affection for comfort. But it was obvious.

Natty avoided eye contact with me as I got a clear picture of what was going on. This was not a one-sided relationship.

# CHAPTER 8

**MY BROTHER AND** I were quiet on the ride back through town to his office. I couldn't help but notice the number of abandoned buildings downtown and the lack of effort to clean up any of the garbage along the street or in vacant lots. This place was an advertisement for the "broken window theory" of government.

When we were inside the State of Mind Tavern and seated at Natty's personal table, he turned to me and said, "There's probably some more you need to know about what's going on."

"No kidding." I just stared at my brother, who remained silent until I said, "I'm listening."

Natty looked around nervously. The bartender who doubled as his bodyguard was used to me by now and didn't pay too much attention to our conversations. Finally, Natty said, "Katie told me she loved me, too. I mean, um, we've developed sort of a relationship. You know what I'm saying."

"Since Pete was killed Friday night?"

"No, it's been going on for a little while. She mentioned to you how they had drifted apart."

"But you said you thought you loved her. Didn't you also say she was faithful to Pete?"

"That's true. It's just how we feel about each other. It's not like we've slept together. She's not that kind of girl."

I appreciated the fact that my brother could still surprise me. I considered his awkward confession and finally said, "You didn't have anything to do with Pete's murder, did you?"

Natty looked hurt. "Do you have to ask?"

"Yes, of course I do. Natty, you're a criminal by trade. You've got a thing for a guy's wife. If the cops knew this you would be their only suspect. So I have to ask if you killed Pete."

Natty looked down toward the table and shook his head. "No, I didn't kill Pete."

I leaned back in the chair, tipping it up on the rear two legs as I looked at my brother and decided I believed him completely. That didn't change the fact that his relationship with the widow of his friend and business associate wouldn't look good if word got out. Deep down I had a feeling I wouldn't express right now: I liked the idea of my brother interested in a nice girl like Katie who wasn't involved in a scam or part of his usual world.

As I was still considering this new information, the front door suddenly opened and the room filled with sunlight.

Mike Tharpe and another detective stepped in the doorway and made a quick scan of the bar. Tharpe walked toward us while his partner faced the bartender. I recognized the good tactical sense.

Tharpe kept standing as he looked at Natty and said, "You're under arrest. You want to make it easy or do you want to make it fun for me?"

I was the one who said, "What's the charge?"

The meaty detective didn't even glance at me. "Homicide. We got some forensics back on a weapon we recovered. It was Pete Stahl's gun."

I said, "So why does that make my brother a suspect?"

"His fingerprints were on it and we think the DNA we're testing now will come back to him. You wanted me to clear this up and this is how I'm doing it. Now you don't have to worry about finding out who killed your friend."

"You didn't know any of this earlier today when we were talking?"

"You made me realize I had to do something, and when I checked with the lab, this is what came back. I want to thank you for doing your civic duty and motivating me." He motioned for my brother to stand up and did a quick pat-down, then handcuffed Natty behind his back. In the big scheme of things, it was a fairly civil interaction, considering my big brother was going to jail.

# CHAPTER 9

**AS THE TWO** detectives led a handcuffed Natty out of the bar, he turned to the bartender and said, "Call Lise." Then he looked at me and said, "Don't worry, little brother. For once, I'm innocent."

I stepped to the door to watch them stick my brother in the back of a black Ford Crown Victoria. Apparently the Newburgh Police Department had gotten a pretty good deal on the model. I stayed on the curb until the Ford pulled down the street and out of sight.

The few people on the street didn't seem interested in a nonviolent arrest.

When I stepped back inside I said to the bartender, "Who's Lise?"

The surly bartender barely looked up from the ledger he was working on and said, "Best attorney this side of the city. She changed everything when she showed up last year. Natty is as good as out on this bullshit. I just called her and she said you can go by her office around five. She'll know something by then, after she talks to the DA."

That was more words than the bartender had ever spoken to me.

I debated calling my mom but wanted to have more information first, so I drove around Newburgh to get a better feel for the city. It had a bad reputation, but I had learned that cities, just like people, rarely matched the way they were portrayed in the media. Almost every other year, Newburgh was listed as the most dangerous city in New York or given some title like "Murder Capital of the State." And to be fair, it had been flooded with drugs, guns, and gangs, in that order. But there were a lot of people trying to make it a better place to live. People who understood that working with at-risk kids could have the biggest payoff down the road. I noticed adults coaching kids in every park and mothers keeping a close eye on their toddlers as they played. They were families, and that meant there was still hope for Newburgh.

I found the law office on Ann Street near downtown. The building was a typical three-story brick, block-shaped structure with a little grocery store stuck awkwardly to the side. Lise Mendez's office was on the second floor, and of course there was no elevator. The building housed a couple of lawyers, an accountant, and a financial planner. It was a drug dealer's dream. When I found the right door, there was no name painted on the glass, just a card taped in the corner. This did not instill confidence as I stepped into the room and realized the reception area was unused and empty except for a couple of chairs. I heard a voice in the inner office say, "In here."

I stepped through the door to find Lise Mendez standing behind a large, ornate desk that didn't seem to go with the office. She had a pretty face and long, black hair tied in a loose ponytail. She was probably thirty-five and radiated that sort of professional confidence that came from a good education and some success in her field.

She said, "You must be Nathaniel's brother." She extended her hand.

"I am." I glanced around to notice that her office, unlike the reception area, was packed with boxes and files, which to me was a good sign because it meant she was busy.

She said, "What's your name?"

"Mitchum."

"Your name is Mitchum?"

I didn't feel like explaining and I wanted to hear about my brother so I just said, "That's what everyone calls me." I glanced over at the wall nearest me and noticed her diploma. I looked at her and said, "Impressive, Harvard Law. Surprised you're not with one of the big firms in the city."

"I was, but I moved back here for family reasons." Now she pulled Natty's file from a stack on her desk and motioned for me to sit down. I noticed my brother's file was pretty thick.

I said, "Natty called me to look into the death of his friend."

"Pete Stahl? I know. I represented him, too. Why did your brother ask *you* to look into it?"

"I'm sort of an unofficial private investigator and he..."

"Nathaniel told me you delivered papers."

"I do both." I decided I wanted to change the subject, fast. "Do I owe you any money for this yet?"

The pretty attorney shook her head and said, "No, your brother keeps me on retainer. Granted, it's normally for narcotics cases, but let's see what happens with this. So far all they have is the gun used to kill Pete, and unfortunately, Nathaniel's fingerprints and, potentially, his DNA are on the gun. There are no witnesses, nothing else."

"Do you believe Natty when he says he had nothing to do with it?"

"I don't have to believe him. I just have to make sure his rights aren't violated, and that means that I'll protect him. If he had nothing to do with the murder and I protect his rights, he'll be a free man soon enough."

"Have you handled many cases like this?"

"A few."

"How many defendants walked free?"

"Every single one who deserved to. This isn't a sporting event where you keep score. I'll do my best. If that isn't good enough, there are other attorneys in town."

I considered what she had said and nodded, then said, "Do you think they'll let me visit Natty tonight?"

"They usually don't at the police department holding cell, but probably when he gets to the county jail." She took a Post-it pad from the corner of her desk and wrote down the phone number for the jail in the western part of the county.

I took the single blue square sheet of paper with an upstate New York logo that said *Adirondacks are not only chairs.*

I looked back at her and said, "What can I do to help?"

"I don't need some half-assed PI on this. Sorry, no offense."

I gave her a quick smile to let her know I had a sense of humor, but said, "Offense taken."

# CHAPTER 10

**IT TOOK MUCH** longer than I expected to get through the Newburgh police red tape and see my brother in his holding cell. First, I sat in a room at the front of the station for thirty minutes. Then they moved me back to a visitors' area near the holding cells.

I'm a big guy at six two and 190 pounds, yet all the Newburgh cops in uniform made me look like a scrawny teenager. I thought back to the offer of a job from Mike Tharpe. Maybe taking on that career would be more of a challenge than I assumed. I could see that the station was bustling. Newburgh in the winter. It was a wonderland.

While I was waiting at the counter by the holding cells, the policemen walked a few prisoners through the hallway behind the counter. Most of them looked like younger Hispanic men and I recognized some of the tattoos on their bodies that told me they might be gang members. Most walked quietly, but there were two that were barking the whole way and pushing back against the cop who was trying to lead them to their holding cell.

Finally, a middle-aged black man in a neat uniform with sergeant stripes stepped out of the hallway and behind the counter.

He said, "You Mitchum?"

"Yes, sir."

He broke into a genuine smile. Not one like the employee from the electric company gives you when you pay your bill. It made me like the guy instantly.

"My name is Bill Jeffries. Pleased to meet you." He stuck out his hand. This was the friendliest Newburgh cop I had ever met.

I shook his hand and said, "Do you think I can talk to my brother for a few minutes?"

"Normally you'd have to wait until he's booked at the county jail before you can visit him. We don't really have the facilities to allow face-to-face contact. But in your case I can make an exception."

I was starting to think Lise Mendez was one hell of an attorney. But then the cop said, "I know your mom, Elaine, from the hospital. She's a good lady and she's always talking about you boys. She's awfully proud of both of you."

"Even Natty?" I didn't mean for it to come out that way.

The man looked at me and put his hand on my shoulder. "Son, one day you'll realize a good parent only knows pride. It takes a lot for any boy to alienate his mother."

I realized this guy had been around, but more important, he knew my mother pretty well. Either way, he was doing me a big favor and I appreciated it.

# CHAPTER 11

**SERGEANT JEFFRIES BROUGHT** Natty out to me in the waiting area. He left him in handcuffs, but neither of us complained. I knew this meeting was a huge breach of protocol. He moved to the end of the counter to give us some privacy, which also made me wonder what his exact relationship with my mother was. It might make for an interesting conversation when I saw her later that night.

It wasn't the first time I'd seen Natty in custody. I know it isn't shocking to think a drug dealer might've been arrested more than once, and Natty had even done a ten-month stint in Ulster Correctional. Still, I didn't like looking at him in handcuffs.

Natty seemed calm enough as he said, "Did you get a chance to talk to Lise? What did she have to say? Will she be at my bail hearing in the morning?"

"She said she'll be there. She also said they recovered the gun that was used to kill Pete and that they have your fingerprints and possibly your DNA on it."

Natty sat back, deep in thought. But he didn't deny it like I was hoping he would. Finally, he said, "I know I played with his 9mm at his house one afternoon. I was visiting Katie and he had left the gun on a dresser."

"Do you know how that will look? That's just not a good explanation for why your fingerprints were on the gun. Plus, no one will believe you weren't sleeping with her."

"It's a better explanation than me using it to shoot Pete."

"But that's the conclusion everyone will jump to. Especially after they discover you and Katie are involved. No one knows, right?"

"No. We were going to tell Pete about it soon and now she wants to wait a respectable amount of time before we take it to the next level or tell anyone. She's really upset about Pete, but their marriage was over a while ago."

"I don't understand it, Natty. I've never seen you googly-eyed over a woman before."

"Katie is different than any woman I've ever met. She could make me a better man. She's honest and decent. That's a lot to say about anyone. She's an occupational therapist who works with autistic kids. That's why she has all the stuffed animals around the house. I could see myself settling down with her."

"Would you keep your current career if you settle down and had kids?"

That made Natty think. Sometimes I wondered if my brother ever considered the future. He looked at me with total sincerity and said, "I think I'd like to try something else. The paramedics are all so nice to me and they do important work. I wonder how hard it would be to become a paramedic."

I let him consider his dream life for a little bit, then brought him back to reality. "What can I do to help you now? Is there anything you can think of that might have led to Pete's death?"

"Just his business with Alton. The stuff I already told you about. Alton Beatty isn't anything like he seems. That's a guy that might be able to provide answers. He just might not *want* to." Then Natty took my arm and said, "I'm not worried. I didn't do it and I have faith in Lise. But Katie won't move on until she knows exactly what happened to Pete. I need you to find Pete's killer for her. That's all that matters now."

# CHAPTER 12

**BY THE TIME** I was back in Marlboro it was pitch-black outside and there was a light snow starting to fall. I don't know if it's because Marlboro is my hometown or that I was just glad to be out of Newburgh, but I felt a sense of relief when I pulled into my mother's driveway.

She still lived in the simple two-bedroom house where Natty and I grew up. She kept our bedroom the same so if either of us needed a place to stay we always had a bed. So far, I'd only taken her up on the offer a couple of times while I was on leave in the Navy. Natty had used the house to escape the police and avoid sticky situations with other drug dealers. I would hate to be the drug dealer who thought he could barge into my mother's house without her permission.

I knocked on the door as I opened it and called out, "Mom?" It's never a good idea to surprise my mom.

She stepped out from the kitchen and said, "Bill Jeffries already called me and caught me up on everything. He even worked it out for Natty to call me and managed to get your brother into a private cell at the county jail." She had a slight hitch in her voice, but was still her usual, efficient communicator. Then she said, "I talked to Pete's mother. She doesn't believe Natty had anything to do with it, either. I told her you'd figure it all out. She's been out of her head with grief. Pete's sisters stayed at the house around the clock to comfort her."

Then I noticed her eyes were red and I realized *she'd* been crying. That was not my mother. I had seen her mad plenty of times. That was terrifying. But I'd never seen her worried or sad before. I always assumed it was her training as a nurse. Natty or I would suffer some sort of injury like a broken arm and she'd talk to us like she was making lunch and never show emotion. This was unnerving.

She came out in the living room and gave me a hug. Then she said, "This is bullshit. They're just trying to clear a case quickly. Murder? No way. Not my Natty."

"But you had no problem believing the narcotics charges over the years."

"That was just business. I'd be a fool to think Natty wasn't a dope dealer."

"Drug dealer."

"What?"

"Nothing," I mumbled, realizing this wasn't the time to debate semantics.

My mom said, "I know exactly what Natty is. He sells drugs for a living. Christ, he even tried to steal some OxyContin once when he visited me at the hospital."

I cringed, imagining what my mother had done to him. When she didn't offer any details, I had to say, "What did you do?"

"I tore that stupid earring he used to wear right out of his lobe."

The image was unsettling, but at least it solved a mystery. I had wondered why he had abruptly stopped wearing the earring. He also stayed down in Newburgh for a while after that. I guess so he had time for his ear to heal and he wouldn't have to answer a lot of questions.

My mom said, "No, my Natty would never kill anyone. He's basically a good boy."

That made me think about what Sergeant Jeffries had said about a parent's pride. I also thought about all the favors he'd done for Natty the last few hours, from getting him a private cell to allowing me to see him at the station. I blurted out, "Are you dating Bill Jeffries?"

Mom didn't hesitate. "Yes. Yes, I am."

I was a little shocked by her honesty. She had always kept her love life hidden from Natty and me. I just stood there, speechless.

She said, "Are you shocked I can attract a man?"

"No, not at all. It's just that I don't think about you and men. I mean, you are my mother."

"Are you too old to start calling someone Dad?"

"Yes. And besides, you were always both to me. A better mom and dad than any man could ever be."

My mom started to cry in front of me. Something I'd never seen. Then she gave me a hug. You're never too old to appreciate a hug from your mother.

# CHAPTER 13

**THE NEXT DAY,** as soon as I finished my paper route, I headed to Tina's Plentiful for some breakfast and a place to think. Thank God my official booth was open, so I plopped down, already considering what I could do to help my brother.

The place was nearly empty this morning because snow was starting to build up on the roads. After a few minutes, while I was still lost in thought, Alicia placed a plate of eggs and ham in front of me and a bagel on the other side of the table. Then she slid into the booth.

Alicia said, "You look like you need some protein and company."

I smiled at her insight.

"You left so fast yesterday I didn't get a chance to tell you what a wonderful thing you did for Mrs. Ledbetter. She and her daughter stayed here an hour, then went back to her house. It was beautiful."

I gave her a smile. This was exactly the sort of thing I

needed this morning. Something light and friendly before I headed down to Newburgh.

Alicia said, "I get off just after lunch today. Are you free? Would you like to do something?"

My guess was that with a face like hers, she rarely had men turn her down. And I wanted to be here when she finished her shift. More than anything I could think of. But I thought of my brother sitting in the county jail and Pete Stahl's mom crying over her dead son, and I summoned the courage to shake my head.

"I'm sorry, Alicia. My brother's gotten into some hot water down in Newburgh and I couldn't face my mother again if I didn't do everything I could to help him."

"Your brother Natty, the drug dealer?"

Finally, someone was up on the current lingo for the job description. I nodded my head, still feeling the regret for turning down an offer to spend time with this beautiful girl.

"I hope you'll give me a chance to make it up to you as soon as I can. Maybe a nice dinner and movie up in Poughkeepsie."

She smiled and patted my hand. "You're a good brother and son. That's more important than an afternoon of wild sex."

My head snapped up at that. I smiled and said, "I wish you hadn't said that. Now that's all I'll be thinking about while I'm in Newburgh."

"That's okay. It was just a test to see how important your trip really was. You passed with flying colors. I'm very impressed."

A smile spread across my face as I realized just how smart and funny this girl was. Plus, I thought I could get lost in those brown eyes.

She grinned and said, "Eat up. You've got crimes to solve and brothers to rescue. Just remember your promise to take me out when this is all finished."

"Then, I'll have to find a way to clear this up right away."

# CHAPTER 14

**DRIVING THE STREETS** of Newburgh, I wasn't really sure why I had rushed away from my breakfast with the beautiful girl who wanted to spend the afternoon with me. Snow did little to hide the deterioration of the city. All it did was keep more people inside and maybe a few cars off the road.

I spent a few minutes watching kids play a game of football in an open field. It was four on four and the two-hand touches were a little on the rough side. They were doing what kids did: having fun.

It made me think of Pete and the things we did and dreamed about as kids. He used to say he was going to be a sports trainer. Maybe work for the Buffalo Bills. We all had dreams. At least Pete realized he wasn't talented enough to play football professionally.

I never knew my limitations. I wanted to be a Navy SEAL. I thought I had all the bases covered. It turned out I'd missed one in order to get there.

I talked to a couple of people on the streets, using my cash sparingly to buy information. When you're a paper-boy and a low-paid private investigator, there's no other way to use your cash but sparingly.

Each person led me to someone else who gave me a lit-tle more information. I wasn't being particularly discreet, but I was starting to get a clear picture of the drug trade in Newburgh.

Finally, later in the afternoon, I pulled up to a bar named the Budstop. This was where Alton Beatty ran his business, which apparently wasn't much of a secret in Newburgh.

I took a second to survey the building and parking lot. It didn't look that much different than the bar where my brother worked. I did notice the rented Cadillac in the park-ing lot and three pickup trucks parked directly in front of the building on the street. I wondered if that had something to do with Alton selling more meth than pot and cocaine.

I waited until all three trucks pulled away from the bar. All three of the drivers, who came out a few minutes af-ter one another, looked like sickly rednecks. They were thin with sallow complexions. I don't know much about methamphetamine, but these guys looked like billboards designed to scare kids away from it.

I parked at the far end of the lot and came into the pub from the side door. I've never been much of a bar guy, and this place looked just like the State of Mind Tavern: dark and musty, and no place to be on a crisp winter day.

After I walked inside, it took a few seconds for my eyes to adjust to the lighting. When the room came into better focus, the big Hispanic guy I had kicked in the crotch was striding toward me from across the room. At least he wasn't reaching for a weapon. That proved that he had some brains.

He said, "You and me got some unfinished business." His voice sounded like a tuba.

I said, "I'm pretty satisfied with our last transaction. Are your balls still swollen?" I have no idea why I threw that last comment into the conversation. Or why I felt like I had to smile at him. It only pissed him off like I knew it would.

He squared off in front of me again. Not much different than he did the first time.

Today I had another test of his abilities in mind. I raised my left hand, just like I had during our first meeting. This time he didn't take the bait and kept his eyes on me and his big hands near his groin.

This was another old trick I had learned. I just balled my left fist and hit him with a wild haymaker across his chin. It was spectacular. I felt his jaw shift and his head snap to the side as he staggered backward, finally plopping into a chair next to an empty table.

Then the bartender and a sturdy-looking guy at a table sprang into action. I saw a flash of metal and realized the bartender had a knife. I didn't have time to reach into my pocket and draw my commemorative Navy knife. I angled my body to give him the smallest possible target and got ready to show some Navy pride.

Then I heard a shout.

"Cool it, everyone."

# CHAPTER 15

**THE MEN FROZE** as Alton Beatty stepped into the room from a rear hallway. He had his long hair in a ponytail and was wearing a simple plaid shirt and jeans. He hardly looked the part of the successful drug dealer.

Both the men froze but didn't retreat at Alton's command. As he stepped closer to me he said, "Jerry, Blade, step back."

I looked at the bartender and said, "Are you Blade?"

He smiled and nodded.

In my experience, a guy usually didn't get a nickname like Blade for no reason. He stepped back to the bar and I breathed a sigh of relief.

Now Alton Beatty was right in front of me. He said, "In all the time I've known Natty, he never mentioned he had a brother."

"I don't brag much about him, either."

"I hear you been askin' about Pete Stahl. Mind telling me why?"

I really noticed his twang in simple conversation. "Where are you from? I mean, originally."

"Outside Cincinnati."

"For some reason I thought you were from New York City."

"I went to NYU and stayed after graduation. I moved here from the city a couple of years ago."

"Excuse me. NYU? Are you kidding me?"

Alton gave me a smile of pride and said, "School of Business." He sharpened his gaze at me and said, "That's just your New York prejudice. Hear a slightly Southern accent and assume a person's stupid. I try to use it to my advantage."

"How did you get into drug dealing after graduating from NYU?"

"Easiest way to learn the metric system," he said, giving me a sly smile.

I looked around the seedy bar and said, "This place is just like the bar my brother works out of."

"You gotta go where the customers are. It's just smart business."

"Like killing Pete Stahl?"

"Don't be a dumbass. I worked with Pete. If you're gonna start throwing around accusations like that, I'll just refer you to my attorney, Lise Mendez."

"Jesus, she the only attorney in town?"

"Only one worth a shit, and who looks like that." He stepped closer to me and put his arm around my shoulder. "Speaking of beauties, how's Pete's wife, Katie? Is your brother still sniffing around her?"

# CHAPTER 16

**ALTON DIDN'T TELL** me a whole lot, and his condescending attitude made me realize it was time to move
on. At least for now. It was late afternoon by the time I
left the Budstop. Dusk comes awfully early in upstate New
York in winter. Especially with the low clouds that threatened more snow. The temperature dropped and I wasn't
prepared for it. I stepped out of the side door and felt
the sharp wind. There was ice across the parking lot, so
I made my way as quickly as I could without losing my
footing.

Alton hadn't given me the impression that he was a
cold-blooded killer. But greed could do crazy things to
people. I still had a lot of questions to ask and work
to do.

I was lost in thought and concentrating on not falling,
so I wasn't paying attention to my surroundings. That's
a mistake in most circumstances and an all-out blunder
when you're investigating a criminal case. I hadn't noticed

anyone else in the parking lot before the man in the ski mask stepped out from behind my car.

I skidded to a stop, astonished. It was a big guy wearing a thick winter jacket. He didn't say a word as I just stared at him. Then he moved his right hand and I saw he had a red crowbar in it. It almost looked like a fireman's tool, but I knew he wasn't here to fight a fire.

I'd like to say I was prepared to fight him, but I was no idiot. My training in the Navy and specifically the SEAL class taught me when to evade. This was one of those times. I quickly spun and intended to dart back into the bar, when I felt the hook of the crowbar around my ankle, tripping me on my first step. I fell to the hard, icy asphalt and immediately rolled to my side, just as a blow struck the pavement where I had been lying.

I was able to scramble forward and gain my footing, but now I was facing my attacker and I didn't have an easy way to run. He stepped forward with confidence because he was wearing decent boots. I feinted left, then tried to jump to my right. The attacker fell for it at first, and swung the crowbar wildly as I tried to slip past him.

It caught my forehead with a glancing blow, opening up a gash. Almost immediately blood started to run down my forehead into my eyes. I took a second to wipe it with my sleeve and before I was finished, the attacker was on me again with the crowbar over his head. This time I jumped back and rolled over the hood of a newer Chevy.

As the attacker swung down with his crowbar, I slid off

the hood, and the curved part of the crowbar punctured the metal, locking the attacker's weapon in place. I knew this was my one chance so I kicked hard, catching the ski-masked man on his left side and knocking him to the ground.

It was a good, solid kick and the only thing that protected him was his padded jacket. I rushed forward, trying to take advantage of my good luck.

The man was able to fend me off and send me slipping back onto the icy asphalt. Then he turned and started to run across the street and out of sight.

I sat there for a minute, catching my breath and assessing my injury. As I stood up, holding my forehead, I noticed a Newburgh police cruiser pulling into the parking lot.

They were a little late, but I was still happy to see them.

# CHAPTER 17

**THE DRIVER OF** the patrol car was a huge, bald black man, and his partner was a scrawny white guy with an odd-looking mustache that tilted at an angle to the right side of his face. They kept their distance as they asked a few questions and the white guy handed me some gauze to put on my forehead.

The black officer said, "We had a complaint about a disturbance in the area. You fit the description of the assailant pretty well."

"Assailant! I'm the victim. Can't you see this blood?"

"There's no law that says a victim can't kick an assailant's ass once in a while. Why don't you come with us and we'll straighten this out?"

"Come where?"

"To our station. There's someone there who wants to talk to you."

"But I . . ."

The big cop grabbed me by the arm and spun me. I

could have resisted. He was strong, but I was fast and bet-ter trained. No way I wanted to hurt a cop. Especially one who was just doing his job. I felt handcuffs across my wrist almost instantly.

He said, "You have the right to remain silent and I hope you have the ability to remain silent for your own good."

Ten minutes later, I found myself in a holding cell in the same area where my brother had been the night before. I understood what the big black cop had meant when he told me to keep quiet. There's a time to be a smart-ass and a time to shut your trap and listen. So far I hadn't heard anything of value, but I hadn't antagonized anyone, either. That was sort of new for me. I was starting to think these two cops were working outside their job description.

When they dumped me in the cell and took the cuffs off, the cop said, "Someone will be here in a few minutes to talk to you. I suggest you listen up."

Then I found myself alone on a hard bench, confused about what the hell had just happened.

I sprang upright on my bench when I heard the lock on my cell turn about fifteen minutes later. I wondered if these cops were bold enough to give me a beating right here in the cell. My whole body tensed at the idea.

At least the gash in my head had stopped bleeding; one of the cops had given me a Band-Aid for it. A big Band-Aid. I considered rushing whoever came in the door and trying to escape. But I knew no one would ever buy the idea that I was arrested on bullshit charges. Come to think of it, I hadn't actually been arrested. I guess you'd call it *taken into custody*. That started me thinking about why I'd really been picked out like this. *Could there be a rat in the police?*

I felt myself lift off the seat slightly, getting ready to charge. But when the door opened my whole body relaxed back onto the bench. Standing in the doorway was my mom's friend, Sergeant Bill Jeffries.

The sergeant gave me a smile and shook his head. "You Mitchum boys have stirred up a lot of shit in the last couple of days here in Newburgh."

"Are you the man I'm supposed to talk to?"

Sergeant Jeffries shook his head and motioned me to follow him. There were no handcuffs or searches involved as we hustled down the hallway. He led me through a door, which took us outside. He pointed to a cruiser and said, "Jump in the passenger seat."

I didn't ask any questions but could tell he was headed back toward the Budstop, where my car was parked.

Sergeant Jeffries said, "I don't exactly know what's going on here. You weren't officially booked. I'm not asking any questions about it, but you've made some enemies in the Newburgh police department. You need to get out of Newburgh and stay away from this case. Let your brother's lawyer do what she's good at."

"Come on, Bill. You know my mom. You think she'd let me drop this case?"

The sergeant chuckled and said, "Then you better start watching your ass more closely. There are a lot of bad people in this town."

# CHAPTER 18

**BEFORE SERGEANT JEFFRIES** even dropped me off at my car at the Budstop, my phone rang. I was surprised to hear Katie Stahl asking me to meet her. I raced through Newburgh, or, at least, drove as quickly as I could in my beat-up station wagon, to where Katie had told me she was waiting: Lise Mendez's office.

As I stepped through the front door, Lise called from her office, telling me to come in.

As soon as she saw me, Lise said, "Is everything all right? What happened to your head?"

My hand rose to the giant Band-Aid on my forehead and reminded me I still had a slight headache. "Just clumsy."

Katie smiled and patted the chair next to her. "We need your signature on a couple of forms for Natty."

"What kind of forms?"

"I'm moving the retainer Pete had with Miss Mendez over to cover some of the expenses for Natty," Katie said. "She wanted to make sure there was no question if anyone asked where the money came from. I'm also trying to get a fix on my cash situation in case Natty gets a bond hearing so I can help him out."

Lise said, "There are a couple of businessmen in town that will help with Natty's bond as well. He's very well respected here in Newburgh."

"By businessmen, do you mean drug dealers?"

"Does it matter?"

I thought about it and shrugged. I couldn't believe how lucky my brother was to have two people like these women in his life. An attorney who was going above and beyond the call of duty and a young woman who trusted him enough to post a bond on a homicide charge. Whatever choices my brother made, he was doing all right in at least one department.

I filled out the paperwork and chatted with the women for a few minutes. Katie stood, slipped on a cute leather jacket, and got ready to leave.

The manners my mother had beaten into my brother and me demanded that I stand as well.

She gave me a quick hug. "Thank you for everything you're doing."

"I really haven't accomplished anything yet. But I'm not giving up." I didn't tell her that now I was prepared to take drastic measures to help my brother and find my friend's killer. You can only put up with bullshit for so long, and I was at my limit.

Once Katie had left, Lise looked at me and said, "I thought I said I didn't need any help on your brother's case."

"I'm not doing it for you."

She shook her head and looked down. "I hope to make some progress at the evidentiary hearing scheduled for next week. If the gun gets thrown out for any reason, your brother will be free to go."

I leaned in and said, "I heard you represent all the drug dealers in town."

"Why does that matter?"

"Because you represent my brother, Pete, and Alton Beatty."

"Alton has me on retainer. But that's really all I can say. Why? Is there something I need to know?"

"Did Pete or Alton ever tell you about some kind of big score they made in the city?"

"As I said, ethically, I can't tell you anything a client has discussed with me. That being said, typically, my clients don't call me unless there is some kind of problem. I don't hear about the successful business transactions."

I thought about how she could discuss this so casually and blurted out, "Does what you do for a living ever bother you?"

"You mean upholding people's rights?"

"I mean figure out ways for felons to get back out on the streets."

Lise said, "Like your brother?"

She hit the target on that last comment. I had no real retort other than to bow my head and say, "Touché."

There was an awkward silence that one of us needed to break.

Lise said, "Natty told me you were in school to be a

Navy SEAL. He said it was all you ever wanted to be. How does a SEAL recruit become a paperboy and PI?"

"I had all the skills. I could run. Was great with weapons. I took karate since I was eight so I knew how to move. There was just one thing I underestimated."

"What's that?"

"Swimming. I could swim, but not the way I needed to. Upstate New York is not the best environment to become a great swimmer."

"You didn't know that going in?"

"I thought I'd get better going through the school in San Diego. Turns out, with everything we had to do, I couldn't keep up. The instructors cut me slack because I could do everything else. That's how I made it until the end of the course. Ultimately, I had to give up that dream and make a new one. I wanted to help people. Contribute to society. That sort of nonsense." I gave her a smile. "That's why I became a PI. Paid or not."

Lise said, "Not that I'm interested, but what's your next move looking into Pete's death?"

"I didn't see Alton Beatty's car at the Budstop on my way over here, so I think I'm going to go get some rest and track him down early tomorrow afternoon. Maybe scare a few answers out of him."

"He's not the simple redneck he pretends to be."

"Neither am I."

Lise said, "Be careful out there. Newburgh is a dangerous place."

"You're the second person today who's told me that."

# CHAPTER 19

**WHEN I START** to concentrate on a case like this, I often lose track of time. The only thing I remember to do is my paper route early in the morning. I got up before dawn, like I do every single day, and delivered my papers. I do it not only because I get a regular paycheck, but because I know that I'm the lifeline to a number of elderly residents around Marlboro. It makes me get up every morning. I like to say hello and chat for a few seconds if one of my customers happens to be outside. I needed a regular, uneventful morning like this.

By midday, I was back in Newburgh and looking for Alton Beatty. The condescending little turd needed to have some answers for me or this would be an unpleasant day. It didn't take long to track down his Cadillac in the parking lot of the Budstop.

By now I had switched modes completely. I wasn't only a private investigator, I was the brother of a guy falsely accused of murder. My mom was depending on me. That meant something. At least to me.

I stepped through the side door of the bar. I didn't see the big bodyguard, but Blade's head snapped up as soon as I came into view. Alton was sitting in a booth reading a *New York Times*. He hopped to his feet as soon as he saw me.

He said, "Don't you know that it isn't polite to drop by without calling first? You Yankees sure don't have the manners of us folks from the Midwest. Why are you bothering me again? I told you everything I knew yesterday."

I glanced around the room quickly and noted that Blade stepped around the bar, ready to take action. "Where's your big bodyguard?"

"At the doctor having his fractured jaw fixed. I ought to bill you for the damage."

"Or invest in a better bodyguard."

"You're wasting my time, Mitchum. I got things to do. What do you want?"

"Let's say I believe you didn't kill Pete Stahl. You've gotta have an idea who did."

"You asking me as the town genius or as someone involved in the industry?"

"I didn't realize you were a genius."

"Not everyone does. Usually I call those people idiots. I'm guessing you went to a state school of some kind."

"I'm asking if you heard anything in your position as a local drug dealer."

"You trying to insult me? It sounds like you're talking down to me. Frankly, you're not smart enough to talk down to me. No one is. I don't appreciate that sort of attitude in my business."

That was one sentence too many from this little prick. "Do you appreciate this?" I grabbed him by the collar of his shirt and pulled him close to me. "My brother is in deep shit for something he didn't do. I think you have information that can help me clear him. And you're gonna start talking. Right. Fucking. Now."

As soon as I released him, Alton took a step away and reached behind his back. Before I had time to act, he was holding a small semiautomatic pistol. Worse, he still had a smirk on his face as if he was absolutely brilliant for walking around with a gun.

I didn't hesitate. That's the key in a situation like this. I used my right hand to slap him hard across the face and at the same time grabbed the gun with my left hand. I twisted Alton's arm, pulling him close to me as I put the gun to his head. We shuffled toward the rear door. I looked at Blade the bartender and said, "Be cool and this will all work out. I don't think you want to blow your meal ticket just yet." As soon as we were outside, I pushed him forward into a brick wall that hid the dumpster.

I said, "I'm out of patience with you. You're gonna start talking or I'm gonna smack you around so hard no one in this town will ever respect you again. They'll have to take you by the emergency room to get this gun removed from your ass."

"You think because you're a big guy and were in the Navy that you know what tough is. Try being the smartest kid in Cincinnati who's only five foot seven. There's nothing you can do to me that will make me talk."

I didn't understand how a guy was so smart and still didn't understand the physics of a pistol. I shoved him up hard against the wall with my left hand under his chin, lifting him onto his tiptoes. Then I screwed the nozzle of the gun into his nostril.

He gave me a hard stare like he didn't think I had the nerve to pull the trigger.

I extended my thumb up and pulled back the hammer of the pistol, so he would hear the cocking sound and see the movement. That did it.

"Okay, okay, hang on one second."

I didn't move. I growled, "Talk."

And he talked quickly.

"Pete and I stumbled onto a new recipe for meth. One of the chemical engineering students from Columbia I used to buy shit from made it. We interrupted his deal with some Canadians and got lucky."

"How lucky did you get?"

Alton said, "Six hundred and fifty thousand."

"How much is the recipe worth?"

"We've been offered a million bucks for it. The Canadian mob is all over this. The Canucks love prescription pills and meth. And this recipe has them drooling."

"Why? What's so special about it?"

"You can make it with ingredients that aren't too hard to find. Not quite as potent, but it can be made on a big scale."

"Who has it?" The whole time he'd been talking I had been releasing my grip slightly, at least to the point where his feet were flat on the ground. Now I stepped back with the pistol still pointed at his face.

Alton was out of breath and sweating as he said, "Pete and I stashed the money and the recipe with the help of another partner. We wanted to make it so not one of us could get to the cash without the other two. It's in a bank up in Poughkeepsie and you need two keys to get into the box, and a code to get into the safety-deposit-box room without any questions."

"What do *you* have?"

Alton stuck his left hand into the front pocket of his jeans and pulled out a flat metal key with a number 68 on it. He said, "Pete had the other key, but I suspect whoever shot him took it."

I stared at the key.

Sensing my interest, Alton closed his fist around it and held it by his side.

I said, "You think I won't take it?"

"You'll have to kill me first. I earned this."

I decided to let it go for the moment. I said, "So who has the code?"

"Forget that. What you need to do is find out who has Pete's key. Whoever has the key probably killed Pete and has the answers to get your brother out of jail."

"I need some direction. You were my best lead."

"A cop picked up Pete on some cheap, narco charge. Pete told me—"

But that's when I heard the first gunshot.

# CHAPTER 20

**I DUCKED AT** the first sound of the gunfire, then rolled to my right when I felt pieces of brick start to fly from the ricochets. I had Alton's little popgun in my hand and brought it up to fire a couple of times.

Alton was on the ground, so I grabbed him by the back of the shirt to pull him out of the line of fire and to cover. As soon as I grabbed his belt, his whole body went limp. As I brought him closer to me, I saw the bullet wound that went in through his cheek and exited the back of his head. His open eyes were already glassy.

Something shiny on the ground caught my attention. The key! I reached forward, trying to stay behind cover. A bullet pinged off the dumpster next to my extended hand. I lurched back. I stuck Alton's pistol around the dumpster and fired once to get the shooter's head down. Then I snatched the key and jammed it in my pocket as I tumbled back behind cover.

I caught a glimpse of someone in a dark coat running

between cars in the parking lot. I left Alton where he was and started to give chase. I could tell it was a male who was pretty big and, most important, still had the pistol in his hand. As he came out on the street, he turned to see if anyone was following him, and I dove onto the asphalt parking lot.

I was up again and running after a few seconds. I needed this guy. He could answer a lot of questions.

Now I was moving across the sidewalk in an all-out sprint. There was a little ice, but at this point I didn't care. There was no one who could outrun me when I was determined.

I took a corner hard, sliding out onto the road and narrowly missing a woman holding two kids by the hand. The woman gave a short shriek of surprise.

The little boy, in a dark-blue tattered parka, pointed down the street.

I gave him a nod of thanks and kept running. As soon as I came to the next block, I glimpsed the man at the edge of an industrial park. He turned and fired two more shots at me.

At this distance they both went wide, so I stayed in pursuit. When I was a little closer, I raised Alton's tiny pistol and popped off a round to keep the guy off balance.

Then I tried to do what the running man wouldn't expect. Instead of going right to where he was the last time I saw him, I cut into the industrial park and started to circle the building in between us. It was a little trickier here because there were workers coming and going in vans, carrying everything from windowsills to sprinkler pipes.

As I darted around the building, I saw what I needed to see. The guy with the gun was crouched behind a parked van, waiting to ambush me from the other direction. Perfect.

I eased into a line of cars so it wouldn't be easy for him to notice me. I wanted to say something clever like "Looking for me, asshole?" But I knew the most important thing was to get the pistol away from him.

When I was still a decent distance away, the man glanced over his shoulder. All I could tell from that angle was that he was a white man. I couldn't identify him specifically. Right now, that didn't matter. He turned and aimed his gun at me as I ducked behind a parked Honda Civic.

The two shots shattered the rear window of the car and made me crawl back farther away from the trunk. Then I heard a police siren.

I had to catch this guy now and get some answers before he was taken into custody.

I squeezed between some parked cars and crawled under one of them until I was close to the place where the man had taken the shots at me. I sprang out with the pistol up in front of me. There was no one there.

I could see the blue lights of the cruiser and I knew it was time to get the hell out of there.

# CHAPTER 21

**I DROVE TO** a McDonald's on the outskirts of New-burgh's downtown. If you ever want good insight into a city, look through the wide windows of a Mickey D's. You see everything. The locals, workers from businesses, and the homeless. This intersection can provide a glimpse into the city's soul. Is it prosperous? Is it a college town? Or is it struggling, ready to chew you up and spit you out?

As I sat in the hard plastic booth, throwing down a hamburger and staring at the key I'd taken from Alton, my mom called. I worked hard to keep my voice calm as I told her there wasn't really anything new on the case. When I was in the Navy and going through the SEAL course, I always tried to paint the best picture. My mom worried about me. At least now, my job was to make her life as easy as possible.

About an hour after my chase through the streets of Newburgh, I decided it was safe to make my next move.

I walked through the front doors of the Newburgh

Police Department, leaned in close to the little circle cut into the thick, bulletproof glass, and asked the receptionist if I could speak to Sergeant Bill Jeffries.

I followed him through the bowels of the police station. He kept quiet. Seemed he was worried about people eavesdropping.

Once in his cramped office, I spun him my somewhat vague story about Alton Beatty and his relationship to Pete Stahl. I didn't give too many details because I still wasn't sure I could trust him.

Finally, he said, "The Alton Beatty you're talking about is the guy who was just shot at the Budstop about an hour ago, right?"

"Exactly."

"And you wouldn't know anything about a shoot-out between two men that lasted for several blocks?"

"Not a thing."

"Unfortunately, the only description of the two men shooting is that they were white males. Not a lot to go on."

I kept my expression blank.

Jeffries said, "Look, Mitchum, I know you had nothing to do with either death. I even know your brother didn't kill Pete Stahl. But there's a lot of weird shit going on. I don't get the sense that you're telling me everything."

"Maybe that's more for your own good than mine."

Jeffries nodded. He turned and typed on a keyboard. He studied the screen, frowning as he scrolled through a few pages.

He said, "As the administrative sergeant, I can get into

any part of our network. It looks like your friend Pete Stahl was arrested about a month ago but never booked. When I peeked into the narcotics squad's notes, I saw that Stahl was brought in on some kind of a possession charge. It doesn't look like he got a chance to call his attorney. That could mean he was cooperating."

I said, "I think I'm following you. One of your narcotics guys grabbed him, then let him go for no documented reason. Sounds like he might've made a deal, all right." I couldn't help but reach in my pocket and feel the safety-deposit key I had taken from Alton. There were too many leaks in the Newburgh Police Department to let anyone know I had it.

Jeffries was taking a few notes from the computer screen and looked troubled by what he saw.

"Who's the cop that arrested Pete?"

"He was on a temporary duty assignment. I was looking to see if maybe he screwed up some paperwork and that's why they had to release your friend."

"Who was the cop?"

"Mike Tharpe."

# CHAPTER 22

**THE ORANGE COUNTY** jail, where anyone held on charges from Newburgh ended up, was an unimpressive, sprawling structure surrounded by a twelve-foot-high chain-link fence. It was also in the village of Goshen, about thirty-five miles west of Newburgh. That's where my brother had been cooling his heels after his initial bond hearing failed to win his release.

The jailers were clearly breaking my balls by making me wait in one room after another while they said they were getting my brother ready for our visit. I stopped one of them, a tall muscle-head with the name Norton on a tag, and said, "Do you know how frustrating it is to wait this long for a simple visit?"

Norton shrugged and said, "Probably feels just as frustrating as it does for the cops when some smart-ass tries to take over a homicide investigation."

That answered my question for sure.

I glanced through a couple of *Time* magazines that were

all more than three years old and got to know the layout of the facility by studying a map on the wall.

Finally, two jailers led me to a narrow room, about twice the size of a confessional, with a Plexiglas partition. Natty sat on the other side in a simple orange jumpsuit. We had to speak over a closed-circuit telephone. Natty gestured with his hands to let me know that the call could be monitored. That was important information. Especially considering all the shit that had happened to me the last couple of days.

The first thing Natty said was, "How's Katie holding up?"

"It's you I'm worried about."

"I'm fine. Could be better. I know a couple of the guys in my dorm. Since I'm in here on a homicide charge, everyone's keeping their distance."

I said, "I need some answers, Natty." I didn't like how tired he looked. Eyes bloodshot and his usually neat hair hanging down in an oily curl.

Natty showed no emotion as he said, "Go for it."

"Do you know any more details on the big score Pete and Alton made about six weeks ago? Like where the proceeds are or how to get them?" I was hoping the answer was no. That meant he was never involved.

He shrugged. "You've met Alton. He's the first one to tell you how smart he is. He was always bragging about one thing or another, but he'd never tell me anything important." Then he added, "I was sorry to hear he was killed."

"Word travels fast, even in jail."

My brother shook his head and said, "We have TVs in here. It was on the news."

I just shrugged. "Was anything unusual going on with Pete or Alton?"

"Pete was acting a little funny. He's the one that was all excited about something they did, but he didn't give me any details. I have no idea about Alton. We were never close."

"Did Pete have another partner?"

"We all work alone. Most of the time we're competition. Pete just focused on meth, so he and I got along well. Even though I knew him as a kid, he would have never told me the specifics about his business. Not a smart thing to do in our field."

I said, "He talk to anyone a lot the past few weeks?"

"The only person he started to talk to on a regular basis in the last few weeks was a cop."

"A cop? Which cop?"

"The guy who arrested me, Mike Tharpe."

# CHAPTER 23

**MY GUT WAS** telling me that Mike Tharpe had something to do with the murder of Pete Stahl. Whether he had pulled the trigger himself or if there were others involved was still a mystery. I found a coffee shop, not a Starbucks but a mom-and-pop place. I always supported family businesses, because I hated the muted taste of anything that came out of a corporate restaurant. But what I really wanted was a Wi-Fi connection to make my phone that much faster as I signed into my LexisNexis account. My teenage cousin, Bailey Mae, had talked me into getting one so that my private investigation business could run a little smoother. That's how I had found Mrs. Ledbetter's daughter near Philadelphia so easily.

After a few minutes on my smartphone, I found the house where Mike Tharpe lived. Or at least the address where he paid the electric bills. The house was in an area called Little Britain, southwest of the Stewart Airport, a few miles from downtown Newburgh, but far enough away from the chaos to make a cop feel secure when he got home.

It didn't take long to find the comfortable two-story on Station Street. It looked like the kind of place where people dreamed about setting up a life. Quiet, safe, and convenient to a bigger city like Newburgh.

The house was dark and I was out of time. I was also running short on common sense and good judgment. Somehow, the idea of breaking into a cop's house didn't even rank as the dumbest thing I had done all week. I'd chased an armed man for the sake of this case, after all.

I took a minute to survey the house from where I had parked up the street. It was completely dark and the next-door neighbors only had a porch light on. If I was going to do something this stupid, now would be the time. I walked casually up the sidewalk, trying to look as natural as possible. People in neighborhoods like this were generally not too suspicious. At least not of a clean-cut guy.

When I turned toward Tharpe's house, I saw the sticker for an alarm system. Often on my paper route, I helped my customers with other problems around their homes. Just quick little jobs to save them from having to pay a professional. One of the most frequent requests was help with alarm systems that the elderly didn't understand well. When I saw Tharpe's sticker for Malloy Security, I knew he'd bought a second-rate system. Malloy was a shitty company that would slap a sensor on your front and back door. Often customers were lucky if they had hooked it up to a power supply at all.

I scooted around to the back door and saw a keypad. This was going to be easier than I expected. I used a trick an electrician showed me when we were working on one of my customers' houses. I pulled my commemorative Navy knife from my pocket, slipped the blade between the house and the keypad, and ripped the plastic contraption right off the wall. Then I crossed the two wires in the back of the box and heard the beep on the inside of the house saying the alarm was no longer active. It never paid to be cheap where security was involved.

The lock on the door was a little more complicated. When you're desperate, though, a few locks can't hold you. I laid my shoulder into the door and it almost came off the frame as it opened up.

I flipped on the light. It was obvious I would never be able to hide the damage to the back door. Now it was all about speed. I bolted up the stairs and rummaged through a few drawers in the bedroom and a little office. I wasn't sure what I was looking for, but I had to find something that would link Tharpe to Pete Stahl.

I worked my way back to the kitchen and had just about tossed the entire house upside down when headlights washed through the living room as a car pulled into the driveway.

I prayed Tharpe would use the front door and not remember if he left the light on or not. The one thing I did know: I was about to get either some answers or a bullet in the head.

# CHAPTER 24

**I HEARD THE** car door and realized my best chance to escape would be to scoot out the back now. But something kept me from doing it. The idea of my brother sitting in jail for Pete Stahl's death kept my feet firmly in the hallway near the kitchen. I had to get to the bottom of this.

I could see the front door over the first few stairs. As it opened, I eased back into a dark nook in the wall that looked like it used to be a linen closet. Like the rest of the house, there hadn't been much renovation there. The door had been taken off the hinges and a few shelves removed. But I felt secure, at least for the moment.

I could barely see the front door as it opened. There was a hesitation as Tharpe stood in the doorway and tried to figure out if he had left the light on in the kitchen. I could see the Marine in him as he surveyed the front room and took a step toward the stairs to get a better view.

My heart was racing as I ran through the options in my head. In that moment, I was a burglar, but if I did much more I'd be considered a home invader. Neither looked good on a résumé. But at least I'd have my brother to talk to in jail.

Tharpe peeked into the kitchen and must've seen the back door busted open. That made him reach with his right hand and draw his service weapon, a Glock semi-automatic. He held it up in his right hand and pointed it up the stairs.

I knew what he was doing. I would've done the same thing. He was listening. He wanted to hear a footstep upstairs or the creaking of a door. He put his back against the wall and let his eyes scan all around the house.

Then I saw my chance. He stepped away from the wall and was about to turn and climb the stairs. I made a decision and acted. That's what the SEALs taught me to do. I stepped from my hiding place and swung my right hand hard, catching him in the side of the head. The blow knocked him off balance and his face hit the side of the stairs as he went down hard.

I immediately grabbed his gun, which had tumbled to the floor. I pulled the magazine and ejected the round left in the chamber. Then I stuck the magazine back into the gun and laid it on the floor near Tharpe's unconscious body. At least he wouldn't be able to pick it up and fire it without racking another round into the chamber.

I rolled Tharpe over to make sure he was breathing

and realized I may have been searching in the wrong place. If I had something portable and important, I'd keep it on me. First, I rummaged through his coat pockets, then I felt his front right pocket. At the bottom, securely in place, was a single flat metal key. I pulled it out and immediately recognized it as the same kind of safety-deposit key I took from Alton Beatty. It had the number 68 etched in it.

I felt like I'd solved everything until I thought about it for a minute. How could I prove where I'd found the key? What kind of evidence did I have to implicate the police officer in anything illegal? How would it help my brother? It would be my word against Tharpe's. Although I knew *I* was beyond reproach, I doubt the legal system realized it.

At least, since I wasn't an official police officer, I didn't have to worry about how I obtained evidence or built a case. What I needed were a few more breaks, but finding this key was a good start.

I knew Tharpe couldn't be the third partner. Neither Pete nor Alton would've trusted him. This key had come from Pete, and I was quite certain the beefy police officer had killed my friend for it.

Tharpe started to stir and I took that as my cue to leave. I scooted out the shattered back door and raced to my car down the street. I backed away so I wouldn't have to pass in front of the house. As I reached the end of the street, I could see Tharpe stepping through the front door and standing on his front porch. That son of a bitch was tough.

Maybe all that Marine bullshit about being tougher than everyone else was true.

I tried to make a stealthy getaway, but when you're in a ten-year-old station wagon, trying to get away from a house you just burglarized, that's a tall order.

At least now I had my suspect.

# CHAPTER 25

**I SAT IN** Tina's Plentiful and downed a hamburger with two beers. After the night I'd experienced, I had earned a couple of beers. I had also earned the right to talk to Alicia, but I was disappointed to see she had a number of customers.

It gave me a few minutes to figure out what I was going to do next. I had two keys to the safe-deposit box that held some kind of crazy drug recipe worth a fortune and at least $650,000 in cash. I wanted nothing to do with the contents of the safety-deposit box, but I was trying to see how I might use it to help my brother.

When it was clear Alicia wouldn't be able to sit and chat with me, I decided it was time to catch my mother up on everything that had happened. At least the stuff that wouldn't scare the shit out of her. I intended to avoid the story about chasing a man with a gun or invading a cop's home.

I pulled up in front of my mom's neat brick house. All the neighbors were home from work and the street and driveways were filled with cars. I rapped on the front door as I poked my head inside and called out, "Mom?"

I stepped into the house and saw my dog, Bart Simpson, on the couch in the front room, wagging his tail at the sight of me. He was comfortable and didn't feel like jumping down to show his affection. I understood that. My mom often kept Bart here at the house if I had to work in the afternoons. She liked the company and so did Bart.

Mom called out, "Bobby, I'm back here."

I cut through the kitchen into the sunken family room and saw she was sitting on the edge of the couch, talking to a visitor at the far end of the couch. As I was about to apologize for interrupting, my mother turned slightly and I saw her visitor. It was Mike Tharpe.

I stood for a moment, speechless. That doesn't happen all that often, but I had to gather my thoughts. When he turned and smiled at me, I noticed his black eye where he'd hit the edge of the stairs. It was a satisfying sight, on a certain level.

Tharpe said, "I was just telling your mom that I think I might have found some evidence that will get your brother out of jail."

"What kind of evidence?" It was clear my mom was buying this bullshit story.

"We think there are two safety-deposit keys that can open a box with the evidence we need. The problem is the keys have gone missing. I was just about to ask her to call you to come over to help me find them. You know, since you're such a good private investigator and all."

He had more subtlety in him than I thought. But I let a smile spread across my face so he knew I had both keys and understood what he was saying. I waited as it sank in and said, "How would that help? Doesn't the district attorney have to be involved?"

Now my mom jumped in, saying, "Don't cloud the issue, Bobby. He says he can help Natty."

I said, "Mom, he can do a lot of things, but helping Natty is not one of them." I could feel the mood change in the room. Not only did my mom stiffen, but Tharpe realized there was no way to do this quietly.

Tharpe stood up and I realized he was still in the same clothes as at his house. He had known that he needed to find me. He must've seen me drive away from his house. *Damn my big clunker.* I had to get a smaller car.

After my mom stood up like she was going to break up a fight between us, I said, "If you don't think my brother is guilty, then who killed Pete Stahl?"

"Does it really matter?"

"More than you would understand. He was my friend and his family lives here in Marlboro. I can't let something like that go."

Tharpe let out a chuckle, but his eyes didn't show any humor. "That's very noble of you, dropout. But it's a big mistake." He stepped to the side and calmly drew his service weapon, letting it point at the ground. Not too showy, but he got his point across.

It was one thing to threaten me, but no one, and I mean no one, threatens my mom.

# CHAPTER 26

**A KILLER HAD** my mom by the arm and I had never felt so helpless. I had to buy time and engage this creep.

I said, "What's your plan? Kill a fifty-five-year-old nurse to cover a drug deal?"

My mom mumbled, "Fifty-three."

Tharpe said, "No one has to die. Just give me the keys and all is forgotten. If not..." He raised the gun to my mother's head.

Suddenly she realized exactly what was going on and let out a little whimper. This was coming from the toughest woman I had ever known. My stomach flipped. Then I realized Mom didn't look scared, she looked pissed off. Right then, I knew I had to act. This jerk wouldn't forget anything. As soon as he had the keys, my mom and I would both be dead and Natty would spend the rest of his life in jail.

My gun was two blocks away in my own house. Then I realized his gun probably didn't have a bullet in the chamber. Had he checked his gun after I'd knocked the crap out of him? My guess was that he hadn't.

I raised my hands slowly and said, "Okay, okay. We can work this out."

I tried to calculate the probability of whether he had checked his gun. Was there a round in the chamber? I shook the idea out of my head. Whatever my calculation revealed, I couldn't risk my mom's life on it. I needed Tharpe's full attention on me. I wanted his anger completely focused on me.

I said, "Typical Marine, threatening a woman." I took a tiny step backward and to the side.

Tharpe looked at me and said, "A SEAL dropout is questioning Marine honor?" He lowered the pistol from my mom's head and pointed it in my direction. "You, a goddamn paperboy, think you can cross me."

I took another step back. The gun followed me and he took a step away from my mother. Now my mom was behind him, and I felt emboldened.

Tharpe said, "I should've taken your head off with that crowbar."

I reached up to feel the Band-Aid that was still stuck to my forehead. At least one mystery was solved.

I said, "You're not even smart enough to hold on to the key you stole."

Now the big cop was mad. That meant he wasn't thinking. I pounced on the moment and said, "I took the bullet out of the chamber when I knocked the shit out of you earlier." I saw the surprise on his face and knew I had been right.

Then he acted. Quickly. His left hand sprang onto the back of the pistol so he could rack it.

I barreled into him, knocking him back and batting away the pistol before it was operational. We tumbled onto my mom's new laminate floor, and I got a good shot on his chin with a closed fist.

He didn't give up. He hit me with an elbow that made me literally see sparkles. I sprang away from him and to my feet. He rolled to one side and was up quickly as well. I glanced around the floor but had no idea where the gun had gone.

We squared off. All I could think was how much I was going to enjoy this. Tharpe had a lot to answer for, and I was about to exact payment. Then I saw movement behind him. I heard a loud *thunk* and Tharpe dropped to his knees, then lay out flat on the floor.

When I looked up, my mom was holding her heavy cast-iron skillet.

She shook her head and said, "That guy is an asshole."

"Tell me about it."

# CHAPTER 27

**I HANDCUFFED THARPE** behind his back and around the legs of a wooden chair with his own set of cuffs. When he came to, he tried to give us a tough expression, but it's hard to do when you're trussed up like a steer at a rodeo. It had no effect whatsoever.

I pulled a chair close, but not too close. I eased into it so he could see that I'd taken his pistol, which I had found under the TV, and tucked it into my belt. I said, "Don't feel bad. You're not the first victim of my mom's frying pan. She clocked my brother a couple of months ago. I don't think he's right yet. I wish she could back me up on the street sometimes."

Tharpe glared at me as he growled, "You understand the deep shit you're in?"

"You think? Let's call the Ulster County sheriff and let them sort this whole situation out." I pulled my phone from my pocket and started to punch in numbers.

Tharpe said, "Wait."

"Why?"

"Maybe we can help each other."

"I'm listening."

"If I get the box and you let me run, I'll give you a video statement that'll clear your brother."

"You think that'll be enough?"

"Yeah. I'll tell them I did it. I'll confess to killing Pete. And then I'll run for the hills."

"Fine," I said. "I have both keys. Do you have the code?"

That surprised him. He didn't realize I'd figured out the details.

Tharpe said, "I have the number of a throwaway phone that I can text. All I have to do is tell them when to meet us at the bank."

I took the phone from his inside coat pocket, and when he had pointed out the number, I texted, Meet me at the Poughkeepsie bank at 9 AM tomorrow. I looked at Tharpe and said, "Any idea who the silent partner is?"

He shrugged his shoulders. "Pete Stahl and Alton Beatty knew. They never would tell me. It was their insurance."

A minute later a text came back that said, 9 AM tomorrow. Okay.

Tharpe looked at me and said, "I'll make the statement right there in the safety-deposit vault, on video, when I have the contents of the box."

I gave him a hard stare. "Then I'll never see you again?"

Tharpe smiled and said, "No one will."

# CHAPTER 28

**IT HAD BEEN** an anxious night at my mother's house. Keeping a Newburgh detective in custody is a complicated matter. At first my mother insisted on calling the local sheriff's office, but then she realized this was the best way to get Natty off the hook. I had snatched a couple of hours' sleep while my mom kept an eye on the handcuffed Tharpe. Now I found myself with the big Newburgh detective handcuffed in the front seat of my car.

We crossed the Hudson to Poughkeepsie in silence. I had taken a couple of passes in front of the north branch of the First Poughkeepsie Financial Services. I'd seen commercials for the private bank in four locations, but I'd never had a reason to visit it before. It operated like a bank, with a savings-and-loan division, and it provided a whole series of safety deposit and financial transaction options. A one-stop shop for drug dealers, money launderers, and divorce attorneys.

I parked in the front lot amid Jaguars and Cadillacs. At

least my sagging station wagon was unique. The bank was a faux-stately one-story building that tried to project an aura of dignified commerce but came up short. The place was used by too many scammers and thugs to ever be dignified.

Knowing the harsh gun laws in New York and not knowing what security was like inside the bank, I made a tough decision. I didn't want a metal detector to get me thrown in jail and ruin my chances of saving Natty, so I hid my gun under the front seat. I was subtle when I slipped it down there and I let Tharpe believe it was still in the pocket of my jacket.

Tharpe had his usual smirk when he said, "Getting nervous?"

"About what? Anything goes wrong and you're the one who's in deep shit."

"What if our partner doesn't show?"

I looked sideways at him and said, "You know something you're not saying?"

"Not a thing."

"Any ideas about who might show up?"

"If your brother wasn't in the can, I'd say him. So it's gotta be some other lowlife dealer. I'll probably recognize him."

We sat in the car for a minute. I checked out the surroundings. Poughkeepsie is a bigger city than either Marlboro or Newburgh and showed signs of growth. There was a completely different vibe here, with new businesses opening and only a few vacancies in the strip malls. A

Poughkeepsie police cruiser passed with two officers in the front seat. It made me remember that technically, I was acting illegally, and I wasn't sure how many people would believe my story about Mike Tharpe being a murderer.

I looked at Tharpe and said, "We're going to wait in the lobby." I patted my pocket where I told him the gun was. "Don't give me a reason to use this. We have an agreement. You make the video statement and I let you take everything in the box. You know I don't want to have anything to do with it anyway."

Tharpe looked at me and said, "And you wait before you tell anyone, so I have a chance to get out of town."

I nodded. "Agreed."

He turned so I could use the key on the handcuffs and free his hands. Then we both eased out of the car, feeling each other out. Tharpe looked tired. It didn't seem like he had any tricks up his sleeve. I let him walk just in front of me as we entered the bank, and I explained to a receptionist, sitting behind a cramped desk, that we wanted to go to the safety-deposit room after our business partner arrived. The pretty, young receptionist motioned us to a small waiting area, where we sat on hard plastic chairs. A velvet rope separated the waiting area from the rest of the lobby, which also served as the entrance to the other sections of the bank.

I looked into the main lobby and evaluated the everyday business the private bank did. There were young mothers with their children and an old couple waiting to speak to a loan officer. Nothing out of the ordinary.

Now I wondered who would show up to meet us. There were too many possibilities to anticipate anything. Tharpe didn't say a word and looked like he was waiting to visit his stockbroker. Every car that pulled into the lot drew my attention.

Then the one car I didn't want to see pulled up. A dark-blue BMW. As I watched out the wide window, I saw Katie Stahl emerge from the car and stroll to the front door of the bank, like she was on a normal errand.

Tharpe smiled and said, "Well, well, well, little miss perfect has a dark secret. It makes me like her that much more."

She hesitated for a moment in the parking lot, staring at us through the window, then regained her composure.

And my heart broke a little bit.

# CHAPTER 29

**BY THE LOOK** on Katie's face, she didn't know who she was going to meet, either. She stood at the edge of the waiting area, right in front of us, brown leather car coat with a fur trim and red Aldo purse draped over her shoulder. Her blond hair hung down her back in a loose ponytail. She wore the same black running shoes my mom did at the hospital. She must've come directly from work.

It felt like the three of us were in an Old West standoff, silently assessing one another as the sounds of normal bank business drifted across the tile floor.

I scanned the tellers behind us. There were no visible security guards and no one was paying any attention to our little moment in the corner.

Katie's eyes cut to Tharpe.

I said quickly, "He's not here in an official capacity."

Tharpe let out a cough and muttered, "That's an understatement."

Katie ignored him, turned to me, and said, "Hello, Mitchum. I didn't expect to see you here."

"Who did you expect to see?"

She gave Tharpe a nasty glance and said, "I don't know. But he doesn't surprise me at all."

I could've explained my involvement to her, but right now I needed this to go quickly. Besides, she didn't deserve to know exactly what was going on.

"Do you have the code?" I asked, hoping she was some kind of a pawn.

She nodded and said, "Do you still intend to split it evenly?"

Tharpe mumbled, "Not as evenly as any previous agreement."

I cut in. "We'll work it out. The only thing I want is for Natty to be released." I just needed Tharpe's statement. After that, these two could negotiate.

Katie considered this. When she nodded, I realized there was no way she'd been more than just a pawn. That didn't just break my heart, it pissed me off.

The three of us walked down the long hallway, past the armed security guard, and met an attendant who led us down another long hallway to the room that held box number 68. The building was designed like a maze, and I stood in the center of it with a guy I hated and a woman who had tricked my whole family. Great. Just another Wednesday in upstate New York.

The attendant, a thin man in his forties with a Boston accent, said, "Who has the code?"

Katie stepped up and faced the keypad on the side of the closed door. She pulled a small piece of paper from her purse and punched in the five-digit code.

The tumblers in the door turned and it popped open.

The attendant looked at me as if I was in charge and said, "Number 68 is on the top row in the corner. There's a table and two chairs. Would you like me to find another chair?"

I shook my head.

He smiled and said, "I'll be right down the hall if you need anything at all."

The three of us entered the room slowly. It was the size of a bedroom. Maybe ten by twelve feet. Up against three of the walls there were boxes of different sizes. Everything was gray. The boxes in the wall, the door. Even the ceiling was a lighter shade of gray. There was no natural light, just a sleek tract of soft LED lights. Ten minutes in here would drive anyone crazy.

I pulled out both keys from my front pocket. Before I inserted them into the round locks on the box, I looked at Tharpe and said, "Let's get your video statement first."

He hesitated, so I let my hand slip inside my pocket where he thought I was holding a gun. He nodded and sat down in one of the two chairs at the table in the center of the room.

I quickly recorded his statement, and when I looked up, Katie was at the far end of the room, holding a gun on both of us.

# CHAPTER 30

**IT WAS HARD** to take my eyes off the gun in Katie Stahl's hand. She clearly had no regard for the gun laws of New York. There was a little tremor in the barrel, but overall she seemed calm and confident. Always bad news for the person facing the gun.

The sea of gray and soft lighting wasn't helpful at all. I felt like I was stuck in a cavern, surrounded by a building.

She looked at me and said, "I'm not enjoying this."

I said, "If it makes you feel any better, neither am I." I tried to read Katie's next move. I'd wait for my chance.

I turned my attention to the box. Mike Tharpe stood to my right and I knew a guy like him had to be calculating the odds of escape. He'd already lost his old life. He'd never be a cop again. Now it looked like he was losing his new life as well. I didn't want him to do anything desperate.

I slowly turned both keys in the lock at the same time. Once they turned all the way to the left, the door unlatched and I pulled it open. I reached inside and pulled out a safety-deposit box that was about the size of a recycling bin. With the lid closed it looked like a big, gray building block.

I plopped it down onto the table. Tharpe was eyeing it like a wolf stalking a sheep. I stepped back to the wall and said to Katie, "You open it." I thought I might trick her into a mistake. Maybe tie up her hands for a second. But I had no such luck.

She pointed the semiautomatic pistol at Tharpe and said, "Let him do it." With her other hand, she gave him a piece of paper with the code written on it. Katie was in control and appeared ready to shoot if she had to. This wasn't how I imagined a pretty occupational therapist would behave.

Tharpe moved forward, cutting his eyes toward me. When he focused on the box, he paused. Then he unlatched the front and lifted the lid like it was the Ark of the Covenant. We all looked on in silence.

There was a leather-bound notepad and a cloth sack. Tharpe picked up the notepad and thumbed through it quickly. Nothing but page after page of instructions and formulas.

He set the book on the table. Then he pulled the cloth sack from the box. It was fairly large, about the size of a kitchen garbage bag. When he pulled open the drawstring, all I could see as I peered over his shoulder was cash. Bundles of hundred-dollar bills. Lots of bundles. Bundles of dreams.

I had never seen that much money. I would probably never make that much money in my entire life. It annoyed me. How could people have that kind of cash? Suddenly I didn't like the idea of Tharpe taking it. It seemed wrong, no matter what deal we had made earlier.

Katie read his intentions, too. She said, "This was everything Pete worked for. He gave his life for it. I can't let it be stolen. Don't make me shoot you."

I noticed Tharpe out of the corner of my eye. He was trying to be subtle and get my attention. As Katie gazed into the box, he used two fingers to make a gun sign. Then I realized he thought I really had a gun in my jacket and he wanted me to shoot her. Even if I was armed, I wasn't going to shoot Katie over this garbage in the box. It wasn't worth it.

I stayed where I was and raised my hands slightly. Part of it was a show of surrender to Katie, but when I turned, my jacket pulled tight and Tharpe saw that I didn't have a gun.

And that's when he decided to make his move.

# CHAPTER 31

**THARPE LURCHED FORWARD,** fast. Faster than I thought a guy his size could. He slapped Katie's hand to one side, then reached across to grab the gun. It slipped out of both of their hands, bounced off the table, and clattered onto the floor. That's when things got really rough inside the tiny vault.

I dove for the gun as Tharpe tumbled over the table to get it. We met on the hard tile floor. Each of us had a hand on the gun. We tried to find the right leverage to pry it from the other man's hands. We rolled on the floor, bumping into the boxes in the wall and the legs of the table. Each bruise made me angrier and angrier.

I was hoping Katie would help me. All she had to do was push the heavy box off the table onto Tharpe's face. Instead, she stepped forward and started to collect the contents of the box for herself. I managed to gain a hold of the gun and struggled to my feet as Tharpe was hanging on as hard as he could.

He had a weight advantage on me and used it well. He twisted hard and jerked me into the wall of safety-deposit boxes. But no Marine was going to get the better of me. I raised my knee and caught him hard in the abdomen, driving him back. Then his fingers tangled in mine near the gun and he pulled it back before smacking it against my temple.

I quickly regained my bearings, and as soon as I did, the gun discharged. In the enclosed space it was like being next to a thunderclap. My brain scrambled for a second.

I let go with my left hand and threw a punch hard into his face. He staggered back.

The smell of the gunpowder hung in the smoky air and stung my eyes.

That was when I saw Katie. On the ground. The blood pumping out of a wound in her chest. I couldn't help myself, and let go of the gun. I dropped to my knee to try and stop the blood pumping out through the hole in her leather jacket. It pooled on her chest.

Tharpe wasted no time grabbing the gun, sack of money, and notebook. He slipped out of the room instantly.

Katie tried to say something. It might've been "I'm sorry," but maybe I was imagining it. No real sound came out. Within moments, I felt her body go still underneath my hand and I knew she was dead.

I heard shouting in the hallway as Tharpe tried to get past the security guard. That's when a shot was fired.

This plan had gone completely to shit.

# CHAPTER 32

**SURROUNDED BY THE** gray walls, I felt my anger rise. I didn't care if Katie Stahl was the mastermind or criminal conspirator. Someone else was going to pay for all of this shit. Right now, the only target I saw was Mike Tharpe.

I stood up and took one more look at poor Katie. Then I noticed the piece of paper with the room code written on it next to her. I plucked it off the floor and raced out of the small room.

I crouched just outside of the door to figure out the direction in which Tharpe had fled. The maze of hallways made it difficult. I could hear people screaming. Then I heard gunshots around the corner toward the front of the bank.

I sprinted down the long hallway, dodging the body of the murdered guard. As I got closer, I could hear the chaos. In the lobby, a young mother clutched her baby and ran for cover. An elderly man fell and just stayed on the tile, reaching up uselessly, like a turtle on its back.

Customers and tellers alike were scrambling past him and shouting. Security had spread around the perimeter of the room.

When I turned to my right, I immediately saw Tharpe crouched behind a heavy planter with leafy branches spreading out above him. This hallway led to the waiting area where we had come from.

Tharpe leaned out from behind the planter and took a potshot at a security guard twenty feet away. Tharpe intended to flee out the front, but this guy held his ground. Good for him.

The security guard was using a column as cover and he had the advantage of time on his side. The police would arrive before long. All he had to do was keep Tharpe behind the planter.

I crept toward Tharpe in his blind spot. When I was about a dozen feet behind him, I tried to signal the security guard by waving my arm. The last thing I wanted was to catch one of his bullets by mistake. Or on purpose, if he thought I was Tharpe's partner.

The guard looked like a deer in the headlights. I had to risk the chance that he saw me.

I made my move.

# CHAPTER 33

**I JUST DOVE** in. Like I was playing football in school. I led with my shoulder. Tharpe made a *humph* sound as I drove him into the planter.

I wrapped both hands around his right wrist to keep him from pointing the pistol in my direction. I jerked him away from the planter, expecting the guard to give me some sort of support. I didn't care if he shot Tharpe while I had him in the open. Instead, I was in dogfight mode. The SEAL mentality was to never lose. This time I wanted to make the loser pay.

I jerked Tharpe closer and head-butted him in the nose. He staggered back, blood already dripping from his nostrils. He managed to hold on to the gun. He even squeezed off a round that kept the security guard behind the pillar.

I stole a peek at the lobby and saw that it was still in chaos. A woman screamed and ran for the front door. I hoped others would follow her.

I focused on Tharpe again and used my legs to drive

him into the wall. He crashed hard. The whole building seemed to shake.

Then I twisted and used my body's leverage to snap his right wrist. He let out a grunt of pain as the bones broke. I could hear them as well as feel them shatter under my hands. The gun dropped onto the tile floor. I kicked it hard with my left foot as if it were a soccer ball. It spun across the floor. I threw an elbow into Tharpe's jaw and felt it break under the pressure. The big cop stayed on his feet. Incredible.

He was done. I had the upper hand, but this was the best therapy I could imagine. I wound up my right arm and balled my hand into a fist. Tharpe didn't even know what was coming his way. Then I heard someone shout, "Police! Don't move!"

I looked to my left and saw two uniformed Poughkeepsie cops with their service weapons drawn and pointed at me. They were both young. A blond woman, who couldn't have stood at more than five foot one, and a lanky guy with a military haircut. His pistol clearly shook in his hand.

The security guard pointed at me and said, "That guy stopped the gunman."

That made the cops focus their attention on Tharpe. Then I delivered my punch. It was a wild haymaker that felt like it came from across the Hudson and landed squarely on Tharpe's nose. He stumbled back and hit the wall again. This time he fell to the ground. That's when I gave him a good, solid kick in the ribs. He grunted and blood poured out of his shattered nose as if it were a garden hose.

The tall cop stepped forward and yelled, "Cut that shit out. Now."

I was already in a stance to kick Tharpe again when I looked over at the cop. He could see I had nothing in my hands and I was no lethal threat. At least not to him. I winked and threw my kick anyway. Tharpe made another satisfying grunt as I felt one of his ribs crack beneath my foot.

I immediately held up both hands and stepped back, mumbling, "Sorry, Officer."

The young patrolman dropped to his knee and started to search Tharpe. The other cop kept her gun trained on me. She had more tactical sense than her partner and didn't step forward.

The cop cuffed Tharpe behind his back, then stood up to face me. He was holding Tharpe's ID case with the Newburgh detective's badge on the outside.

He said, "What the hell is this?"

"That's something he doesn't deserve to carry."

# CHAPTER 34

**THREE HOURS LATER,** I found myself back in Newburgh. I tried to process everything that had happened. The Poughkeepsie police had a lot of questions. They weren't particularly happy with me. There wasn't much they could do. It was a mess and there was no chance to spin it in a positive way. A cop had gone bad, and because of him, there were bodies in both Newburgh and Poughkeepsie.

I didn't knock when I entered the law office of Lise Mendez. There had been some vague reports on the news from Poughkeepsie. I figured she didn't have any of the details yet.

She didn't seem surprised to see me as I stood in her door. She looked up from her desk and gave me one of those dazzling smiles. "Hello, Mitchum. What are you doing here?"

"I just came from Poughkeepsie."

"What's going on in Poughkeepsie?"

"You can try and play this cool, but I think we're past that."

She elected to remain silent.

"I know you sent Katie Stahl to collect the money."

"I have no idea what..."

"Save it." I held up the piece of paper that Katie used to read the code for the safety-deposit-box room. It was a blue Post-it note with the logo across the top that said *Adirondacks are not only chairs*.

Lise froze in place.

"When I saw this Post-it with the security code, it took me a minute to remember where I'd seen this logo before." I started walking across the room, slowly.

Lise didn't move. She followed me with her eyes.

I said, "You were the perfect partner for drug dealers. If the cops ever had questions, you could've claimed attorney–client privilege. And Pete trusted you." I stopped at her desk. I saw the Post-it pad with the same logo near her pen in the corner of her desk.

I stared at her, waiting for some sort of response.

She finally said, "That's hardly a basis for an indictment, let alone a conviction."

"Not by itself. Phone records will help. Maybe your handwriting on the pad. Who knows. Good cops can be persistent."

There was no panic in her voice when she said, "I suppose the money is still at the bank."

Now it was my turn to keep quiet.

She said, "What can we do?"

"You think you can make some kind of deal?" I took a step back so I wouldn't be tempted. "It's a great idea. Make Katie do the dirty work. You get a big wad of cash and get to remain Newburgh's top criminal defense attorney. Pretty sweet deal."

Then the front door opened and Sergeant Bill Jeffries walked in with three other Newburgh police officers. One detective already had handcuffs ready.

I looked at Lise and said, "The problem is there are still a lot of good cops in Newburgh. For your sake, let's hope there's at least one other good attorney."

# CHAPTER 35

**THE GRAY CLOUDS** that hung low in the sky over Woodlawn Cemetery in New Windsor matched my mood exactly. The cold crept into my bones as I stood next to my brother. The crowd of friends and family listened to a Presbyterian minister say a few words over Katie Stahl's grave. Her family wanted nothing to do with Natty and that suited him fine.

It had been six days since the "shootout in Poughkeepsie," as the newspapers called it. Katie had been listed as a victim of a cop gone bad. That was better than I had hoped she'd be represented. The media tended to focus on the more sensational aspects of a case like this, so naturally, they wanted to talk about the corrupt cop in this sting. That caught people's attention. Not the fact that other cops jumped to make the case against Mike Tharpe and set things right as soon as they found out about it. All anyone talked about was a single bad apple.

If I was mentioned in any story, it was always as

someone trying to help his brother who'd been charged with a murder. I was worried someone would use the phrase "private investigator," and I'd have to explain myself to the New York Department of Business and Professional Regulation. There may not have been a specific charge about impersonating a private investigator, but I'm sure someone would have charged me a decent fine, and my days of helping the residents of Marlboro might be over.

Some of the news stories liked to show photos of Lise Mendez and talk about the pretty attorney who'd been involved in a drug conspiracy. She was now being held without bond on a slew of charges.

As for Mike Tharpe, he pled guilty to the murders of Alton Beatty and Katie Stahl, after I'd handed in his confession tape for Pete's murder. That would help reduce his sentence, but he'd still be away for a long time.

After the service, we walked to Natty's leased red Chevy Camaro with its extra-wide twenty-two-inch rear wheels. It looked like something a seventeen-year-old would drive.

As I slipped into the passenger seat I said, "You know, I could've driven."

Natty let out a short laugh and said, "I can't be seen in a car like yours. Sorry, no offense."

We drove through Newburgh on 9W in silence. I noticed Natty was pushing it and we were cruising at over seventy.

I said, "We're going a little fast, aren't we?"

"I thought you were a fake private investigator, not a fake cop."

I chuckled and mumbled, "Funny."

Natty pushed the sleek car a little harder and took it up over eighty as we left Balmville. Then he said, "I really did love her."

It was the first time he'd talked about Katie since he'd gotten out of jail the day after she was killed.

I said, "I know. She was a great girl. She just got caught up in something she didn't understand."

"It makes me think about my profession and lifestyle. I never knew what it was like to lose something as precious as Katie."

I did know, but I kept quiet. I liked seeing my brother grow up right in front of me, even if it was a dozen years later than everyone else usually did.

Natty said, "Who would've thought that after all these years, you'd be the one to understand what I'm going through? You're the person I can count on the most."

I shrugged and said, "I figured I'd have to bail you out of trouble sooner or later."

Now Natty smiled and said, "You're an asshole, but I love you."

"I love you, too." Then the car hit ninety and I added, "Asshole."

# MALEVOLENT

JAMES PATTERSON
& JAMES O. BORN

# CHAPTER 1

**I PAUSED FOR** almost a full minute on the porch of the house on Kerry Street near the town of West Nyack, New York. I was here as part of my private investigation business, but it wasn't like my usual chasing down drunken husbands or figuring out why elderly women were charged three times too much for air-conditioning units. This had the potential to be a real case. With a real payday.

Ellen Guidry had paid me $500 up front to find her daughter, Elizabeth. She also promised me another thousand if I got her out of the crack house where she'd supposedly been living and back home to Marlboro, about twenty minutes north of Newburgh.

My brother, Natty, offered to come. Although we'd had our differences as adults, he'd really matured in the last year. He'd given up his shady employment—selling dope from a bar in Newburgh—and was currently enrolled in paramedic school. I didn't want him missing any class time to come on some crazy adventure like this.

So here I stood. A pistol tucked in my waistband. Another first for this job. I was hoping I took this assignment for the right reasons. Save a girl stuck in a drug den. Reunite her with her mother. But in reality, I was starting to hurt for money. My job delivering newspapers had spiraled downward in the last few months. Everyone wanted their coupons and information in electronic form. Even my eighty-two-year-old neighbor started getting her local news on her iPad. I needed a reliable, secondary source of income.

I looked out over the patchy grass and clumps of weeds scattered around the dirt yard. There was an abandoned shopping cart with no wheels stuck in one corner. A couple of trees looked like they hadn't been trimmed in years. Their limbs grew out to unusual lengths and dipped so low they brushed the earth. A giant oak stump loomed like a barricade in front of the house.

I thought of different ways to gain entry, but decided knocking on the door was my best course of action. I'd wing it after that if I had to. It wasn't like I was a cop. I had no real authority.

I knocked three times. Steady. Too loud, and they might think I was a cop. Too soft, and they might miss it. I was thinking about what I was going to say, not paying as much attention as I should. I thought I heard something inside. Just some movement.

Then came two quick gunshots from inside the house.

As I heard the shots, two holes burst out of the door. At the same time that I heard the shots, I scrambled off the cement pad in front of the door. I scurried a dozen feet to the oak stump. I yanked the pistol out of my belt as I tried to catch my breath. The stump was big enough to cover most of my body.

My heart pounded as I held the gun, ready to return fire. I glanced behind me to make sure no one was trying to sneak up on me from another direction. Not only was all clear, no one in the neighborhood seemed to have noticed the gunfire. Were things really this bad in West Nyack?

I heard a voice shout from one of the windows. "What the hell are you doing here?"

I hesitated. Should I shout the girl's name? I decided I had nothing to lose. "I'm a friend of Ellen Guidry. She sent me to check on her daughter."

There was a long pause. I knew there was a discussion going on inside.

I was surprised when the door opened tentatively. A black man in a collared oxford button-down stuck his head out cautiously. His hair was cut neat with a little fade.

He glared at me next to the stump. "You almost got your head blown off."

"No shit." I stuck the gun back in my pants and stood up slowly to show my hands were empty.

The man motioned me to come forward. He had nothing in his hands, either.

As I reached the cement threshold, he said, "We didn't know Lizzie's mother was worried."

He didn't sound like a drug dealer.

I was still pissed. "Why'd you guys shoot at me, dammit?"

"We've had some trouble. Local gang is catching onto us. Thought that might show them we mean business."

I glared at him.

The man shrugged and said, "We aimed high on purpose. Didn't figure you'd be so big. Sort've came a little close. Sorry."

I stuttered for a moment. "I, I, um, is Elizabeth here?"

"Who the hell are you?"

"Like I said, I'm a friend of her mom's. She asked me to check on her."

The man stepped to the side so I could look inside the house. Elizabeth Guidry stepped from one of the rooms in the back. She wore a clean and respectable sundress with a pretty pastel sweater. And held a chromed, semiautomatic pistol in her right hand.

I said, "You're the one who shot at me?"

She nodded sheepishly. "Sorry." Her brown hair lay across her shoulder in an intricate braid. "I thought it would scare you off." She gave me an odd look, then said, "I know you, don't I?"

She motioned me inside. I stepped through the front door that hung at an angle. I was shocked at what I saw in the house. It was immaculate. It was beautifully furnished with an Ethan Allen couch. I glanced in the kitchen and noticed all new stainless-steel appliances. What the hell?

I rotated my head in every direction, looking for pieces of this puzzle. I turned and stared at the couple. I noticed she was now holding the young man's hand. The gun was nowhere in sight.

She said, "Now I remember you. You're Mitchum. You deliver newspapers up in Marlboro."

I nodded and said, "I'm a little confused. To be perfectly honest, your mother asked me to *rescue* you. She thought you were in some kind of a drug house."

They both started to giggle. She said, "This is my boyfriend, Eric. Does it look like I'm being held against my will? Or that I'm on drugs?"

"No. No it doesn't."

"We met at Hamilton College. All we did was use our business classes and accounting seminars to start a business."

"What kind of business?"

"I can't say out loud. Let's just look at it hypothetically. Say we rent two apartments in the next block. One of them sells crack and one of them sells pills and synthetic drugs. Between them, we're bringing in about $25,000 in cash a month. Pure profit."

"So why do you live here?"

"We don't want the police to seize our personal property if they raid one of the apartments. Now all they get is whatever cash is there and they make the arrest of one or two of our employees. So far, we've had no problems in almost four months of operation. We figure another year and we can retire to a legitimate business. Does that satisfy you?"

"So you're not a victim, you're drug kingpin."

The smile spread over her face. "That's very flattering, but I'm hardly a kingpin. I have five employees and we move a fraction of what real drug dealers do. But that's their weakness. They're greedy. They have no business plan." She waved her hand around the beautifully decorated interior like she was a model in a home show. "And we don't flaunt our money. That breeds jealousy. That gives people incentive to snitch on us. We've really thought this through. I hope you're not going to screw it up for us."

"I'm only worried about my assignment. I have no idea what I can tell your mother."

"Don't bother. We'll drive up to Marlboro this afternoon. I'll show her I'm safe and healthy. I'll just tell her I'm living with Eric. That should be enough to keep her away."

I liked her mischievous smile and attitude. She clearly had a head for business.

My phone rang and I noticed it was my brother. A *former* drug dealer. At least that's what he told me while he was in paramedic school. I answered it quickly.

"What's up, Natty?"

"Meet me at the hospital in Newburgh. Mom's been hit by a car. It looks serious."

# CHAPTER 2

**I RACED THROUGH** the front door of Saint Luke's Cornwall Hospital. The hospital is on DuBois Street, about a mile south of where I-84 crosses the Hudson. I slid to a stop in front of a uniformed Newburgh police sergeant. It took me a moment to realize who it was.

"Hey, Mitchum. You got here fast."

"Bill, how's my mom?"

Bill Jeffries was a sergeant with the Newburgh police department. He also dated my mom occasionally. He had the kind of naturally calming voice you hoped you'd hear when things went bad. The look on his face told me everything I needed to know. Nothing I *wanted* to know, but that's how bad news usually hits you.

Bill said, "She's still in surgery. She's got a broken left hip and possibly some internal injuries. They're also worried about the way her head hit the curb. We're waiting up on the third floor. I thought it might be best to catch you down here before you stumbled into the situation."

He calmly led me to the elevator and up to a waiting room where my mom's best friend, Dolores Hackmacher, sat next to my brother. She held Natty's hand like he was a fifth-grader. I wondered if I sat on the other side of her, she'd hold my hand, too.

After settling in, I tried to make a little small talk, asking my brother how paramedic school was going and if Dolores's granddaughter got into Syracuse. I really didn't care about Dolores's granddaughter. And I knew my brother was doing well because I checked on him almost every day. It's tough to make changes like my brother had. He went from a successful drug-dealing career to trying to make something out of his life. If I didn't realize how difficult that transition could be, I did now. And as much as he frustrated me, I was really proud of him.

Hospital waiting rooms are a scary prospect. Not only are you there because something's gone wrong with someone you love, but you have plenty of time to think about it.

When Bill Jeffries sat down next to me, I asked him if he had any details about what happened to my mother.

"Nothing, really. She was exiting through the back of the hospital. She likes to park high up in the lot in case it rains. Just one of her cute little quirks. She was hit on Johnson Street."

I could tell by the careful tone of his voice that he had stronger feelings for my mother than he let on. I wondered if it was mutual. I just wanted her to be happy. He seemed like a decent guy. There's not much else a son could ask for his mother than her meeting a decent guy.

Bill cleared his throat, then said, "Two eyewitnesses said a blue SUV came down the street kind of fast and hit your mom. The witnesses said the SUV didn't slow down. We got half the Newburgh Police Department out searching for an SUV with front-end damage."

I said, "Did the witnesses get a look at the driver?"

Bill shook his head. "They couldn't even agree on the exact color of the SUV. One said it was a lighter, bright blue. The other witness swore it was a dark blue. No plates, can't ID the driver, and already looked at any security footage on the backside of the hospital. The cameras don't cover much more than the walkways to the main doors."

I may not have ever been a cop and didn't have any formal training as a private investigator, but something inside me said this was no accident. I had to get some time to think where I wasn't worried about my mom or how other people were reacting. I needed to figure this out.

My brother, Natty, joined Bill and me in the corner of the waiting room. Bill said, "I've never seen you visit the hospital before, Natty."

He shrugged and said, "Mom sort of banned me a few years ago."

I was impressed that Bill had enough sense not to ask any more questions. My mom told me she caught Natty trying to steal some OxyContin to sell. She'd ripped an earring out of his ear on the spot and issued his lifetime ban. I'll admit I thought it was funny when she told me the story.

I also think Natty learned his lesson. The fact that he was trying to change his life was a great step.

A man in green surgical scrubs and cap stepped into the room. He had black and gray stubble on his chin and his eyebrows bristled from underneath the edge of the cap.

He had no hint of a smile and said, "Which of you are related to Elaine Mitchum?"

No one moved for a moment, then I said, "We all are."

That seemed to satisfy the surgeon as he plopped into an empty chair and looked at Natty, Dolores, Bill, and me.

After a few seconds of silence, Natty blurted out, "You're killing us, Doc. What are you waiting for? A musical intro?"

Score one for my brother.

# CHAPTER 3

**IT WAS ALMOST** two hours later when the hospital staff allowed us to join my mother in her private room, one of the nicest. Apparently, the hospital was trying to take good care of one of its own employees. A fifty-inch Samsung TV hung on the wall, already tuned to an ESPN talk show my mom loved. She followed the Giants and the Bills on *NFL Live*. Then she'd watch *Around the Horn*, followed by *Pardon the Interruption* with Tony Kornheiser and Mike Wilbon, every weekday evening. She knew the line on every game and could no longer participate in the hospital football pool because she won it three weeks in a row.

She seemed content. The room looked like a resort, except for the view. No tall building in Newburgh had much of a view. Unless you consider crumbling old buildings and dead trees a great view.

Once Natty had gotten the doctor talking, he didn't seem to shut up. But the long and the short of his explanation was that my mother would recover. I almost didn't hear the other things he said about her bruised kidneys, broken hip, and concussion. All I heard was that she would make a full recovery. I almost cried I was so relieved.

A nurse, about twenty-five, managed to slip between my brother, Bill Jeffries, and me as he set my mom's IVs and equipment.

My mom let him work for about two minutes before she started giving him orders. I would say she was giving suggestions, but she sounded more like a drill sergeant.

"Put both the IVs over on this side so my sons don't trip over them. I don't think I need the EKG running all the time. It's distracting."

The nurse shot me a quick, confused look. He was used to doctors ordering him around. Now it was a patient. But he knew exactly who she was. And he listened to every word she said.

My mom said, "Tell everyone at the desk, I'm a customer now. Don't treat me like a coworker."

As soon as the nurse was finished with all of his adjustments and my mom's orders, he fled the room like a Giants fan slinking out of the stadium after a loss.

My mom looked at Natty and me. "C'mon, Bobby and Natty, give your mother a kiss." Her voice was just a shade weaker than normal, but her tone was just as sharp. It gave me hope.

My mom was the only one who ever called me by my given name. Even my brother called me Mitchum. All my cousins call me Mitchum. I'm sure a few of them don't even know my first name. I'm so used to being called Mitchum that sometimes I forget to answer when someone calls me Robert or Bobby.

A doctor walked in a few minutes later. He was a good-looking guy with blondish hair. He glanced down at a chart and said, "Looks good."

That comment seemed to give my mom some energy. "Looks good! Looks good." The outrage grew with every word. "Listen to me, Doogie Howser. It looked good yesterday. Today I'm a mess. I was run down by a truck." Then she looked at me and Natty, standing in the corner of the room, and added, "On purpose."

Apparently, this was the theory she had floated already to Bill Jeffries. He didn't react but I wanted to hear more.

I said, "Mom, are you saying someone hit you intentionally?"

"That's exactly what I'm saying. And when I find out who did it, they'll wish they only get arrested."

I had to chuckle, as even lying in a bed, with a hundred medical devices attached to her, my mom's threats were still scary. If she ever catches whoever ran her down, I wouldn't want to be in their shoes, especially if they did it on purpose.

My mom turned to Bill and said, "I know that what I'm about to say will make me sound like Bobby with his conspiracies, but it's the truth. I heard the engine rev just before the truck hit me."

The doctor was clearly trying to extricate himself from

this conversation. He casually said, "We'll get a good view of your hip and pelvis with a CAT scan tomorrow."

My mom said, "I can do it right now."

The doctor said, "Let me check the schedule," and he scooted out of the room faster than the nurse had earlier. Everyone but my mom knew he wasn't coming back today.

I looked around the room and ran some numbers in my head. This was going to be an expensive stay. Really expensive. Even with her insurance.

I had never really worried about money. I made enough in the Navy to be happy. I lived in a comfortable but tiny house, and until recently, I had money coming in. Now I considered what my mom would need even after she was released.

Money might be one of my new worries.

# CHAPTER 4

**IT WAS LATE** by the time I got back to my house. I ran by my mom's house to make sure it was secure, and I grabbed her mail. Mostly bills except for her copy of *Sports Illustrated* and her church newsletter, *The Marlboro Message*. Her house is only a few blocks from mine. I sat on my threadbare couch, with my dog, Bart Simpson.

He looked like a cross between a Boston terrier and a bulldog, but I knew he was just a mongrel. There was no intentional breeding to make him come out like this. He considered himself royalty. At least that's how he was treated. My mom baked homemade dog treats for him. Unfortunately, I found out she was doing this when I stole one from a tray in her kitchen thinking it was some kind of holiday treat. She used some kind of natural fiber to help Bart Simpson's digestion. I can say it works pretty well.

We had the news on, but we weren't really watching it.

Bart's head lay across my lap and I rubbed behind his ears. There were a couple of brochures spread on the couch and on the coffee table in front of me. One was from the Newburgh Police Department, designed to recruit new officers. Bill had tried to sell me on it several times.

I looked into law enforcement jobs. It seemed like a natural fit for a Navy vet who wanted to help people. I was amazed at the good pay and the benefits, including a great retirement. But I didn't think I had the right temperament for it. I was never big on following too many rules. That made it tough on me in the Navy. Besides, it was pretty dangerous to be a cop nowadays. Just stopping someone for a speeding ticket could lead to an ambush. Timmy Jones, my childhood friend who worked for the sheriff's office now, told me about a couple of his close calls. I didn't think I could live my life worried about stuff like that.

I picked up a business card sitting on the coffee table. The top said "Non-Metric Solutions." There was a photo of Neil Armstrong planting the American flag on the moon. Underneath that, it said "Metric system? Whose flag is on the moon?" Next to the photo was my friend's name, DP Lampkin. We'd been in the Navy together. He was one of the smartest, funniest guys I'd ever met. Now he worked for a military contractor coordinating people in Afghanistan.

DP was one of the most interesting characters I knew. Raised in Los Angeles, he now had a home on the coast of Oregon. He said his wife didn't mind him working overseas as long as she got to live as comfortably as she did. He loved to laugh about her saying that. I'd met her a couple of times and knew she'd stick by DP's side no matter what.

I'd put off calling him about a job for months now. I dialed the number with an Oregon area code and waited as it routed through God knew how many satellites. At the other end of the line, I heard a groggy "Hello."

"DP, it's Mitchum. Did I catch you at a bad time?" Then I remembered the crazy time difference. "I'm sorry, what time is it there?"

"Six thirty in the morning. I thought it was my alarm."

I heard him laugh and that made me smile. I said, "It's ten o'clock at night here. How's it six thirty there?"

"Like everything else in this country, their time zone is screwy. It's eight and a half hours ahead of the Eastern time zone."

"I didn't know there was such a thing as a half time zone."

"Trust me, there're a lot of odd things over here."

We chatted for a few minutes and I finally asked him how he liked his job.

DP said, "Mitchum, I swear to God, I fell in it. This is the best gig I could've ever imagined. You really need to come work with me. Non-Metric Solutions, purely American."

"What sort of stuff would I be doing?"

"We're only contracted for patrol and security. No detention. Other companies handle that kind of stuff. I can take you on anytime you want.

"There's a little bit of training, some medical screening, but that's about it."

I nodded as I listened. "I'm seriously considering it."

"I could use a guy like you."

The whole conversation kept me from sleeping very well. But it was nice to know I had a fallback if I needed it.

# CHAPTER 5

**THE NEXT DAY**, I knew I wouldn't be allowed to visit my mom until after nine o'clock. I made my usual stop at the only place I'd eaten besides my house for most of my adult life. A diner named Tina's Plentiful. Tina had been in school with me and now ran the place that virtually everyone in town stopped at several times a month. It was also my unofficial private investigator's office.

I usually took the booth in the back and no one minded if I talked to clients over breakfast.

My cousin, Terry Mitchum, worked in the kitchen. He'd lived in the city for a couple of years but decided he was more of a small-town guy. Like me. That was the only thing we had in common.

The real reason I was here this morning had nothing to do with my office or my dorky cousin. The real reason flashed me a beautiful smile as she bumped backward out of the swinging kitchen doors, holding two plates of pancakes and eggs. Alicia Sosa was as graceful as a ballerina. If that ballerina was carrying food to hungry customers. Her brown hair tied in a ponytail made her look younger than twenty-seven.

Once she delivered the food, she came by my booth. She did a quick glance around the restaurant then leaned over and gave me a kiss on the cheek. She said, "The other night was fun. We should do it again soon."

A grin spread over my face. I said, "I agree. One of the best nights I've had in a while."

"We did a lot that night, but there's a whole lot more to go."

I said, "How many more seasons of *Game of Thrones* are there?"

"It took us four days to binge the first season. There's like seven more to go. At least."

I didn't have to order. I liked when Alicia surprised me with breakfast. She was more health conscious than me and shied away from pancakes and waffles.

I said, "Do you have class today?"

"Nope. I went by and said hello to your mom after class yesterday. Considering what happened, she looks pretty good."

I thanked her and watched as she put in an order for an egg-white omelet and whole-wheat toast. That would not have been my first choice. Or my second. But I'd eat them and probably feel better for it later on.

Alicia was an impressive woman. She moved back to Marlboro to help care for her father, who has been recovering from a stroke. She also continued her nursing education by enrolling in Mount St. Mary College in New-burgh. She already had her BS in biology from SUNY Binghamton. Alicia had said she looked up to the most famous Binghamton grad: Tony Kornheiser from ESPN. I knew him from my mom's obsession with New York sports.

I didn't know how she put in the early hours here at the diner and went to school or studied the rest of the day.

Before my food arrived, I was surprised by an unusual visitor. I didn't notice when the front door opened. A moment later, the shadow fell across the table forcing me into a friendly mindset. When I looked up and realized it was my brother I realized I didn't have to be friendly at all.

I said, "I never see you in here. I never see you this early in the morning."

He slid into the booth across from me. "I used to sleep late every morning. Now I usually have to be at class early. Except Tuesdays and Thursdays."

A minute later, Alicia was back and seemed happy to see my brother. She even grabbed an extra cup of coffee and sat down with us while things were a little slow.

I'll admit I felt a twinge of jealousy when she slipped into the booth next to Natty and not me. I knew it was innocent and probably just an easier way for her to keep an eye on the two customers sitting at a nearby table, but it still stung a little. I'm also a little envious that my brother is lean, whereas I'm considered anything but lean.

It didn't matter that I worked out and stayed in shape, my brother looks that way naturally. And now that he had stopped smoking and started working out, he looked even better. That sucked.

I even noticed Alicia checking out his newest tattoo on his left bicep. A little devil in a paramedic's uniform.

Natty charmed her with tales of becoming a paramedic.

I couldn't resist saying, "Certainly better than your last job."

Alicia knew what he used to do; I just wanted to remind them both.

I said to Alicia, "What time do you get off today?"

"About eleven. If Larry shows up on time. Then I'm just going to crash and study for a while."

"Why don't you let me buy you lunch at the Bristol Pub? It opens at eleven and it's always pretty busy."

The smile on her face gave me a warm feeling. That is, until she turned to my brother and said, "What about it, Natty, want to join us at the Bristol Pub?"

The day was not starting out like I wanted.

# CHAPTER 6

**AFTER BREAKFAST, NATTY** and I raced down to see my mom at the hospital. We only got a couple of minutes with her before they took her for a battery of tests. She still looked good, although now some of the bruises on her face and arm were turning a sickly blue and yellow.

On our way back to Marlboro, I said to my brother, "You don't have to hang out with us at the pub. You have the whole day free."

"I'm looking forward to a beer and a burger. Besides, Alicia clearly wanted me to come or she wouldn't have asked me."

"Unless she was being polite."

"Or she thinks you're a clueless putz."

I would've kicked him out of the car except he was driving his rented Chevy Impala. It was a big step down from the sports cars he went through as a drug dealer. But it was a big step up from my ancient, decrepit station wagon that I used to deliver newspapers.

Alicia had changed into jeans and a throwback Phil Simms Giants jersey. When she saw us, she smiled and said, "I decided I needed to dress properly for the sports bar."

It was a pleasant conversation over pretty good food. Natty made some comment about how important it is to work for the community.

He looked at Alicia and said, "That's why I'm in paramedic school. That's why you're in nursing school. That's why Mitchum…" He didn't even have the decency to smile like it was a joke. "I guess that's why Mitchum delivers newspapers. Or whatever he can deliver now one or two days a week."

I said, "I remember when you first got community spirit. Wasn't it ordered by a judge? I bet with all the court-ordered time you've done on the side of the road, you've picked up a record amount of garbage." It was childish, but satisfying.

Natty wasn't done, either. "I'm selling you short, Mitchum. You did your time in the Navy. Even if you didn't make it into the SEALs like you wanted. What ended that dream? Oh yeah, you weren't a good enough swimmer. Pretty much the one thing every SEAL is known for, you didn't practice."

I didn't come back with anything. One reason was it was accurate. That was exactly why I washed out of SEAL training in the final week. The other reason was that it was clear Alicia wasn't enjoying this exchange. She was too nice to appreciate typical burns that brothers laid on each other. Especially brothers trying to impress the same pretty girl.

She said, "I probably need to get home to study."

She only lived a couple of blocks away from the pub. I offered to walk her home, claiming that it was an easy walk to my car at the diner after that.

Natty didn't push it and said his good-byes inside the pub. As Alicia and I strolled down the quiet streets of Marlboro, I turned to her and said, "I'm sorry for my childish behavior in there. Natty and I tend to be competitive. It really is harmless. We get along better now than we have in years."

"Why's that?"

"He appreciates what I do as a private investigator and I appreciate that he gave up drug dealing. I just hope he stays the course."

Alicia laughed and said, "At least he changed course, even if it only proves temporary. But I have a good feeling about your brother. I think he'll make it."

We stopped on the street in front of her cute apartment building. The two-story brick building had been around since I was a kid. Now it was divided into apartments. Two big ones downstairs and four smaller ones upstairs.

She turned to me and said, "Thanks for a lovely time. I could've wasted it watching TV."

"What about catching an episode of *Game of Thrones*? After that, you can study till your eyes fall out."

She smiled. "That's a lovely image."

Just then, the world seemed to turn upside down. For

a split second, between the noise and the concussion, I thought it was an earthquake. As I stared almost directly at the window to Alicia's apartment, a roar of an explosion and a flash of flame shattered the glass. The concussion made me take a step back just in time to catch Alicia as she lost her balance.

Glass and debris made a clanking sound on the front walkway of the apartment complex. Smoke poured from Alicia's window.

The front door to the building burst open and a couple of people rushed outside screaming and crying.

I had to make sure there was no one else inside.

# CHAPTER 7

**I RACED TO** the front door of the building. Just as I stepped inside, a woman handed me a child. A screaming little girl about two years old. The woman was coughing violently in the haze of smoke billowing down the stairway. I led her out the front door, and Alicia met us halfway down the walkway. I handed her the little girl and turned back to the building.

There wasn't a roaring fire, but the smoke was blinding and made it difficult to breathe. I pulled my shirt over my mouth and ducked low as I scrambled up the stairs. An older woman I knew from the diner stumbled out of her apartment at the end of the hallway.

"Mrs. Siddiqui, are you okay?"

She coughed and looked at me. She said in a re-markably normal voice, "Mitchum, how is your mother doing after the accident?" Good manners become part of someone's being, even in a crisis.

I heard someone moan down the hallway. I told Mrs.

Siddiqui to wait right there. The smoke poured out of Alicia's apartment. The door had been twisted off the hinges and lay in the hallway. That's where the moaning was coming from.

I flipped the door off the man on the ground. It was the super of the building. He was a tall man with dark hair, graying at the temples. I'd seen him around over the years. I thought his name was Mike.

He looked up, but his eyes didn't focus well. I didn't have time to worry about spinal injuries. I had no idea what had exploded and if something else was going to blow up.

I shouted, "Mike, we're on the clock. I gotta get you out of here right now. I'm going to lift you up. Do you understand?"

He nodded weakly.

I started to pull him upright and realized he was much heavier and sturdier than I expected. I draped him over my shoulder like a long piece of limp lasagna. Now I had him in a classic fireman's carry.

I waddled down the hall and reached out with my left hand to guide Mrs. Siddiqui carefully down the stairway. Every time something popped or a new wave of smoke floated past us, I jumped. I expected something horrendous to happen.

At the landing, halfway between the first and second floors, Mrs. Siddiqui needed to stop for a moment. She was coughing and I gently pushed her toward the floor and out of the thickest smoke.

I said, "Can you make it? I can come right back for you."

She waved me off. Then she stood up and started down the stairs, this time leading me.

By the time we reached the first floor, I could hear sirens in the distance. My eyes felt like someone had splashed Clorox in them. I could hear Alicia calling to me from the front door. She had someone's dog by the collar and a wriggling black cat in her right arm.

We all came through the front door at about the same time. Coughing and sputtering. The cat squealed and jumped from Alicia's arms. It scampered toward the edge of the yard.

The little dog yapped.

Mrs. Siddiqui stepped in the grass and hacked, trying to clear her airways. Alicia stepped over to help her.

I struggled down the walkway with the big super across my shoulder. He started to cough as well. That was a good sign. At least he was breathing.

I set him down gently on the swale in front of the apartment building. A small crowd started to gather.

I felt a little dizzy from the smoke and the exertion. I plopped down on the grass next to the super. When I looked up, Natty was running toward me.

"I could see the smoke as soon as I got to my car. Something told me you'd be involved." He turned and checked the super. He spoke in a comforting tone, telling the man to relax and breathe.

Now the fire engines were arriving. Two paramedics raced to the fallen super.

The older of the two said, "Look, it's Nat Mitchum from the academy."

The other paramedics said, "Great job, Nat. Looks like you're a real hero."

I just lay on the grass next to them, hoping I didn't vomit.

# CHAPTER 8

**IT TOOK A** little convincing, but I finally agreed to sit in the back of a paramedic's truck and breathe oxygen through a clear, plastic mask. Natty sat with me for a while but decided to look important by stepping up to one of the paramedics and suggesting he help in the search of the building. I was glad. I didn't feel like talking to him anymore.

Alicia was obviously upset that her apartment had been utterly destroyed. Thank God she had no pets. Someone from the sheriff's office ran her over to her father's apartment so she could rest and break the news to him carefully.

My friend from the sheriff's office, Timmy Jones, came walking from the building toward me. Timmy knew me well enough to know my first question.

He said, "The super is going to be okay. He really owes you one. I don't even know how you carried him. The son of a gun must be six foot six."

"Do you have any idea what happened?"

"The super had a complaint about someone smelling gas. He figured out it was coming from Alicia's apartment, knocked on the door, and when he got no answer, he used his master key. It was just about then that the gas leak ignited and blew the shit out of anything near her stove. The door protected the super from the blast. And he was lucky a big moose like you happened to be the guy who found him and was able to carry him."

I asked, "Did anybody see anything suspicious?"

"Buddy Wilson, from the gas company, said it was a nick in the pipe."

My eyes popped open at that comment. I said a little more harshly than I meant to, "Butt-crack Buddy? What else is he going to say? What about the state police?"

"They're busy with the shooting in Poughkeepsie. My boss told them to never mind." Then Timmy looked at me. "Mitchum, it was just a freak accident. Let it go."

"Or is that what someone wanted us to think?" I could tell by his sigh that not only did he not agree with a theory like that, he didn't want to discuss it.

"C'mon, Mitchum, don't start with the crazy conspiracy theories."

"I just think it's a coincidence, a weird coincidence, that my mom is a victim of a hit-and-run and then my..." I thought about the term carefully. "Sort-of girlfriend is almost blown to bits. What are the odds of something like that?"

"That's why it's called a coincidence. Very high odds.

But not impossible. In fact, given where we live and what you do for a living, I think it's highly unlikely. Extraordinarily unlikely. Incredibly, unbelievably..."

I held up my hands in surrender. "I get it, I get it. It's not likely."

"In fact, it is *unlikely*. Don't make me go through the whole story again."

Timmy sat down at the back of the truck with me. We watched as the first responders made sure the building was secure.

I mumbled to myself, "Alicia's got no place to stay."

He said, "What's wrong with your house?"

"I don't want her to think I'm trying to take advantage of the situation."

"I thought you said she's your girlfriend."

"I said, *sort-of* girlfriend. We're not officially dating. Or exclusive."

"Have you spent the night at her apartment?"

"Never. I've been there a couple of times in the last week just to watch *Game of Thrones* with her."

He scratched his head and said, "Sounds like you and I have different definitions for girlfriends. I watch *Game of Thrones* with my dad. I'm not judging." He gave me one of his sly smiles.

This was something I'd have to talk over with Alicia. After I thought about it a little while longer.

# CHAPTER 9

**I SPENT THE** afternoon at the hospital with my mom. I didn't tell her exactly what happened at Alicia's apartment, just that she couldn't stay there for a while.

My mom had a brilliant idea. She said, "Do you think she'd stay with me while I recover? She'd have her own bedroom, and I wouldn't make too many demands."

"So you're saying you'll treat her differently than you treat everyone else?" I was sitting a little too close and she was able to reach out and rap me on the hand with her knuckles. It made me flinch.

I calmly said, "I will forward that idea. I think she'd love it. She already spends a lot of time caring for her dad, but he only has one bedroom."

I rolled back home about sunset and didn't realize how tired I was until I plopped on the couch and Bart Simpson jumped up to sit next to me. Rubbing his head allowed my mind to wander.

I just couldn't accept that the explosion at Alicia's

apartment was purely an accident. Even though Buddy "Butt-crack" Wilson from the gas company said it was just a simple gas leak, I couldn't let it go.

I'd worked with explosives a little bit in the Navy. I was by no means an expert, but I did know modern buildings with decent pipes don't just explode. I dozed off right on the couch.

The alarm on my watch woke me at four-thirty. It was still pitch black outside. This was one of the few days I could still deliver newspapers and I jumped on it. By eight o'clock, I'd finished my wide route that covered several small towns in our area. Mostly I delivered small advertising circulars, but there was one town that got its own newspaper once a week. Those were easy to chuck out of the window of my station wagon onto driveways as I barely slowed down.

When I was finished, I didn't even go to Tina's Plentiful. I knew I had to clear a few things up and satisfy my own curiosity before I got back to my regular routine. I drove directly to Alicia's apartment building.

The fire department had allowed the other residents to return. I wandered through the front door and could still smell the smoke embedded in the cheap carpet and wallpaper. Eventually, they'd have to change all of that.

Alicia's apartment had a piece of plywood nailed across the doorway, covered by police caution tape. I pictured how the blast had knocked the door off the hinges and saved the super's life.

I was startled to hear someone call my name. I turned and saw the super coming down the hallway. He only had a couple of Band-Aids on his forehead and cheek.

I said, "Hey, Mike. Should you be back at work so soon?"

The tall man shrugged. "This is my only source of income. I'm not only the super, I own the building. I can't afford to take a day off."

"Did anyone come up with any answers?"

He shrugged. "The cops explained that we're just a small town. They don't have the resources or experience to do an in-depth investigation. They were certain enough that it was an accident. I agreed so the building wasn't shut down for a long investigation. That's good and bad. It's good because my insurance company should pay off fairly easily. It's bad because it makes it look like I don't take care of my building."

"Do you mind if I look around a little bit? I won't damage anything or cause any problems."

"You're a private investigator, so as long as you don't charge me, I don't see why not. Besides, I owe you. Bigtime."

I brushed off his praise. I was also about to correct him and explain that I wasn't an official private investigator. I had no license and hadn't been vetted by the state. But I had some experience with explosives and a real interest in this case.

Mike said, "The door and some of the debris from the apartment are in the dumpster."

I clapped my hands together and rubbed them as if I was trying to keep them warm. "There's nothing like starting your day off by climbing in a dumpster."

The tall man laughed and patted me on the back as I headed around back.

# CHAPTER 10

**THIS WAS OUTSIDE** my normal duties as an unlicensed private investigator. Usually, my job had a lot to do with finding people or interviewing people. This was the rare occasion where I was looking for evidence of a crime. Something that wouldn't be obvious.

I had to pull a lot of garbage out of the dumpster to examine it. Also, the door was wedged beneath much of the debris. After more effort than I really wanted to expend, I had the debris laid out in the parking lot next to the dumpster the same way the FAA laid out parts recovered from a plane crash. I was hoping I might see a pattern.

The nature of the blast, one giant wave of heat, left very little smoke damage on most of the debris. Finally, I got to the door itself. It was intact. The hinges had been ripped from the jamb and were still attached to the door.

I ran my fingers around the door handle and lock. I didn't see anything unusual. Then, on closer examination of the deadbolt, I saw some odd markings on the outside of the lock. There were several scratches around the key-hole. I touched the marks carefully with my pinky and could feel the ridge with a minuscule amount of metal roughing the edges. These were fresh markings. At first I thought it was from the blast. Then I realized they looked like the markings from someone picking the lock. I'd seen it in training with the Navy. After I had washed out of SEAL training, I went through a number of criminal investigation courses. One of the instructors set up a crime scene to teach us how to determine if someone had entered a file room at the law enforcement training center in Arizona.

The first clue in the training exercise looked exactly like the marks on this lock. The instructor had explained how hard it was to pick a lock. This concerned me.

I continue to examine the door and found one other thing out of place. At the very bottom of the door, on the inside, a piece of clear Scotch tape about the size of my thumbnail was carefully placed on the corner.

I had to think about this and what it meant.

After I was done with the dumpster, I talked to Mike about security video or any other security devices on the property.

He showed me his homemade security center in the corner of his own apartment.

Mike said, "The cops glanced at all of these. There's really nothing to see prior to the blast. For some reason, the light in our parking lot was out. That's the only way the video picks up anything at night."

He walked me out to the parking lot and showed me the camera and the light.

I borrowed a ladder and carefully set it against the eighteen-foot-tall light post. It only took me a moment of examination to realize someone had shot the light out with a BB gun. A single, tiny hole showed me that someone knew what they were doing. And it gave them a way to enter the apartment building unseen.

Mike let me look through seven days of security video. Most of it was mind-numbing. I recognized many of the tenants as they came and went, including Mrs. Siddiqui, the woman I helped from the building after the blast.

I noticed something at the edges of the parking lot where the camera caught a bit of the street. I watched the video three different times. At approximately two in the afternoon, three days prior to the blast, a blue SUV drove past on the street. It almost looked like surveillance.

I watched the video of the night before the explosion. At the far corners of the dark video, I saw a person moving about five a.m. That would've been just after Alicia left for work.

It was just a smudge. Almost like a ghost in a horror movie. From the size of the person, I guessed it was a man. That made me think as well.

Then I started to put it all together. Surveillance of the area. They probably saw me coming over to watch TV with Alicia. The light knocked out by a well-placed shot from a BB gun. It could be kids fooling around. But what if it wasn't?

The marks on the deadbolt made it appear to me that someone had entered the apartment. If they were just trying to cover their tracks from a burglary, it seemed like a huge amount of effort. Especially to burglarize a nursing student. And what criminal in their right mind would elevate a simple burglary to a possible murder?

The final piece of the puzzle was the tape at the bottom of the door. Somewhere in the recesses of my mind I recalled an easy, old-school way to ignite a booby trap. In the training scenario I went through, it had to do with gasoline on the ground. And securing an easily ignited match, like a giant kitchen match, on the bottom of the door would be a good flashpoint.

If there was enough natural gas in an enclosed space, a match would be an easy way to ignite it. And putting it on the door meant it would be ignited by the person with the key.

All of this together pointed to one unsettling theory: whoever did this was a real pro. Even with the crude step of using a match taped to a door. I felt like it was all intentional. Someone purposely used household items to create the explosion. I had to figure out how to stop them.

# CHAPTER 11

**A FEW DAYS** later, I was no closer to finding an answer to my questions. I hadn't told Alicia about my concerns because I didn't want to scare her, and I didn't want to look like some kind of conspiracy nut.

I was in an upbeat mood because it was time for my mom to come home. I had already helped Alicia get settled in the second bedroom at my mom's house. She was thrilled with the chance to help my mom, who she knew from the hospital. She was also grateful she had a comfortable place to live.

I drove my mom in her big Buick LaCrosse. I was jumpy. Every time I saw any sort of SUV, I checked it out carefully. I was starting to see blue SUVs everywhere.

When we got to the house, I pushed my mom in a wheelchair up the ramp Bill and I had built the day before. Just simple plywood, but knowing my mom, we painted it the same color yellow as the house. It looked natural.

Just as we got to the top of the ramp, my mom turned and motioned me closer. She patted me on the cheek and said, "That ramp is beautiful. It looks like a professional did it. Thank you so much."

Instantly, I was transported back to second grade, when my mom made me feel like I would definitely win the science fair with my in-depth look at the differences between green beans and lima beans. She had always made Natty and me feel like we could do anything.

We got her settled comfortably on the couch. She barked at Natty to bring her the TV remote. She wanted to watch all the *Jeopardy!* episodes that had been saved on DVR. I noticed Bart Simpson was quiet, sitting carefully at the end of the couch. He sensed that she was injured, but he didn't want to be too far away from her.

Dolores Hackmacher had made some Toll House cookies. Natty and I both tried to steal several, only to be caught by my mom. She ordered Natty to come closer to the couch. When he stepped over to her, she gave him a little smack on the cheek and said, "Act your age."

Natty held his cheek and said, "Jesus Christ..."

That earned him a serious slap.

Natty said, "C'mon, Mom, what was that for? You curse all the time."

She calmly said, "First of all, I don't curse all the time. Secondly, you boys are usually the cause of it. And thirdly, don't take the Lord's name in vain."

We both knew that tone. She was deadly serious. And if I thought about it, she occasionally dropped the F-bomb or a "shit," but she never used "goddamn" or "Jesus Christ." I knew to steer away from that minefield.

Bill said good-bye to my mom and nodded for me to follow him out on the porch. Once we were alone, he said, "I know you've been asking around about the blue SUV and you think the explosion at your girlfriend's apartment was deliberate."

I was going to say something, but he held up his hand.

"Learn from my experience, Mitchum. Conspiracies just don't happen much. It's easy for people to think in conspiracies. That makes our ordinary lives more interesting. It keeps us from thinking about the real things we have to face every day. That's why people want to believe it was a conspiracy to kill JFK or Martin Luther King. In real life, at least in police work, I found the simple answer is usually the right one."

He made sense, even if I still thought there was some conspiracy at work around me and my family. He was trying to comfort me and give me the benefit of his experience. It was one of the first times someone had actually acted like a father toward me in this town.

When I walked back inside, my mom was chatting with Alicia. The two of them were giggling about something I was sure made fun of me. That was no conspiracy theory.

When Alicia left for her training shift at the hospital in Newburgh, my mom patted the edge of the couch. She made no effort to distinguish calling me or calling Bart Simpson, and we both listened.

She said, "That girl is a real find. She's smart, pretty, and takes no bullshit. She's a real keeper."

When I didn't answer immediately, my mom said, "It doesn't matter if you see it. She'd work out just as well for Natty. But I think you're the one she's interested in."

Just what I needed. More things to think about.

# CHAPTER 12

**THAT NIGHT, I** decided to do a little surveillance around town. I had listened to Bill about conspiracies and decided I was too immature to learn from his experience. I'm sure he'd understand.

All I really did was tool around town in my station wagon. I'm not even sure what I was hoping to find. A blue SUV with a dented front end. Someone I didn't recognize who looked suspicious. All I knew is that I couldn't sit around and do nothing.

Bart Simpson had elected to stay at my mom's house. He had a good sense for how much she needed him at the moment. My mom said he could be her service dog for a few weeks. She promised not to put him in a purse like the rich ladies in the city.

Until I provided her with grandchildren, my mom would have to make do with a dog that slobbered and had terminal flatulence. That was okay with me.

The first thing I realized during my surveillance was

that I lived in the quietest town in America. I knew it was small and comfortable, without the normal noise of a big city, but this was ridiculous. There was no one on the streets. I passed a car about every three minutes. I'm not even sure why the town incorporated. It also made me realize I knew virtually everyone in town by name. Or, at least, I recognized them on sight.

After a couple of frustrating hours, I decided it was a waste of time. But I wasn't ready to go home. I had a boatload of nervous energy. For no real reason, I headed south on Route 9 toward Newburgh. I still found myself really examining every vehicle that passed me.

Once I reached the city limits of Newburgh, I considered running by the hospital and visiting Alicia. That was something I'd never done before. Never even considered it. Did my mom's little talk have more of an effect on me than I realized? Alicia was definitely special. Like my mom said, she was a keeper.

When I thought about it, I decided I would only be a nuisance if I went by the hospital. I'd see her in the morning when I visited my mom. Or if I ate at Tina's Plentiful.

Instead, I turned toward my brother's new apartment. He'd recently had to downsize because as a student, he didn't have the cash coming in like he did as a drug dealer. He'd given up the rented Corvettes and Camaros for a rented Impala. He had moved from a house in the suburbs to a reasonable apartment on the edge of the city. It was one of the few decisions I couldn't fault him for.

I parked on the street next to his Impala and called him to let him know I was coming up.

He said, "It's not a great time, Mitchum. I'm studying."

"Then take a break. I'm already here." I ended the call before he could protest any further.

I knocked on the door and waited longer than I expected before I heard him yell, "Come in."

He sat awkwardly on his couch. There were no books open and the TV wasn't on. He looked stiff and stilted with his hands folded in his lap.

I stepped into the apartment. "I thought you were studying."

He didn't answer. That was weird. Even for him.

His eyes shifted to the hallway behind me. I looked over my shoulder and froze.

I stared at a man pointing a gun at my face.

# CHAPTER 13

**WHAT DO YOU** do when a man is pointing a gun at your face? Instinct kicks in. In my case, I raised my hands and backed away. At this point, I wasn't even thinking about fighting back. That's how complete the surprise was.

I carefully eased backward until I bumped into the couch where Natty sat. Then I realized that of all the possible plans, that was the worst. Now we were bunched together and easy targets for the man with the pistol.

I shifted to my right to get a little distance between my brother and me. A trickle of sweat ran down my forehead. I still hadn't said a word. It felt like my brain snapped into gear a moment later. I worked hard to stay calm. At least now I was thinking a little more clearly. Unfortunately, the first thing I thought about clearly was having a bullet strike me in the face. That was disconcerting.

A man stepped forward, out of the shadows of the hallway. It was hard to tell his age because he had a shaved head. He was powerfully built, with heavy muscles across his shoulders. That's when I realized I recognized him. For just a moment, I thought he might be a famous wrestler. His dark mustache drooped over the corners of his mouth and I could see him going by the name of "The Ringmaster" or "Mr. Clean."

Then it hit me. The Mr. Clean image stuck in my head. That's what we called him when we found him in the hidden prison on the outskirts of Marlboro.

He had a smirk on his face, as he looked me over like a piece of meat. Then he said in that deep voice, "Hello, Mitchum. Been a while."

I was at a loss for words. A few months back, in the dead of winter, my fourteen-year-old cousin, Bailey Mae, had gone missing. It turned out she had stumbled into a plan this asshole and a couple of others had to run a secret prison in an old mining facility not far away.

While looking for my cousin, I exposed the facility. Once the feds arrived and carted everyone off, I thought the whole thing was over. Apparently, I was wrong.

I couldn't stop myself from mumbling, "I know you."

His smirk turned into a smile. "Somehow that's gratifying. Considering the last time you saw me, you had stuffed me in a cell in a freezing mine shaft."

"You mean after I released the dozen men you had already stuffed in that cell in the mine shaft?" I paused for a minute, starting to feel anger replace my fear. "And a teenage girl. No one ever told me what you guys planned to do with her. I can only imagine."

That seemed to hit a nerve. The man said, "We didn't

want her there any more than she wanted to be there. We were trying to figure out how to keep the national-security aspect of the detention center intact. No one was looking to do anything weird with your cousin."

"You mean weird like locking her up in a mine shaft?"

Now he stepped forward. It felt like the conversation was over. I had to wonder what else was over. The muscular man held the gun with confidence, even if my arrival surprised him. He showed no nerves. His voice was calm and even.

Dammit, I hated professionals.

I took another step away from my brother. Now my mind was starting to work clearly. I needed the man to focus on my brother for just a moment. I just needed a momentary distraction. Anything to occupy the man's attention.

# CHAPTER 14

**NOW THE MAN** was completely in the living room with my brother to his right as he focused on me to his left.

Like anyone familiar with weapons, the gun moved wherever his eyes did. I didn't like that. He wouldn't be tricked easily.

I engaged him. I wanted a conversation. The longer something like this went, the less vigilant the gunman usually is. It was human nature. I had nothing to make small talk with. Finally, I said, "What was your name again?"

He let out a laugh. "Jackson, Rick Jackson. I don't think you'll forget it again."

"How'd you get out of jail?"

"What jail?"

"You were arrested for the shit you've pulled at the mine shaft. I mean, you kidnapped my teenage cousin. That's a crime by itself."

"I didn't kidnap anyone. I was just doing my job. I was hired by the government. The US government. My job was to maintain a detention facility. I didn't question who came into it. Your cousin wasn't harmed. She had food and water. I didn't even throw her in a cell with anyone else. I was never arrested. I just got a ride from the feds."

That pissed me off. I felt myself make the full shift from being scared to being angry. I said, "You never spent a day in jail."

He smiled. "Not in my entire life."

"So nothing happened to you guys at all?"

"We lost a huge contract. We lost one of our most valuable employees. Our computer guy is in custody because of the old couple he shot. You have any idea how hard it is to find a decent IT guy? You ruined a sweet gig our little company had. And worst of all, you pissed me off. I've stewed about you and your stupid meddling for months. And now I'm here for a little payback. Sort of my own little therapy, only a lot more fun."

"So your plan has been to shoot me. Why bother my mother or blow up my girlfriend's apartment?"

He stepped closer into the room. I was clear of the card table my brother used as a dining table. I calculated the distance between Jackson and me.

Jackson said, "The plan wasn't to just shoot you. It was to screw up your life. And it's gonna get worse. And there's not a damn thing you can do about it." He laughed.

This crazy son of a bitch enjoyed this. He didn't want it to end anytime soon.

Now he was stuck between Natty and me. It had been a long, calculated shift. I don't think this guy was used to facing multiple threats. Most people would take one look at him and decide to do what he said.

Jackson said, "I saw you poking around the girl's apartment. I purposely taped the old match to the door so the cops would figure out it wasn't just an accident. I was going to watch you squirm as you tried to figure out who would do this to you. What I didn't expect was for the local cops to not investigate at all. I could've just used a military device, maybe some kind of electronically detonated IED. But I wanted someone to realize I put some effort into it."

"All that effort because I cost you a little money?"

"My partner, Dave Allmand, told you to just walk away. He said he was doing you a favor. He wasn't kidding. Aside from the money, you let a lot of potential terrorists return to society. I think that deserved some kind of answer. Maybe teach you to mind your own business."

I snorted. "People have been trying to teach me that for years. What makes you think you could succeed?"

He smiled. "Because I've got a plan."

# CHAPTER 15

**I HAD NO** real plan. This asshole was holding a gun on my brother and me. If I didn't do something, one or both of us was going to be dead. And I was hoping my brother would pick up on the fact that I was maneuvering. But he didn't. And I couldn't blame him. It wasn't like he'd ever had training in anything like this.

So I did the next best thing. I turned to Natty and said, "You remember this jerk who looks like a giant penis? He was one of the guys that kidnapped Bailey Mae."

Natty had no idea why I was antagonizing a man with a gun. He tried to participate. He nodded his head slowly. He said, "I remember." It wasn't genius, but he was giving the effort. I had to cut him some slack. Then he added, "Those men looked like something from a concentration camp."

That made Jackson more angry than any insult I had hurled at him. He glared at my brother. "Those weren't men. They were terrorists. Maybe not directly, but they were funding terrorists. So don't give me any of that..."

He stopped short when my full 230 pounds slammed into him. He felt like one of the tackling dummies from high school. Except he was harder. His abs hurt my shoulder. Now we were a little more equal.

He slammed against the breakfast bar. The cheap bar rattled and creaked. A two-liter bottle of Mountain Dew fell to the floor and exploded. Sticky clear soda sprayed the small kitchen.

Somehow, Jackson managed to hold on to the pistol. All I could do now was grab his right wrist and make sure the pistol didn't point at me. I felt like I had a giant snake by the neck. I couldn't let go and couldn't move fast enough to get away.

Jackson was strong. That was an understatement. He somehow managed to make it back to his feet even with me hanging all over him. I used my left elbow to slam him in the head a couple of times. It had no effect.

Then I got lucky. I slammed his arm against the corner of the refrigerator and the gun flew out of his hand. It bounced off the stove, then slid across the floor under some cabinets in the kitchen.

Natty came across the room to help. As soon as he entered the kitchen, Jackson kicked him in the side of the leg so hard it knocked him into the flimsy wall and he tumbled onto the hardwood floor.

Now Jackson and I faced off against each other in the kitchen. I couldn't spare the concentration to wonder what sort of injuries my brother had suffered. If I didn't win this fight, it wouldn't matter.

The problem with knocking the gun out of Jackson's hand meant that he had two hands to fight with. He swung at me hard. The first punch glanced across my chin. It was mainly luck that I was moving and it didn't catch the full force. Then he gripped both of my wrists. I felt like a child in his grasp. My hands almost immediately turned purple.

Then he head-butted me. Hard. I'd seen this in training a dozen times. I lowered my head so that I took most of the blow on my forehead instead of my nose where he was aiming. It still dazed me.

I lifted my right leg, hoping to throw my knee into his groin. He twisted and blocked the kick, but that made him release my wrists. I stumbled back to the counter next to the refrigerator. I reached out blindly and found a jar of peanut butter on the counter. As Jackson charged me, I swung the jar wildly and caught him on the side of the head. Too bad modern peanut butter jars are plastic.

The blow still slowed him down, but not by much. The lid blew off and the jar cracked down the side, covering Jackson's face and neck with peanut butter. He looked like a radiation victim whose face was melting. I swung hard with my left hand, hoping the peanut butter was blocking his vision. It wasn't.

He blocked the punch and hit me with a counterpunch that sent me onto the cheap floor. I slid across it and slammed into the cabinets.

Now Natty was up, catching his breath. He threw himself at Jackson before Jackson could stomp on me. His body looked spindly next to the older, muscular man.

Jackson threw him like a rag doll against the wall, then dove onto the ground, aiming for his pistol.

I rolled over to stop him. We both reached for the pistol at the same time. All of my strength seemed to go into my hands as we fought for the gun.

It went off three times. *Bang. Bang. Bang.* Like a metronome keeping time for a deadly waltz. It was deafening. But I hoped it might bring some help. One of the neighbors had to have called the cops.

Somehow, I managed to wrestle the pistol away from him. I couldn't believe it came free. He scooted away from me and sprang to his feet. He was the fastest big man I'd ever met. He turned and sprinted out the door before I could even aim the gun.

I rushed to the door to give chase. I froze when I heard my brother moan in the kitchen. I turned and saw the spreading stain on his shirt.

One of the bullets had struck him.

# CHAPTER 16

**IT FELT LIKE** an eternity between when I called 911 and the paramedics arrived at Natty's apartment. At least they let me ride in the back of the ambulance as I held Natty's hand and talked to him.

I said, "You're going to be okay, Natty." I didn't know what else to say. Who does?

He looked at me, but didn't answer. He'd been panting, trying to keep the panic at bay. I answered the questions the paramedic asked me on the way. How old was he? Any allergies? I didn't know much about emergency medicine, but I knew my brother's blood pressure was low and dropping.

At the apartment, waiting for help, I'd done my best to hold direct pressure on the wound that was on his upper chest, almost to his shoulder. Just like I'd been taught in the Navy. I didn't think the bullet had caught a lung. That didn't mean my brother's color or respiration looked good.

I'd been in the waiting area outside the emergency room

at the hospital in Newburgh for about two hours when my mom hobbled in on crutches with Alicia trailing behind her.

She continued on her crutches, unchallenged into the emergency room. Alicia didn't know what to do, so I followed her. My mom stopped short of surgery.

My mom said in a loud voice, "Someone tell me what's going on. I'm still a customer. That means I'm going to be very demanding."

I heard one of the orderlies behind me mumble, "What else is new?"

A nurse, about my mom's age, stepped over and put a gentle hand on her back. She said, "Elaine, if you're a customer, you can't be back here. Your son's in surgery and they're doing everything they can."

What happened next was a real shock to me. My mom started to cry. Not just a sniffle or a tear, but a sob. Followed by more. The nurse wrapped her in a loving hug and patted her back.

After a few seconds, the nurse steered her toward me. I held her and let her cry on my shoulder. I could count the number of times I'd heard my mother cry during my entire life. And never like this.

Once we sat down, Alicia sat next to me and took hold of my hand. Then she let her head drop onto my shoulder. It was a quick slice of heaven. Then she said, "I have to clean up. My shift will start soon. I'll come by to visit as soon as I can." She kissed me on the lips. I tried to calculate the kiss. It was more than a peck and not a full-on girlfriend kiss. It was enough for now. She managed to energize me when I thought I might not make it through the night.

Almost an hour later, in the waiting room, Bill and a couple of Newburgh detectives came to talk to me. Bill was good about getting me away from my mother. Very patient and calm.

My mom said, "Can't you talk to him here? I don't want to be alone."

Before he could answer, Alicia popped into the waiting room in her uniform. A tiny badge on the pocket said STUDENT. She said, "I can stay with you for the next hour."

That made me sad I'd miss time with her. I knew now that I needed to show Alicia how much I cared about her.

I talked to the cops in an empty office a few corridors away. Bill sat in the back and let the detectives do the talking. The Newburgh Police Department and I had a little history. One of their detectives had gone bad and murdered a local drug dealer. I set the trap that caught him. The cops may not like crooked cops, but they don't like people doing their job, either.

A detective, who had identified herself as Sue Koteen, said, "I read the statement you made. It just sounds a little far-fetched. We think whoever did this was a drug-dealing rival to your brother."

"My brother is in paramedic school. He doesn't deal drugs anymore."

The detective laughed. "I've never heard that one before."

"Have you heard the one where the cops find the man who shot someone in their own apartment?"

The detective wasn't flustered. "I've read your entire statement and I find the whole private-prison revenge theory ridiculous. I'm not sure what you expect the Newburgh police to do about it."

"My experience with the Newburgh police tells me not to expect you to do anything at all."

Bill realized it was getting a little heated. He stepped forward quietly and placed a hand on Detective Koteen's shoulder. He said softly, "Susie, can you give us a couple of minutes?"

The detective gave me one more glare, just to make sure I understood I was pissing her off.

I gave her a goofy grin. Just to make sure she understood I was *trying* to piss *her* off.

As soon as we were alone, I turned to Bill and said, "She thinks I'm some kind of conspiracy nut."

"She's not alone." He waited until he had my full attention. "I've heard the story about the private prison from you, your brother, and your mom. I believe you. But think about it from a regular person's perspective. There was no news coverage, no public outrage, nothing that most people could relate to. If this is the reason your brother got shot or your mom was hit by the car or your girlfriend's apartment blew up, you might have to deal with it outside the police. But don't ridicule a dedicated detective like Susie Koteen."

I nodded. He made sense. I wanted to get back to my mother in case there was any word about Natty.

# CHAPTER 17

**IT WAS ALMOST** the next morning before we had our first positive update on Natty. They had removed a 9mm bullet and he had lost a lot of blood. But he would recover fairly quickly. Most people didn't realize that if a bullet didn't strike an organ or tear up veins or arteries, the victim could deal with daily life in a matter of days. They couldn't climb Mount Everest, but they could function. The doctor estimated that Natty could return to class in a couple of weeks if he didn't participate in anything too strenuous.

Alicia popped into Natty's room just as we heard the good news. I held her as I looked into her eyes. I didn't say anything. I just kissed her. And she kissed me.

She leaned in and said, "Where has this guy been?"

Before I could come up with a witty reply she said, "I hope you have this kind of energy and interest when I get off work."

I just smiled. I kept smiling until she went back to her rounds.

Now that I had a pretty good idea of who was trying to screw up my life, I had to make a stop here in Newburgh. My mom refused to leave the hospital until she could talk to a conscious Natty. I borrowed her car and found a convenience store a few miles from the hospital.

There was nothing unusual about the store. It had a couple of gas pumps and a brightly lit interior, filled with the essentials marked up a mere 300 percent. As I pushed through the glass door, a chime announced someone had entered the store.

The clerk turned from whatever he was doing behind the counter and started to greet me. When he looked at my face and recognized me, he froze. I just stared at him.

Then a huge smile spread across his wide, friendly face. He didn't say a word as he rushed from behind the counter to embrace me.

Finally, he said, "Mitchum, my friend, how are you?"

"I am well, Hassan. And you?"

"My brothers and I are all fine. Thanks to you."

"Did you or any of the other men from the hidden prison ever testify against the men who held you?"

Hassan shook his head. "Aside from an interview with people from the government the next day, I have heard nothing. No one who was with us has heard anything. And we all stay in touch with each other. My brothers and I were in that hellhole for almost seven months. No one has told us anything other than the money we were sending home went to fund terrorists."

I wasn't sure how to phrase this. I thought about it for a moment then just blurted out, "The bald man who ran the prison was not arrested."

Hassan was floored. All he could manage to say was, "No."

"He's here in Newburgh somewhere. He's trying to ruin my life."

"Like he tried to ruin our lives?"

"Not quite. He ran down my mother with a car. He tried to kill my...friend. Last night he shot my brother. I have no idea what he's up to, but I knew I had to warn you."

"How is your brother?"

"He'll survive."

"Everyone from the prison lives between here and Boston. I will get word to each of them today." Hassan was about to say something else, then he stopped short.

I put my hand on his shoulder and looked him in the eye. There was no one else in the tiny store with us. "What is it? You can tell me."

"You know that there were men among us who planned attacks against the US."

"I know that four men were transferred to regular custody. But they didn't cause us any problems the night we set you all free."

"There are ten of us who owe you our freedom. We can help you if you need it."

"Right now all I need is some answers. The government's not big on spilling its secrets to a guy like me."

"The government is made up of people. Mostly good

people. If you found the right person, they might give you some honest answers."

That made me think. I grabbed his upper arms and almost shouted, "Hassan, that's a great idea."

He flashed me a smile and said, "If I knew what you were talking about, I'm sure I would swell with pride."

# CHAPTER 18

**HOWEVER UNINTENTIONALLY, HASSAN** had pointed me in a new direction. I checked on Natty and brought my exhausted mother back to her house. As soon as she was settled, I ran home and immediately got on my computer.

I thought back to the night we found the hidden prison and how federal agents from the Department of Homeland Security swooped in and took the men and woman who'd been running the prison.

I still got a chill when I thought about the woman in charge of the Homeland Security people. She was threatening without having to make explicit threats. That was a real talent. Her name was Cheryl Kravitz. That's who was going to give me answers. All I had to do was find her.

My first step was to search the internet for any new stories that might mention her. She popped up in five different stories. In every story, she had declined comment. That wasn't what I was interested in.

Three of the news stories dealt with cases in the New York area. One of the cases was in Maryland and the other in Pennsylvania. That meant she was probably stationed in New York or Washington, DC. The most recent article was three months old and covered a case in Jersey City, New Jersey.

My next step was to log on to my LexisNexis search account and run her name. I was surprised there were several Cheryl Kravitzes on the east coast. Seven in New York alone. Thank God LexisNexis gives a lot of extra information. I guessed at her age and then matched it to one woman listed in the public records section of the site and saw that she had a house on Staten Island. It seemed to add up.

By dinnertime, Bart Simpson and I strolled over to my mother's house. I thought I was being sly. But as soon as I stepped in the door, my mom, lounging comfortably on the couch, said, "Look who got dressed up to come visit his girlfriend." She gave me a smile and a wink.

She also immediately made me self-conscious about the fact that I was wearing a nice, collared, button-down shirt and new Dockers. I was going to argue, but arguing a point had no effect on my mother. And in this case, she was right. I was hoping to hang out with Alicia for a while.

My mom said, "Alicia's training shift at the hospital just ended, and she's visiting Natty."

For some reason that news disturbed me. "Why's she visiting Natty?"

"Probably because his brother hasn't been to see him since he was moved to a regular room."

"That happened about an hour ago."

"Three hours ago. And that's why Alicia is being nice and polite by visiting your brother."

"I was going to go by and see him tonight." I hated to lie. That meant I'd probably make the trip down to Newburgh sometime before nine o'clock to pop in and say hello to my brother. But if I did that, I'd miss Alicia. She'd be on her way back here.

Then I had an idea. I looked at my mom and said, "I'll go see him right now. Are you okay here alone for a couple of hours?"

"I'll be asleep sooner than that. Don't worry about me. Go see your brother."

I raced down to the hospital and caught Alicia just as she was saying good-bye to Natty. I talked her into staying a few minutes longer, then convinced my brother he was exhausted and got him to fall asleep.

When I suggested coffee, Alicia said she was tired. "I only have class until noon tomorrow. Would you be free to hang out then? Maybe in private somewhere."

I felt a rush at the offer. An offer I didn't take lightly. This beautiful girl, smart and considerate, who wanted to spend time with me. Alone. That was great. I knew I was grinning, but couldn't stop it.

Then I thought about my plan.

Alicia read it on my face. She said, "What? What is it? You can't do it, can you?"

"I, er, I have to talk to someone in the city. It's important. Really important. But I hope to be back midafternoon. That is, if you'll still meet me."

She hesitated. As she caressed my chin with one finger, she said, "I guess we'll see."

# CHAPTER 19

**THE NEXT MORNING** I was rolling early. I had a huge bucket of guilt over missing Alicia as soon as she was out of class. This was one of the harder choices I'd made since leaving the Navy.

I didn't trust my station wagon to make the trip into the city so I borrowed my brother's idle Impala. I knew right where I was going. The Jacob K. Javits Federal Building off Broadway in lower Manhattan. If my logic was correct, Cheryl Kravitz worked somewhere in that building. If I wanted to find answers, she was the only one I could think of who could provide them.

I had to park blocks away, which turned out to be good. The federal building was well protected and there was no parking anywhere close. It was best that I approach on foot.

There were barriers along the sidewalk to keep anyone from driving into the courtyard or up to the building. A detachment of NYPD strategic operations members sat in one corner of the courtyard.

I noticed food carts lining the sidewalk just outside the barriers. Everything from Philly cheesesteaks to falafels were offered from the vendors and their trusty carts.

There was heavy security at the front, which included a metal detector. I wasn't sure I wanted to be seen inside the building. I grabbed a chicken gyro from a woman whose cart was dead center in front of the building, then sat on a low planter where I could see the front door. I was still far enough away to not attract attention, but I noticed everyone coming and going from the building. My hope was that Agent Kravitz didn't use some secret entrance.

I finished the gyro and grabbed some French fries and a Coke, then returned to my uncomfortable seat on the hard cement planter. An hour later, I ate a hot dog. This kind of surveillance was deadly boring. I appreciated chatting with the different vendors and sampling a variety of food.

About twelve thirty, while I was eating what was supposed to be roasted steak on a stick, I saw Agent Kravitz coming out the front door. Just as she walked past me, I wiped my face quickly and stood up.

I said, "Hello, Agent Kravitz. Remember me?" I could tell the way she faced me, with one hand in her purse, she was always on guard. I respected that. She didn't have an easy job. And there were a lot of nuts in the world. I guess I didn't realize she considered me one of those nuts.

The forty-something woman, at least five foot ten, stared at me for a moment. Slowly, recognition dawned on her. Then she said, "You're the busybody from Marlboro.

The guy that demanded we answer his questions. What's your name again?"

"Mitchum."

She smiled. "Are you like Cher or Madonna? You only go by one name."

"Something like that."

"Why are you stalking me?"

"You mean waiting in front of the building where I knew you worked? You call that stalking?"

"Yes."

"I guess, when you think about it, it could be considered a little creepy. But all I want is to talk with you for a few minutes. Let me buy you some souvlaki. I know a place just over there." I pointed to a large, hairy man I had spoken to earlier.

Agent Kravitz glanced over at the man, then shook her head. "We have nothing to talk about."

"Are you sure, because I feel like we do."

She turned and said, "Good day, Mr. Mitchum. I have a busy schedule." She said it without even looking at me. I had been dismissed.

I thought quickly and said, "That's fine. I'll leave. Do you happen to know the address of the *New York Times*? I got a buddy over there. John O'Neil, you know him? Hell of an investigative reporter. Never mind, I'm sure I can find it."

When she stopped walking and just stood there for a moment, I knew I had her.

# CHAPTER 20

**AGENT KRAVITZ MOTIONED** me to follow her, and I have to say, even for a tall man, I had trouble matching her pace. Despite me wearing Asics cross-trainers and her wearing attractive pumps, she moved with a determined energy that was hard to match. She also didn't say a word. Or look at me. I just went with it. Stayed a few steps behind and kept my mouth shut.

In the next block, Agent Kravitz turned into a place called Potbelly Sandwich Shop. She nodded hello to a couple of people in the crowded chain restaurant.

I passed on a sandwich, and, after she had ordered her turkey on whole wheat, we sat down.

She said, "Are you on a diet?"

I chuckled. "I had a snack or two while I was waiting for you in front of the building."

"You've got my attention for the next five minutes. Make it count."

"Clearly, the only reason I'd be talking to you is about what happened up near Marlboro. Something the government kept very quiet. Something I haven't spoken about to many people."

She was listening, that's all I could ask for. She said, "Go on."

"You left the prison site with four people in custody. The injured woman, the stoner who shot the Wilkses, and two other men who seemed to be in charge."

"I remember. You're using up your time on useless information."

"One of the men you took, a bald guy named Rick Jackson, is back."

"And the problem is?"

"Shouldn't he be in prison somewhere? I can't imagine someone involved in shit like that, which included a couple of murders, is free to just roam around."

"The things you can't imagine would fill several large books, I'm sure. The fact is, only one person was actually arrested for violating US law. The man who shot the couple who found the prison site. And he's currently in custody. The others were working on a contract from the government. The contract was canceled, and they were released. Mr. Jackson is a US citizen, free to travel anywhere in the country. It doesn't matter if you or I agree with the decision. That was the final resolution."

"So you don't care that he ran down my mother, tried to blow up my girlfriend, and shot my brother."

"On the contrary, I think that's terrible. But it sounds

like a local law enforcement issue to me. Have you filed a report?"

That was enough. I just stared at her. I slid my chair back to make her think I was leaving. I said, "I thought you guys took some kind of oath to protect the Constitution as well as citizens of the United States. Tell me how your operation in the hills behind Marlboro, and ignoring the men who built it, is helping this country? You kept claiming the terrorists were a threat. I think *you're* the threat. You're a disgrace."

She put down her sandwich. We sat in awkward silence for a few moments. She made an assessment. An assessment of me. I could tell this was someone who did this kind of thing all the time. Could I be trusted? Would I do something crazy? I just gave her some time.

Finally, she said, "Tell me more about what happened to your family. Are you sure it was Jackson?"

I told her everything. From the blue SUV striking my mother, to my certainty that it was Jackson because he introduced himself at gunpoint. Just to give her a fair assessment of the situation.

We had another silence between us as she checked something on her phone. Then called a couple of different people, conducting very short and cryptic conversations.

Finally, she focused on me. She looked me right in the eye. She still hesitated. "Look, I believe you. I understand what you're going through. But I'm limited by a number of things. Not the least of which, I'm not assigned to this sort of operation anymore."

"So you believe me, but you're sorry that I or some of my family have to die."

Agent Kravitz sighed. "What if I told you, hypothetically, that the men who ran that prison were released by us. All except the man who shot the old couple. The others were held, temporarily, by another agency. And now..." She glanced around the sandwich shop to make sure no one was listening. "Now they might hypothetically work for a private contractor who deals with the US government."

"Is that something I could track down? If I swore out a warrant, would someone look for Jackson?"

Now Agent Kravitz leaned in close. "They work for a company called Deep River. The company does everything from patrol to detention work in Afghanistan. Jackson is possibly on Bagram Air Base."

"But if there's a warrant for Jackson, you could do something, right?"

"No one's going to care about a warrant from some little town in upstate New York. And no one will look for this guy. But I'll make you this deal: if you find him, I mean exactly where he is, I'll do my best to get a warrant. A federal warrant. Especially if we can get him back to the US."

She talked with me a little longer. I was so interested that I lost track of time. When I glanced at my phone, I couldn't believe it was after noon. I wouldn't make it home in time to see Alicia.

# CHAPTER 21

**I TRIED TO** explain the situation to Alicia, but she wasn't interested. When I told her I could be home in an hour and a half, she said, "Don't bother. I told my dad I'd take him to physical therapy. You should visit your brother."

I'd made a mess of it with Alicia. It was a familiar story with me. I took her advice and stopped in Newburgh. I made it to my brother's room at the hospital just after sundown. The first thing I heard as I walked in the room was, "How could you disappear for a full day?" Of course, it was my mom.

I started to offer explanations, but she wouldn't understand. And I didn't have the energy left to fight her. I just shrugged and mumbled, "Sorry."

My mom said, "And you managed to piss off Alicia, too. Poor girl thought you guys were going on a date or something."

That hurt worse than my mom's guilt trip.

At least my brother looked much better. The news was pretty good as well. He'd be coming home in a couple of days. Looking around the private room with all sorts of medical devices beeping and blinking, I knew this was another expensive visit to the hospital.

A couple of hours later, using my laptop to research Deep River, I looked up DP Lampkin's company, Non-Metric Solutions. Unlike Deep River, about which there was very little information on the internet, Non-Metric Solutions didn't seem shy about posting anything.

I still liked their logo. Neil Armstrong planting the flag on the moon, the photograph captioned, "Metric system? Whose flag is on the moon?" That sounded like my friend's sense of humor. I wondered if he had anything to do with the logo, or if that's what attracted him to the company.

I called DP and told him I could start soon as they needed me. I was shocked how quickly he arranged the weeklong training at their base in Alabama. This clearly was not the US government.

DP said, "Don't get me wrong, Mitchum. Afghanistan is no picnic. But it's calmed down a lot in the last few months. I think you'll like the work. And I know you'll like the pay."

I woke up the next morning with an odd combination of anxiety and relief. Whatever the outcome of my adventure, I was going to see the world again, just like they told me in the Navy. I never thought I'd see Nevada while I was in the Navy, but I did. Same with Arizona and Cincinnati. I never considered them huge duty posts for the Navy.

I drove my mom to the hospital in Newburgh because we were going to bring Natty home. At least to my mom's home. She was very excited.

I wasn't terribly happy that my brother would be living under the same roof as Alicia.

I'd carefully considered the best time to tell my mom I'd taken a job that was going to ship me to Afghanistan. Just the sort of topic to start the day off on the right foot. I considered doing it at the hospital in front of people so my mom wouldn't fly off the handle. But waiting in the car, I realized it was time. I was as hesitant to start this conversation as anything I'd ever done.

I said, "Mom, between your stay and Natty's stay at the hospital, the bills are going to be outrageous."

Staring out the window, she let out a snort. "Tell me something I don't know."

"Okay, I will: I've taken a job with a security company and I'm going to have to go to Afghanistan for a couple of months." Just like removing a Band-Aid, I decided to rip it off.

The silence was chilling. I tried not to speak, just to see how long she'd go. After a full minute, I had to say, "Did you hear what I said?"

Now her head twisted to face me. It reminded me of something from *The Exorcist.* I focused on the road with my eyes straight ahead.

Finally, she said, "You'd desert your family at a time like this?"

Ouch. She didn't waste time getting right to the heart of

the subject. I said, "I told you who shot Natty and ran you down. I've got a contact with the government who told me where the guy probably ran to. And that's Afghanistan. What good can I do my family here in New York? No one believes any part of my story. Not from the hidden prison to this lunatic shooting Natty. This is my only option."

My mom toned it down and said, "It's a hard story to swallow. I lived it, and I still doubt it. But we don't need you risking your life. We need you here, with us."

She didn't say much more until we got to the hospital. Alicia greeted me coolly. She was starting her shift. "I just visited Natty. He's happy to be coming home. I told him I'd make brownies for him tonight." She looked very seriously at my mother and said, "If that's all right with you?"

My mom loved the deference. "Of course, dear. My house is your house. And now it's Natty's house, too."

My mom wandered down the hall to chat with someone. I took the moment to lean in close to Alicia. "I am so sorry about yesterday."

She didn't say anything.

"I swear I am, and I'll make it up to you."

Now she took a moment and said, "Will you take me to a movie and dinner Friday? Like a real date."

"This Friday?"

"Yeah. Is that a problem?"

"I—er—"

"You seem to stammer a lot when I ask you questions. What's so important that you're busy Friday night?"

"I'm kinda leaving for Alabama tomorrow."

"What's 'kinda leaving' mean?"

"I got a new job and I have to leave for training."

She stared at me. "When will you be back?"

"That's a tough one. I'm not really sure."

Before I could give her more details, she said, "I have to get back to work now. I'll talk to you later."

She turned and stomped off so quickly I couldn't even say good-bye.

My mom came back from the counter where she had spoken to another nurse. As we waited for the elevator, I gauged my mom's mood. I was still reeling from Alicia. I said, "Do you think Natty and Alicia are attracted to each other?" It had been nagging me for too long. I had to get someone else's opinion.

"Of course they are. They're both attractive, nice people. But you're starting to sound like the conspiracy nut the Newburgh police think you are. Alicia is just being nice. She'll be a great nurse. You need to grow up. She's a keeper."

"So you don't think I have anything to worry about?"

My mom turned to me with a smug smile. "Not if you stay here."

I smiled and said to my mom, "Good effort. But I'm still leaving tomorrow."

# CHAPTER 22

**WHEN I COULDN'T** reach her, I left a message for Alicia. I tried to make it simple and to the point, but no matter what I said it sounded lame. I ended up with, "I'm sorry I have to leave. I'll be back. And things won't be as screwed up around my house. I'll call you when I get there."

Certainly not the grand, romantic message I wanted to leave, but it would have to do.

I was short on time and virtually out of money. Non-Metric Solutions was now my only option.

I caught a flight to Atlanta then a bus to Huntsville, Alabama. I figured I could use a week of orientation and training. I had no idea what to expect. The first day was mostly filling out something like three thousand forms. And I had a cursory medical exam. Emphasis on "cursory." I'm not certain the doctor administering the test would've noticed an artificial limb. I was breathing and I could walk in a straight line. That seemed to be the bar.

We took a fitness test, which included a two-mile run, maximum push-ups and pull-ups completed in a minute, as well as a couple of other events. I didn't notice anyone failing because of the fitness test. Don't get me wrong, there were plenty of people barely strolling across the finish line of the two-mile run. I guess Non-Metric Solutions had too many openings to be too selective. It was almost the opposite of the SEAL training I'd gone through.

I met some interesting people. A retired cop from Tampa named Greg Stout was there because he found himself bored with the free time. He'd work in Non-Metric Solutions' investigations division, which looked at thefts and crimes that didn't involve military personnel.

The jovial, retired detective had an endless stream of jokes. That's an important guy to have in a place like Afghanistan. Just before we started our two-mile run, he said, "I'll see you at the finish line in about forty minutes."

"C'mon, you can do better than that."

Stout said, "I just had a physical. The doctor asked me if obesity ran in my family. I told him *no one* ran in my family. I'm going to stick to that."

I met a retired Secret Service agent named Jason Roche. He and Stout were also friends. Roche was a solid guy. The kind of person you could trust if someone started shooting at you. Calm and alert. But we all parted company on the last day.

At the end of our training, Stout said, "Why don't you

fly with Jason and me out of Miami? We stop in Dubai, then into Kabul."

I held up my hands. "I don't have a good pension coming in. I can save money by using some of my contacts with the military and catching one of their flights."

Roche said, "They gave us a stipend to travel."

"Which I'm going to save and send home to my mom for medical expenses."

Stout slapped me on the back. "You're a good kid. I hope you can stay out of trouble in Afghanistan."

I caught a series of Greyhound buses to get to Dover, Delaware. That's where I was promised a flight to Bagram Air Base. We had to stop in Germany on the way, and I wasn't guaranteed plush seats or a specific timeline. But it was free.

I showed my paperwork from Non-Metric Solutions at the gate to Dover Air Force Base. The airman standing guard was more impressed by my Navy ID and the fact that I had actually served in the military.

I waited in the tiny terminal and noticed a group of elderly people, as well as a few service members, starting to fill the area. As I sat there watching the crowd grow, an Army master sergeant, about thirty years old, took the seat next to me. She looked at the crowd, then back at me, and said, "I can tell the difference between a contractor and a tourist."

I smiled. She was attractive with blond hair tied up tight to her head like the military preferred. She said, "Every time I travel to Europe on a C-17 there are at least a dozen retired service members and their spouses grabbing free airfare to Germany. If you're not on a schedule, and you don't mind the web seats, it's a great deal."

"What makes you think I'm not a tourist, too?"

"You're twenty years too young to be a retiree, look to be in good shape, and you've got everything packed in a military duffel. Let me guess, you were in the service, got out, and life's not as exciting or you don't make enough money. Usually one of the two. You're now a contractor."

"What are you? An Army psychologist?"

She held out her hand. "Vicki Jensen, logistics."

I shook her hand. "You got me. Mitchum, Non-Metric Solutions."

"Is Mitchum your first name or your last?"

I smiled again. "Both."

That seemed to satisfy the master sergeant. She said, "Headed to Bagram?"

I nodded.

"There are a ton of contractors there. From all over the world. There's not a lot to do."

"I'm from upstate New York. There's not that much to do there, either."

She had a dazzling smile. "Sounds like you're going to work out just fine."

"What's the worst that could happen? They don't like me and send me home? I can deal with that."

"Technically, the worst that could happen is that you're blown up by an IED or shot by a sniper."

"Believe me, I've considered all that. But this was my

best choice." I was relieved I didn't have to go into any of my backstory. She seemed happy to wait out our extended stay in the terminal. The Air Force calls it "Showtime." That's the time you have to arrive to get on one of the flights. And it's always hours before takeoff.

There were worse ways I could've spent my afternoon.

# CHAPTER 23

**WE LOADED ON** the giant C-17 cargo plane. The first thing I noticed and appreciated was the fact that no one complained. The seats were just pulldown web seats on the sides of the plane. The center of the jet was crammed with some kind of IED minesweepers. They looked like they hooked under the front of a vehicle. I didn't see any engine on the minesweepers. Most of the civilian, retired military passengers were in their seventies. All of them looked thrilled to be on vacation. It was great to see.

The aircrew was an Air National Guard unit out of Memphis. I was happy when Vicki Jensen decided to sit next to me. At least I'd have someone to talk to.

We chatted on and off for the first several hours of flight. I dozed off for an hour or two, but for the final three hours, I was wide awake and sitting in the straight-backed web chair. Not the most comfortable way to fly.

Vicki had been lying on a bedroll she brought with her.

I noticed all the active military people had something similar. You had to grab sleep where you could. She woke up an hour before we landed and sat next to me again.

She said, "I didn't join the Army to be in logistics and work on computers."

"Why'd you join? Avoiding a prison term?" I gave her a smile in case she couldn't tell it was a joke. But she could.

"I wanted to serve my country. A lot of people still understand that terrorism is a major threat to our way of life."

"Okay, that's a really good answer. But what, specifically, did you want to do in the Army?"

"I wanted to fly helicopters. Black Hawks to be specific. I thought I had it all down. I was in great shape. I don't mind studying. I had one flaw I didn't know about."

"What's that?"

"I have a minor, visual-spatial issue. Nothing I'd ever noticed growing up."

"So you have problems judging distance."

"You're one of the first people to grasp that. So instead of just quitting, I applied my talents to the vital job of logistics. As a result, I get to fly in helicopters a lot. I know half the Army pilots at Bagram. I can make up some kind of minor errand and have my choice of five different helicopters to fly me there. Not as good as being a pilot, but still pretty sweet."

I smiled. I was always amazed at the enthusiasm young military personnel put into their jobs. It was something most people didn't see.

Vicki said, "What'd you do in the Navy? Why did *you* join?"

I let out a laugh to cover my embarrassment. I just shrugged and said, "I joined because I lived in a little town in upstate New York. I wanted to see the world." I hesitated, and decided to tell the truth. "I wanted to be a SEAL, but it didn't work out."

"Training too hard?"

"Something like that."

"And now you're going to make your fortune in Afghanistan."

"Something like that."

"This will be my third deployment to Bagram. I'll show you around. It's a giant place. And can be confusing. At least for the first couple of days."

I settled into the seat as one of the aircrew yelled out to us, "We're making our descent into Ramstein, Germany." We had an overnight stop in Ramstein, then tomorrow on to Afghanistan.

# CHAPTER 24

**BECAUSE OF THE** time change, we landed at Bagram about five in the morning. At least, on this leg of the flight, I stretched out on the hard floor and dozed off for a few hours.

I was still stiff and tired when I checked in with the base contractor coordinator. The clerk issued me a room, which was a shipping container welded to several more shipping containers. There was a tiny, whirring air conditioner designed to take the edge off the heat.

At least I had no roommate for now. I took the lower of the bunk beds against the back wall. I had a cheap, pressboard dresser with two drawers to place everything I'd brought with me. My whole life in Afghanistan fit in the dresser easily. When I thought about it, there wasn't much more absolutely *needed* from my house. Maybe Bart Simpson and a few books.

Then I walked over to the offices for the different
contracting companies. There were dozens. One place
contracted cleaning and maintenance facilities, another company contracted for certain types of food, another for equipment. There were several for security and
detention, and the very last one in the row of offices was
Non-Metric Solutions.

Sitting behind the only desk in the sparse office was my
friend, DP Lampkin. His official nameplate read DENNIS
P. LAMPKIN. I'd called him DP for so long that I think I'd
forgotten his first name was Dennis.

DP jumped out of his seat and gave me a hug. He was
about four inches shorter than my six foot two frame.
He'd stayed in good shape and had an easy smile that
still put me in a good mood. He was sturdy and looked
ten years younger than his forty years. He now had the
kind of shaved head that only buff black guys can carry
off well.

"What's with the clean head look?"

He ran his hand across the bare skin. "There was a lot
of gray coming into my tight 'fro. My kids suggested the
look. Definitely a lot easier here."

As I sat down, I noticed his Kindle. "That replace the
fifteen books you carried everywhere?"

"I still usually have a few books around, but I've got a
ton on this baby." He patted the Kindle.

DP went through some of the possible assignments
with me. Most were pretty basic. Standing a post, riding on patrol, or a little executive protection. I wasn't

worried about any of the assignments. I was worried about finding Rick Jackson and the Deep River contingent.

I casually asked about other contractors. I didn't mention Deep River by name.

DP gave me a quick rundown of all the non-security contractors. Then he said, "There are five major security contractors. You'll see their guys around. There's no real rivalry. In fact, there's more work than we can all handle. We trade people back and forth all the time."

"You mean I could end up working for another contractor?"

"It's not like you'd have a different job. We all do similar stuff. But yeah, it's possible. And we all bill each other so everyone's making money."

I had to sign a pile of new forms and show off my marksmanship on the range so I could be issued a Beretta 9-millimeter.

When I came back to the office later, DP looked like a proud father of a newborn. He said, "Looks like you're ready to go. I can probably get you a cushy job on the interior of the base."

I was staring at a map on the wall of the giant base. I pointed to a set of buildings far off from anything else. "What's that?"

"Nothing we have to worry about. It's a detention center where they sort out who's going where. Deep River handles that entire contract. The closest we get is patrolling the road in front of it."

"I wouldn't mind doing that. Just driving patrol around the perimeter. Sounds like it's just what I need."

DP shrugged. "Shifts are long and boring out there. You'll be lucky if you talk to two people a shift."

"You got anyone else asking to do it?"

DP chuckled and said, "That's why I wanted you to work here. No hassles and you do a good job. Glad to have you aboard."

# CHAPTER 25

**AS SOON AS** I got settled in my room, I went looking for Greg Stout and Jason Roche. It would be comforting to see someone I knew from the States. This place was so alien to me. The base was a hard and dusty plain surrounded by the Hindu Kush. Sometimes, when the wind blew from the mountains, it was like getting a blast of air conditioning.

It wasn't hard to find the two retired law enforcement men. I led them over to a coffee shop near the PX where Vicki had said to meet her. I made the introductions and everyone exchanged numbers. Mainly, I was showing off that I had made some friends.

Stout insisted on giving me a quick walking tour of the base. We left Vicki with her week-old copy of the *Chicago Tribune* and headed out.

I could tell the pleasant, retired detective had already lost weight in the few days he'd been here. Their direct commercial flight was a lot more efficient than my free military flight. They were already old pros working on Bagram Air Base.

Stout pointed over the cement barriers that surrounded the entire base. "Over there is the ancient town of Bagram. It may not look like much, but it was here before London was much of a going concern."

I'd seen a bunch of contractors, some in company uniforms, but most in regular clothes. The one thing they almost all had in common was a sidearm. I had to ask, "What's with all the guns?"

Jason said, "Every contractor has the option of carrying a personal weapon. They have to go through training and prove they know how to use it. I think it goes back to an infiltration where the terrorist was able to shoot a number of contractors. Whoever runs the administration decided it was better to have more weapons than fewer."

"Doesn't that lead to violent confrontations between the contractors?"

Roche smiled. "I asked that same question. They told me none of the contractors would risk getting booted from this kind of job and pay. Besides, without alcohol available, it seems like everyone stays relatively calm. What's that old saying? A well-armed society is a polite society."

Stout pointed out a relatively short air traffic control tower in the center of the base, nowhere near a runway. "That's the old Russian air tower when they used the base during their invasion of Afghanistan. There are some more Russian buildings way out on the corners of the base.

Most people just call them the Russian ruins. The tower now hosts ceremonies and parties."

Roche laughed. "The other ruins are way the hell out by the detention facility at the perimeter."

That caught my attention. But I didn't say anything. I needed to get as much information as I could before I started making overt inquiries about Rick Jackson and the contingent from Deep River.

I said, "So the two guys in the tower by that entrance are also contractors?"

Both men nodded.

"I figured they weren't US military because they both have AK-47s."

Stout said, "All the Ugandans carry AK-47s. They pretty much cover the perimeter. You can see there are a couple of American contractors where the gate opens. The men on top are just extra firepower."

We looked around a little more near the gate where the Ugandans stood on top of the twenty-foot metal towers.

Roche pointed to the area beyond the perimeter and said, "Sometimes, at night, you might hear some explosions without any of the warnings over the loudspeaker. That means a rabbit, or maybe a deer, stepped on one of the old leftover Russian land mines. They're scattered all over the area around the base."

I shuddered at the thought of some poor, Afghan kid inadvertently stepping on one of the mines. Before I could say anything, I heard someone shout near the gate. Suddenly there was more shouting.

Stout mumbled, "Oh, shit."

I saw the half-ton truck barreling toward the gate down the road on the outside. It was clear they didn't intend to stop. Someone shouted for them to do it anyway. The truck kept coming.

The two men on the towers leveled their AK-47s and started firing at full automatic. The men at the gate pulled their handguns and added to the fusillade.

It didn't seem to have an effect. I looked around for cover.

# CHAPTER 26

**NOW OTHER CONTRACTORS**, clearly not security people, drew their own pistols and started firing. It made me realize I had a Beretta on my hip. I pulled the gun and scurried across the dry ground until I could duck behind a low concrete barrier.

Just as I leaned around the barrier and aimed the pistol, the truck veered to the right. It smashed into a civilian Humvee parked just outside the gate. The force of the truck knocked the Humvee ten feet into some light poles.

The two men in the towers raced halfway down the ladders, then jumped the rest of the way to the ground. Instead of checking if the driver was still alive, the two men, along with the contractors near the gate, started running away.

I was confused. I stood up cautiously, scanning the area. Then I realized why everyone was running. The truck was packed with explosives. As I stood in the open like an idiot, the truck exploded. I instantly dropped to the ground behind the barrier. I could still see the fireball that climbed more than forty feet into the air. The concussion of the explosion rocked my insides and blew shrapnel and loose rocks everywhere. Luckily, the barrier I was behind took most of the blast.

Sirens started to blare all around the base. A voice came over the loudspeaker, but my ears were ringing too badly for me to understand what was being said. I was on my hands and knees so I shook my head, hoping to clear it. No one from the truck had survived that blast. I wasn't worried about anyone rushing through the gate. I was worried about a possible concussion or hearing damage. A trickle of blood dribbled out of my nose.

All I could do was sit with my back against the barrier for a moment. I opened my mouth, trying to clear my ears. It helped a little. Then things started to come back into focus.

A shadow fell over me and I looked up, still in a daze. Greg kneeled next to me and asked me if I was okay. All I could do was nod. He helped me up slowly. My legs were still a little shaky.

The first thing I did was turn toward the destroyed gate. One of the towers where the Ugandans had been standing was just a twisted mass of metal. It looked like an arthritic hand reaching up into the sky.

There were several bodies closer to the gate. People were rushing forward to help the wounded spread out around the gate. No one tried to extinguish the fire still burning brightly and melting what was left of the truck.

When I had my footing, I turned to Stout and said, "Where's Jason?"

Stout shrugged and we both started looking for him. He'd been standing near us when the truck came into view. I glanced at the wounded, then breathed a short sigh of relief when I saw he wasn't one of those being treated.

Then I saw the look on Stout's face, twenty feet ahead of me. I raced to him. I froze. On the ground, right in front of us, was retired US Secret Service agent Jason Roche. A piece of shrapnel had hit him in the lower back part of his head. There were several exit wounds on his face. He still had a look of shock. His eyes staring straight ahead.

He was dead.

# CHAPTER 27

**IT'D BEEN A** tough start to my assignment. Greg and I stayed with DP as he called the US office of Non-Metric Solutions. Someone had to tell Roche's wife and daughters as soon as possible.

I was still down the next day as I tried to make sense of what had happened to my friend. Even running into Vicki didn't cheer me much.

She said, "I heard about your friend. I'm really sorry."

All I could do was nod.

She was very patient and gentle. "How would you feel about a tour of the whole base in a vehicle? Maybe it'll give you some perspective. At least it might take your mind off your friend."

I agreed, and after an hour or so, she turned out to be right. There was so much to see, it was overwhelming. I had to remind myself why I was here. I had to find Rick Jackson. I had to protect my family. I also realized that everyone here took the same risk as Jason Roche.

The vehicle hardly looked like standard military issue. It was a silver Toyota Hilux with a sunroof. The truck was only a couple of years old but it had seen some rough duty. Almost every section of the body had a dent, and duct tape held part of the rear window together.

Vicki handled the truck like a pro. Throughout the tour, she avoided all potholes and the occasional piece of road debris.

She said, "It's fairly cool this time of year, but mainly because we're up at about five thousand feet. Roughly the same elevation as Denver."

"I bet most people prefer Denver."

"There really is a TripAdvisor page for Bagram Air Base. It gets three and a half stars. My favorite review said, 'avoid if possible.' That one made me laugh out loud. But when you've got up to forty thousand people on a six-square-mile base, not everyone's going to be happy. All of Afghanistan only has about thirty-five million people. The capital has about a tenth of the population right there. As far as Afghanistan goes, this is the place to be."

I was curious about the population. "Anyone speak English?"

"Sure, some. Most everyone speaks Pashto. Farther south, they tend to speak more Dari. On the air base, it's a little harder to figure out languages. You'll meet up with soldiers from Estonia or Cyprus or half a dozen other countries you've barely heard of. It surprised me how many of them don't speak much English. And the contractors come from every country imaginable."

"How many contractors are on the base?"

"More than a quarter, probably between eight thousand and ten thousand. There's something like thirty-five or forty countries participating in Operation Resolute Support. Sometimes it's hard to tell who's military and who works for one of the contractors."

"Ever heard of Deep River?"

"Yeah, sure. They're a pretty big outfit. They get some support from my office. They also run the detention facility out near the Russian ruins."

"Who do they hold at the facility?"

"Enemy combatants until they decide if they should go to Parwan prison. Both of them are tough places."

She drove a little farther, then stopped the Toyota. She pointed to the prison, off in the distance. "That's the detention facility run by Deep River. Doesn't look like much, but they hold twenty or more prisoners at any one time. I know some of the guys with the company. They seem okay."

"Ever heard of someone named Rick Jackson?"

"I've seen the name. He's a supervisor or something. Why, do you know him?"

"We've met."

# CHAPTER 28

**AFTER OUR TOUR**, Vicki took me to the main dining hall, named Dragon. The Dragon dining hall was the largest of the four free eating establishments. We had a choice of several locally flavored cafés as well as a regular Pizza Hut. I guess that was there to keep the US servicemen from getting too homesick. I didn't see how that was even possible.

The place was busy, but not overwhelmed. I saw men and women in every conceivable uniform. Usually, the only way to identify them was by the patch on their arm. Slovakia, Serbia, Denmark, Italy, the list went on and on. It was impressive so many countries decided to throw people into this conflict. It didn't matter if it was a large force or just a token group of participants. It was still inspiring.

I followed Vicki through the line with a tray. The choices were astounding. There was trout with the tail still

on to show how fresh it was. I looked over the burger section, Mexican food, and the usual cafeteria-style stew or
casserole. It was nothing like the chow I ate in the Navy
years ago.

We found a place at the end of the table filled by burly
soldiers from the Czech Republic. None of them appeared
to speak English. And certainly none of them took notice
of us.

Vicki was clearly an active Army master sergeant and
my jeans and polo shirt gave no clue as to who I was.
I'm sure most everyone assumed I was a contractor, but I
could be a US service member off-duty.

We chatted for a little bit. Vicki told me about growing
up south of Chicago with two sisters and two brothers.
Then she got the idea she wanted to fly helicopters and
that was her only focus.

Vicki said, "I have more than eighty semester hours I've
earned toward a college degree since I joined the service.
When I rotate back to the States, I'm hoping to be near a
university so I can buckle down. Money is always an issue. Even here in this godforsaken wilderness, you never
seem to have enough cash."

I had to laugh. "Why do you think I'm here?"

"I've been wondering that. Why *are* you here? I mean
why are you *really* here? I've gotten a sense from the
very beginning that you're nothing like you appear. I was
thinking you were some kind of quality-control person for
your company. Maybe they sent you over here to see how
things were running without raising any suspicion. Now

I can't figure out why you're going to go on patrol in the most desolate part of the base."

Man, was she sharp. Beautiful, sharp, and dedicated. That was a powerful combination. I didn't answer immediately. I quickly considered the pros and cons of an honest confession. Just thinking about it made me feel better. I had to talk to someone.

I sighed deeply and said, "It's a really long story. And I doubt you'd want to get mixed up in it."

She leveled those pretty blue eyes at me. I could imagine many men wilting under her gaze. "We are on an air base half a world away from home. I'm stuck here for a minimum of six months. I have plenty of time. I can also decide what I do and don't want to get mixed up in."

"Well stated and fair enough. I didn't mean to make you think I was being secretive. I just didn't want to bore you."

She let out a little growl. "Just tell me already."

I gave her an abbreviated version. I didn't go into details about the hidden prison. Just that a contractor here named Rick Jackson had tried to destroy my family. When I was finished, I realized the story was a little far-fetched. Maybe I owed the detectives at the Newburgh Police Department an apology.

Vicki just stared at me like she was trying to make up her mind whether I was crazy. I'd seen the look before. Sometimes my mom gave it to me. I just gave her some time.

Then she surprised me when she said, "I can help you."

"What?"

"I mean, I have access to all the contractor records. I can tell you exactly where this Jackson guy works and when he'll be there. Provided he's on the base at all."

It was one of the few times in my life I didn't mind not finishing a meal.

# CHAPTER 29

**VICKI'S OFFICE WAS** on the second floor of one of the hardened buildings that had been on the base for many years. These were generally filled by US military personnel and considered a big step above almost any other structure.

There was even decent air-conditioning that kept the place comfortable. At this time in the evening, there was almost no one in the building. It could've been any mid-level company in the US. Nothing fancy like a tech company. Not Facebook or Google. But maybe the head-quarters for Home Depot or Macy's. Lots of paperwork stacked on top of standard, identical wooden desks.

Just like in the US, the break room had a TV and a coffee set that looked like someone brought it from their living room.

Vicki's office held two desks. The other one was occu-pied by an army corporal who was supposed to be her as-sistant. She said, "He's more work than he's worth. A nice kid, but he gets distracted by everything. I'm also not sure about his reading comprehension. He's from Indiana." She smiled.

"I'm sure that's none of your Illinois bias coming out."

"Of course it's not. I can't help it if we're smarter than anyone else in the Midwest."

Vicki logged on to her computer and, shortly, looked up and said, "You're right. Rick Jackson is a supervisor for Deep River, assigned to this detention facility." She read the screen for a moment more and said, "Looks like this guy's been around. He was in the Marines ten years ago. Very impressive."

That's when I heard an alert tone over the loudspeakers. Then the familiar, computer-generated voice that said, "Take cover, take cover, take cover," in a quick, even tone.

I just looked at Vicki and she said, "Missile attack. We've got to get down to a bunker. My captain would freak out if she heard we just stayed in the office during an attack."

She calmly led me down the stairs next to her office and out the back door. No one seemed to be running willy-nilly. It was the most organized emergency I had ever seen.

She led me to one of the many bunkers dug into the ground and covered with sandbags. It was about the size of the inside of a narrow step van, maybe six feet across and fifteen to twenty feet long. There were simple wooden benches on each side of the bunker.

We slid onto the bench with a few contractors sitting on the other end. No one looked too alarmed. Then I heard an explosion in the not too far distance. Almost immediately, more people started spilling into the bunker.

Vicki leaned in close and said, "Usually, the missiles fall way out near the airfield. No one here is used to hearing the impacts." There were two more thuds as missiles detonated in the distance. More people poured in, until both the benches were packed, and people were spread out on the ground between them.

I'm not proud of this, but for more than a moment, I was hoping a missile might hit the prison and kill Rick Jackson. I didn't give any thought to the other employees or the prisoners. All I thought about was getting to go home immediately. I missed my home. I worried about my mom and brother. I missed Alicia. Although the idea of making some extra money here was appealing.

Vicki slid so close to me, she was partially on my lap. Now the whole place was getting a little stuffy and close. I noticed a couple of people in workout clothes and realized some of the stench was coming from them. What could you do? You flee a workout during a missile attack, you can't be expected to take a shower first.

I think it was mostly to break the tension as we all waited for the "all clear," but Vicki said, as she was crammed on my lap, "So, are you seeing anyone?"

I also realized it was a genuine question that required an honest answer. Unfortunately, I hesitated and all I could come up with was, "Umm, ahh, yeah, I guess."

"You guess? I think I feel sorry for the girl back home. What do you have? Commitment issues?"

I just shrugged. I knew my feelings for Alicia were real. I was also still getting over the death of my fiancée years before in a car accident. I figured I'd just leave it at the shrug.

Mercifully, the "all clear" came a minute or two later.

# CHAPTER 30

**SO FAR, SINCE** I'd arrived in Afghanistan, I'd been through another orientation, signed forms to the point that I stopped reading them, then helped DP in the office. It was his hope that I'd like working in the office and give up my crazy request to work patrol along the perimeter near the detention facility.

Today was the first day on patrol. Even though my plan was not just to work for Non-Metric Solutions, but to find Rick Jackson, I was kind of excited. The same kind of excitement I felt whenever I started any kind of new job. I was also slightly nervous. Not just about the job. There was a lot that could go wrong when I found him.

DP showed me the tan Nissan Frontier with a Colt AR-15 in a secure holder by the front seat. The rifle, which didn't fire in automatic, was only in case of emergency. If I broke the seal holding it in place, I had to write a report. My main weapons would be the pistol in a holster on my hip and an ASP I carried in my back pocket.

DP quizzed me as he checked over my clothing. I had 511 cargo pants, a ballistic vest that felt like it was a castoff from a police department, a Kevlar helmet, and work boots I'd brought from home.

He said, "You hear a warning siren, any kind of siren, and you seek cover. This truck wouldn't stop a rubber band, and besides, Nissans are hard to come by out here."

"I'll stay alert."

"You do that, but an occasional mortar round dropping over the wall, or missiles, is about the most action that area sees. I swear I don't know why a smart guy like you wants to work out there. It's the middle of nowhere, inside the middle of nowhere."

I felt like a bird leaving the nest and DP, my nervous mother. I had a map of the whole base and a second map of my patrol area. With all the checkpoints, there was no way I could get lost.

I spent an hour dutifully driving along my patrol route. My orders were to stop and question anyone I saw out there. I had no idea how anyone could get this far from the main part of the base without a vehicle.

It got boring fast. Initially, I loved the beautiful Hindu Kush in the distance with snow and ice on the mountaintop and the brilliant blue sky behind. I could see the far-off detention facility when I made my turn back toward the base. I made up games to keep my interest. I tried driving at exactly seven miles an hour.

Finally, I parked on the side of the road and pulled out the new phone I'd bought here on base. It was preloaded with 120 minutes of phone time I could use to call the US.

I thought about calling Alicia but realized I needed to call my mother first. By my calculations, it was about eight o'clock in Marlboro, New York. She answered on the second ring.

"Hey, Mom."

"Bobby, how are you? What do they have you doing? Are you safe? I haven't seen anything in the news about Afghanistan. What's the food like? Are you eating enough? Are..."

"Mom, Mom, calm down. I'm safe, the food is surprisingly good, and no one cares about Afghanistan in the US anymore. It would take something spectacular for anything to be on the news. How are you guys doing?"

"Somehow we're surviving without you. Alicia and your brother are like kids around the house. Always laughing and getting into something."

Before I could say anything about that kind of outrageous behavior, at least between my girlfriend and my brother, my mom cut me off.

She said, "I guess that's not true. I thought for a moment you might come home if you heard something like that. In fact, Natty is recovering fine and Alicia has been at school most days since you left."

I filled her in on everything going on, purposely leaving out anything about my friend Jason Roche's death. That was probably something she'd never hear.

My mom said, "I was worried about Natty getting lazy.

I went by the academy and grabbed books and some assignments for him. Since they consider him kind of a hero after the explosion at Alicia's, they didn't have any problem with him studying at home for a while."

"Did you get the money I deposited into your account?"

"Yes, I did. I appreciate it, Bobby, but I don't want you to leave yourself short."

"Everything is provided for here. And they're paying me really well. Use the money for the medical bills."

My mom hesitated then said, "Have you found the man who shot Natty?"

"Not yet, but he's here."

"Good. Pull off one of his nuts for me."

I flinched.

She continued. "And feed it to a chipmunk in front of him."

"Mom." I almost shouted.

"What?"

"There aren't any chipmunks in Afghanistan."

Her rant left me in a better mood.

# CHAPTER 31

**ON THE SECOND** day of patrol, things weren't any more interesting. I tried calling Alicia but got no answer. She probably didn't recognize the number. Or even what country it originated from.

I called Natty to see how he was feeling.

"I've already put on six pounds eating all the shit Mom makes every day. How is she not obese?"

"If you notice, she rarely eats what she cooks. Plus, she's got good genes. And fat is probably afraid to stick to her for too long."

"That makes sense." There was a long silence, then Natty said, "We miss you here, brother. I don't have anyone to pick on me when you're not around."

"And there's no one here nearly frustrating enough to get me riled up. I miss you, too."

"How's the search for the asshole who shot me going?"

"I'm close. You have no idea how close. He works in an

isolated building on the base. I wrangled it so I would be patrolling near that building."

Natty said, "If you know he's there, isn't that enough? Can't you tell someone and they'll arrest him?"

"It's not enough. I intend to confront him. Maybe fight him. Then both of us can get sent home. He'll get shipped back to the US. Once he's back home he'll have a harder time weaseling out of anything."

"You think the scary federal agent will come through, if you find him?"

"I think she's embarrassed by what happened in the mine shafts. I don't think she likes these guys at all. So I'll find him, identify him personally, rough him up in a scuffle, then call her."

"What are you going to say when you find him?"

"I'm not in a movie. I don't have to say anything witty."

"C'mon, Mitchum, I'm your brother. Don't hold out on me."

I had to let out a laugh. Finally, I said, "Okay, I'll probably say something like, 'My brother sends his regards.'"

"What about, 'You shouldn't have left me alive'?"

We chatted a little longer. The connection to home was revitalizing. Then he said, "There is one thing. I probably shouldn't even mention it."

"What is it?" I tried to keep the edge out of my voice.

"Mom thinks someone might be following her still."

"Did you tell Bill? He could figure it out or get the right help if he needed it."

"She hasn't left Marlboro. It's not in Newburgh. He and

I talked about it. He's been by the house more and he's checking. I just thought I'd let you know." He paused, then said, "I'm telling you because you don't have enough to worry about."

We both laughed at that.

I needed the stress relief of a good laugh. My brother told me to be careful. And I told him to get well. For a change, we both meant it.

I went about my patrol route. Endless laps around the narrow, blacktop road. Then it happened. I noticed a beat-up Chevy pickup truck leaving the detention facility. I was about a half mile away, but on that flat, wide-open plain, I could see everything.

I didn't even have to hit the gas to reach the road about the same time the truck came out of the access road from the detention facility. The blue truck had a faded Deep River logo on the driver's door. The windshield was cracked and the tailgate missing altogether.

I pulled in behind it and hit the cheesy blue light stuck on the dash of my Nissan. The Chevy pulled over immediately. As I climbed out, I was surprised to see the driver was none other than Rick Jackson. I couldn't wait to see the expression on his face when he saw me here. This was going to be sweet.

As I walked along the side of the truck, the driver's door opened, and Jackson stepped out like it was no big deal.

I had my hand behind me, holding the end of my ASP. I could pop the expandable baton out in a split second and crack him right over the head if I needed to. First, I wanted to hear what he had to say when he saw me.

He glanced back toward me and recognition spread over his face. He actually smiled. Then he surprised me by saying, "Hey, Mitchum, you got here a lot faster than I expected."

# CHAPTER 32

**JACKSON COULD NOT** have been more relaxed. That pissed me off. He shouldn't get to look so smug and satisfied. He leaned on the side of the Chevy, then casually put his hands into the pockets of his windbreaker. It was like we were chatting during a break at work.

I started to say, *my brother sends his regards*. Then I caught myself. If being silent rattled him, he didn't show it. We just stared at each other for a minute.

I expected to square off. Maybe have a good old-fashioned fistfight. At least this time I'd be mentally pre-pared for it. Instead, I stood at the rear of his truck, my hand on the handle of the ASP.

I knew that Agent Kravitz needed me to positively iden-tify Jackson and provide his exact location. She never said she could arrest him. She said she would *try* to get a warrant for him. I wasn't sure I liked those odds.

My other options were decidedly less legal. The easiest thing would be to shoot him in the head right now. Then

I'd have a lot of explaining to do. Instead, I decided to hear what he had to say. What else was I going to do with my day?

A breeze from the Hindu Kush blew across the valley. For a few seconds, it dropped the temperature by at least ten degrees. Jackson huddled in his windbreaker. He gazed around the open base and then looked at me.

Jackson said, "As pleasant as this is, catching up with someone from the States, I'm afraid I have to get back to work."

I laughed at that. "It's ironic that over here they have a criminal running a prison."

Jackson looked hurt for a moment. "Me, a criminal?"

"You don't think so?"

"Maybe, if you stretch it, I'm a criminal in the US. But this is Afghanistan. Believe me when I tell you, no one cares. Not one person." He still wasn't worried that I had the drop on him. "Even the damn Afghan Army doesn't care that much about beating the Taliban."

I said, "I think you're underestimating how people feel about someone running down a woman or shooting someone in America."

This time he laughed. A belly laugh. "It's a big world, Mitchum. Lots of threats. People in the US said, 'never forget' after 9/11. But we forgot. In fact, there are some who want to blame *us* for the attack. Can you believe that? They want to remove the responsibility from the terrorists. That's how screwed up the world is. All I'm doing is trying to keep an attack like that from happening again."

"And getting rich while you do."

"That's not at odds with what America is all about. Ask yourself. If we're going to fight terrorism, would you rather we did it at home or over here?"

I glanced around, making sure no one was driving toward us. It was an unwarranted concern. There wasn't a person visible anywhere. Just the detention building far off in the distance.

As if reading my mind, Jackson said, "No one will come by, Mitchum. My men are at the holding facility. That's what we call it. It's not a jail, or, God forbid, a prison. It's just a holding facility. Have to watch out for everyone's feelings. Even terrorists'."

"And you run it?"

"Very efficiently."

I shook my head and muttered, "Talk about the inmates running the prison. I still can't believe they let a criminal like you do anything."

Jackson said, "Here, I'm just a contractor, even if you think that I may be a criminal."

"What do you mean, 'may be'? You shot my brother and ran down my mother."

"Are they dead?"

"No."

Jackson smiled. "And that hot piece of ass? The one whose apartment I remodeled. What about her? How's she doing?"

He was trying to get me to do something rash. He was playing mind games. He wanted me to punch or jump on him. I resisted. All I said was, "She's fine."

"Then no one will care about me or what I did. Besides, I know something you don't."

"Really? What?"

"This." Jackson casually removed his right hand from the pocket of his windbreaker. It took me a moment to realize what he was holding. By the time it dawned on me that it was a Taser, he turned and fired.

Before I could do anything, fifty thousand volts locked up every muscle in my body. I fell to the hard, dusty ground.

I was conscious, but couldn't move as Jackson kneeled down next to me. I didn't even feel the needle he stuck in my arm.

Jackson said, "Not to worry. This is just a tranquilizer. It's made for horses, but the effect is the same. You're a big boy. I don't want you acting up. This will give you a nice little nap." He tapped my cheek like we were buddies.

The last thing I remembered was the round orb of the sun. Then nothing.

# CHAPTER 33

**I WOKE UP** in a cage, with a very clear memory of what had happened. Now I had to figure out where I'd been taken after Jackson shot me full of some kind of horse tranquilizer. I was careful not to move so no one would notice me. I could hear people in the room and caught glimpses out of the corner of my eye of someone walking past me.

The ceiling was white panels with brown water stains from leaks like we had in elementary school.

My vision wasn't perfect. I felt fuzzy. Really fuzzy. Finally, I tried to sit up. It was considerably harder than I expected. I suspected I'd be sitting for a while before I felt well enough to stand up.

My eyes focused and I saw that I was in a fairly big room with boxes stacked in every corner and files on top of several empty desks. At the desk directly across the room from my cage, Jackson worked at a computer.

After a minute, he noticed me sitting up. He turned in his comfortable-looking leather office chair.

Jackson said, "I was holding you up here in the office to be safe. Away from the real prisoners. They'd love a shot at an American. Especially one as wholesome looking as you."

I had a million questions, but I couldn't form any. All I could work out was, "What are you going to do with me?"

He remained cheerful and said, "Let me show you the first part of my plan. You'll appreciate this, I'm sure." He picked up an ancient rotary phone and dialed four digits. I could only hear his side of the conversation. And I didn't have the energy to shout or distract him in any way.

When someone on the other end of the phone answered, Jackson said, "Hey is this Non-Metric Solutions? This is Rick over at Deep Water." There was a short break and he said, "Hey, DP, how you doing today? Good, good to hear. What's the DP stand for? Dennis Paul, I see. I see your name all over the place and always wondered about that." There was another decent break.

This time Jackson used a professional tone as he said, "Can we borrow one of your people for about a week? Ten days at the most. You can bill us one and a half times the rate if you want. His name is Mitchum. I'm not sure about his first name. Robert, really? Just like the actor?" Then he closed it out with, "Yeah, we could really use him around the holding facility. He said he didn't mind. Probably use him on some transports down to Jalalabad, too." He gave DP some numbers for billing then said, "Thanks so much,

DP. We're all in this together, and I appreciate this kind of support."

Jackson hung up the phone then turned and smiled. He didn't say a word. He winked at me. Without another sound, he went back to working at his desk. And I started thinking about how to get out of this cage.

# CHAPTER 34

**I HAD LITTLE** contact with anyone else the rest of the day. Sometime during the evening, a surly-looking employee with a tattoo on his forearm of the Philadelphia 76ers logo dropped a can of beans with a plastic spoon on the floor next to my cage. I was hungry enough that it was as good a dinner as I'd ever eaten.

I kept wondering about my mom's concern that someone was following her in Marlboro. What would happen if things went wrong here? Would they hurt my mother? It was a disturbing thought.

I also noticed the constant noise coming from the rest of the building. Jackson hadn't been lying to me when he said there were other inmates. When I first heard the organized sound late in the afternoon, Jackson had turned to me and said, "It's prayers. Or *calls* to prayers. Lots and lots of prayers. You get used to it. It's like hearing someone speak in tongues. There's a comforting rhythm to it after a while." He stood up and walked across the room. When he sat a few feet from my cage, he said, "Think of it this way: if they're saying prayers, they're not thinking about killing you or me or other Americans."

I slept in fits during the night. I awoke to the sound of someone calling for morning prayers. Someone had set another can of beans on the floor just outside my cage. I ate them quickly.

Rick Jackson was back at his desk. He turned and said, "Not as easy to sleep without the tranquilizer, is it?" He chuckled.

Now I had all my senses. I said, "You never answered me. What's going to happen to me?"

"There's something big going on. Something that would really help us out, and you're the key to success."

"Me? How?"

Jackson smiled. "A little surprise is good for the soul."

"Is that why you have someone following my mom? To avoid surprises?"

"We like to keep tabs on people. Now that you've co-operated so nicely and come all the way over here, we'll probably call off our assistant. Provided you behave."

"I hate to ruin your plans if I'm the key to them."

Jackson shrugged. "Don't you worry about it. It'll work out. You cost us a lot of money and one of our really good IT people is still in jail in New York."

"It sounds like you think he shouldn't be in jail."

Jackson just shrugged.

I just stared in silence at him. After a while I said, "Someone will ask questions about me."

"Someone already did."

I perked up.

He laughed and said, "Your friend DP Lampkin. He asked how many hours you'd be working per day. I told him we would max you out. That means more profit for Non-Metric Solutions."

Jackson had gotten ahead of this thing and would have plausible deniability. I was on my own. Unless some miracle happened.

Jackson taunted me, making a crying sound and changing his voice. "Why am I here? Why are you so mean? What's going to happen to me?" Then he switched to his real voice. "Jesus Christ, Mitchum, I'd think a former Navy man would be tougher. You sound like a lost kid. Sit back and think of this as an adventure. You never know how it might turn out." He laughed and added, "I bet it doesn't turn out that well for you."

Then I heard a woman's voice in the outer office. I listened for a minute and realized it was Vicki Jensen.

I was saved.

# CHAPTER 35

**I FELT A** burst of adrenaline as soon as I recognized Vicki's voice. She stepped into the office with Jackson. She shot me a quick look in the cage, then followed Jackson over to his desk.

She looked official, in uniform and her hair pinned up. She frowned as Jackson talked to her by his desk. They started to argue in low tones. Then Jackson stepped into the back of the holding facility and left us alone for a moment.

Vicki casually stepped over to my cage. She leaned in close and said, "Are you okay?" She reached through the bars and gently took my chin in her hand. She turned my head in each direction, checking for any sort of marks. She wanted to be sure I hadn't been beaten.

When she was satisfied I hadn't been mistreated—*obviously* mistreated—she sat on a hard wooden chair near my cage. She scooted it in close.

Vicki said, "I've never been inside this place before. It's nothing like I imagined. More cramped and messy."

"This is just the administrative office. The real prisoners are held in the back." I couldn't wait to ask questions. I knew Jackson could come back at any moment. "Who else is coming to help you?"

Vicki ignored my question and said, "Did you really release a bunch of Jihadis from a jail in upstate New York?"

I almost couldn't comprehend the question. All I could say is, "What?"

"I asked you if you released men being held at a jail. It's a yes or no question."

A little panic crept into my voice. "When are you getting me out of here? This guy is crazy."

"I think you're probably where you need to be. I've had friends killed both here and in Iraq. Having someone like you, with no clue about what we're doing, release potential terrorists is dispiriting. It's bad enough that no one even thinks about the military and the risks we take without people actively hurting us."

I just stared at her.

She sighed and said, "Mitchum, I'm not getting you out of here. You shouldn't even be in Afghanistan."

Just then, the door from the back opened and Jackson strolled back into the office. He barked at Vicki, "Get away from there."

She jumped from the chair and backed away from me.

I had hoped she was going to go off on this asshole.

Now I realized I was alone. I waited but they just talked quietly. I couldn't even pick up what was said. Then Jackson handed Vicki an envelope. Even from across the room I could see the cash when she opened and checked the contents.

All I could say in a whiny voice was, "You warned him?" It was completely demoralizing.

She turned to me and said, "We're *fighting* terrorists, not releasing them." Then she pulled out a stack of cash from the envelope and said, "Besides, a girl's got to party." Now she was smiling. Enough so her dimples showed.

I managed to stand and wrap my hands around the bars. "You're not going to leave me in here, are you? There's no telling what they're going to do to me."

Now she stepped right next to the bars. I noticed Jackson keeping a close eye on her from across the room. Vicki reached up and stroked my cheek with the back of her hand.

She said, "Don't worry. You'll be home soon. Jackson told me they're just going to ship you back. They don't need another screw-up like you caused in New York. And I'll have some extra cash."

I said, "You don't understand."

"I understand enough." And she held up the cash again and said, "Enough to know I'm going on a serious spending spree on Amazon. And you're right where you should be. If it were up to me, people like you would have to serve real jail time."

She turned and nodded to Jackson and marched toward the front door. As she grabbed the door handle, she turned to me. "I hope one day you'll understand what you did."

Then she was gone.

# CHAPTER 36

**I DOZED THAT** afternoon. It was my only defense against a feeling of hopelessness. After Vicki left the building, I saw no way to escape.

I awoke to a hood being slipped over my head. I was hurried out of the building and twenty minutes later found myself on a ten-passenger prop plane. Just Jackson, me, and the thin Afghan pilot.

I couldn't keep from looking around the airplane with an eye to escape. I had no idea how, but I knew I had to try.

Jackson sat in the seat across the row from me. "Not so sure of your plan to capture me, are you?"

"I still know where you are."

Jackson laughed and waved me off. "You don't even know where *you* are. We could touch down anywhere. Even Pakistan. And you wouldn't have a clue."

I decided it was best to keep my mouth shut. I also decided to keep my eyes open. I watched Jackson when he worked his way up to speak with the pilot. The tiny plane made him walk at a funny angle to get past every seat. The handle of his pistol caught on the seats over and over.

I glanced out the window and noticed we were over wide-open areas. I guess I'd call it a desert, even though technically it wasn't. Occasionally, I'd see a compound on the ground or maybe several vehicles parked together. But there wasn't much else.

Jackson came back toward me and plopped down in the seat across from me again. He turned to me and started to speak. "You know, we're going..."

Then an alarm started to beep throughout the whole cabin. I had never heard an alarm on a plane like that before.

The pilot became frantic.

I had to look at Jackson and finally ask, "What's going on?"

"Ground radar is lighting us up. Some ragheads with old surface-to-air shoulder missiles think they can get an easy kill."

Just then, the plane made a wild looping turn to the left. The pilot was good. He banked the plane so hard that I almost fell out of my seat. Then I saw the missile. It zipped past the window right next to the wing. I could hear it as it swooshed by. The pilot's crazy maneuvers had worked. At least for now.

Jackson ignored me and started screaming at the pilot. "Get us out of here! Don't fool around! Just haul ass—now!"

The pilot leveled the plane, but yelled over his shoulder, "They're about to launch again." This time the plane did the same maneuver in the opposite direction. The force of the turn threatened to drop me out of my seat again. Then I realized the position I was in and let go of my grip on the seat in front of me holding me in place.

It was like I was in zero gravity when I slipped out of the seat, but barely moved. The pilot forced the plane into another turn and I landed on top of Jackson like I had planned.

My hands were still cuffed in front of me, but my full weight had landed directly on the former Marine. It was satisfying to hear the noise that came out of him when my 230 pounds landed squarely on his stomach. It sounded like an exaggerated effect Al Pacino would make in a movie.

It was hard to twist and use my elbows effectively with the handcuffs on my wrists. That didn't mean I didn't try. I enjoyed throwing my right elbow into his jaw. I expected some blows back my way, but between landing on him and catching him across the jaw, Jackson was completely dazed.

The plane leveled out and I stood up. It took me a minute to get my legs under me and feel confident about walking up the aisle toward the pilot. I was going to have him turn around and land back at Bagram. I didn't care what sort of security forces showed up when we landed.

When I was about halfway to the cockpit, the pilot leaned out from his seat. He had a dark mustache that looked like something out of a fifties noir movie. His left incisor was capped in gold. It was clear when he smiled. And he was smiling as he pointed the small automatic pistol at me.

Before I could think of another way get to the pilot, I felt the pain in my shoulder next to my neck. Suddenly the world started to spin. As I toppled to the rubber mat on the floor of the plane, I saw Jackson standing behind me.

It wasn't until I hit the floor and rolled onto my back that I saw he was holding an empty hypodermic needle. A trickle of blood was running from the corner of his mouth.

Jackson smiled. "Looks like someone's going to take another nap."

# CHAPTER 37

**I WAS AWAKE**, but groggy as the plane landed. I had been unconscious for a while. My hands were secured behind my back this time. The bump of the small plane landing on the runway knocked me awake.

I looked around the plane's small cabin and the first thing I saw was Jackson's smiling face. He was sitting directly across from me, just like before. He grabbed me by the arm and held me upright in the seat.

He said, "We didn't have much tranquilizer left. I didn't even know if it would work. But you got a twenty-minute nap out of it. How do you feel?" He slapped me on the shoulder, like we were old drinking buddies.

In truth, I felt like I had a hangover. But my curiosity overrode any of my instincts to close my eyes and put my head back down.

I managed to croak, "Where are we?" I noticed the plane taxi toward a compact Honda sedan at the end of the runway instead of going to the small terminal. There was no sign on the terminal building and gray duct tape held two of the windows together.

Jackson said, "We are in the lovely city of Jalalabad. Ever heard of it?"

I just shrugged. I knew the name, but it hurt my head to talk.

He continued. "Technically, we could've landed at the US Forward Operating Base Fenty a few miles away. We decided to use the municipal airport to get you to our special holding facility here in the city. I'm not sure the Air Force would be particularly happy about us transporting a US citizen in handcuffs. No matter how much of a dumbass he is."

A man with dark hair, dressed in civilian clothes, drove the Honda Civic I was thrown into. Jackson slid into the seat next to me and said, "You don't need a hood here. No one in the city would recognize you. More importantly, no one in the city would care what was happening to you. They have their own problems. Less than twenty miles from the Pakistani border, everything comes through Jalalabad. Including terrorists and the Afghan army chasing them."

As we drove through the city and into a residential neighborhood, I thought the place looked like the bad areas of Phoenix, Arizona, or somewhere in New Mexico. Brownish sand with very few plants to break up the monochrome color. Mostly smaller, run-down houses with the occasional well-kept two-story. The climate felt about the same as well.

Jackson said to me, "This is the center of the world as far as Afghanistan goes. Kabul may be the capital, but this is the crossroads. One of the few cities with daily bus service to both Kabul and Pakistan. And we've got a sweet house not too far away."

We rolled into the driveway of an ordinary-looking house. We pulled into a carport and entered through the side door, directly into what looked like the living room. Only now the room was crammed with desks, boxes, and other shit laid out in a loose arrangement.

Jackson led me down a hallway and I looked in each room quickly, just getting a glimpse. In each room, three or four portable cages looked almost like a person-size kennel. That made each of the rooms crowded.

We hesitated at the last bedroom. Jackson stepped inside and pulled me along. There were two empty cages in this room. A man sat on some blankets inside one of the cages. He wore a white shirt and baggy white pants. He had no shoes on. He just stared at me with dark eyes. Then a smile slid across his face.

Jackson let out a laugh. "Probably not such a good idea to put you inside with these guys. I don't have enough people to make sure you're safe. We'll have to set up a cage in the main room for you."

# CHAPTER 38

**THEY STUCK ME** inside of a cage in the first bedroom temporarily. There were three men already in the room. They all stared at me silently. I nodded because my hands were still cuffed behind my back.

Two of the men started to speak in Pashto. The third man laughed at whatever they said. One man dragged his finger across his throat in a slashing motion. I didn't take it to mean they were welcoming me to their home.

I glanced around the room. The windows were blocked up with drywall, the only light a single fluorescent on the ceiling. My guess was from the outside the window looked natural. It was only from in here that you couldn't get to it.

I leaned against the bars of my cage and tried to think. My head had been clearing since we landed. The effects of the second dose of tranquilizer didn't last nearly as long as the first. I didn't know if that was from forming a tolerance to the drug or just that he didn't have much left to inject me.

As far as workers here at the jail, there was Jackson and the man who drove us. Every indication was that a third person worked in the house. There was no way I was going to overpower three men. Especially when one of them was Jackson. I doubted I could handle him by himself.

As I started to think about all the possible ways someone might find out about me, I felt something on my shoulder, then my whole body jerked back to the bars of the cage. I couldn't breathe. It took me a moment to realize there was an arm around my throat.

The man in the cage next to me had reached between the bars and grabbed me, hard. I squirmed, but couldn't get out of his grasp. The other two men were whispering encouragement to him. It was in Pashto, but I got the gist of their encouragement. They wanted to see a dead American.

There wasn't a whole lot I could do right now. My hands were cuffed behind my back. I wiggled my head, hoping to be able to bite the arm around my throat. But I got nowhere.

Then the man with his arm around my throat pulled harder and whacked my head against the bars. I saw stars for a moment. I still wasn't getting any air. I felt his grip get tighter.

I had to do something, and it had to be quick. I squirmed, hoping to break his hold. No luck. All I could think to do was stand up. I pushed up with my legs, but the man just rose with me. Oddly, so did the other two men in the other cages. They all stood up at about the same pace I did. They were following the action like they were watching a cricket match.

When I was upright, I bent as hard as I could. I jerked forward with all of my abdominal strength. My butt braced me against the bars. When it didn't work, I did it again. I jerked down savagely, hoping to break this guy's grip and hurt him in the process.

This time his arm came from around my neck. With nothing holding me upright, I fell facefirst onto the floor of the cage. It was the first time I noticed the cages were sitting on nice hardwood floors. This had been someone's home once.

I rolled onto my side, panting, trying to take in as much air as possible. I got a glimpse of the man who choked me. He had a satisfied smile as he stared at me from his cage.

Jackson's bulky body filled the doorway. "Are you boys roughhousing?" He laughed out loud when he looked down at me.

He opened the lock on my cage, then he roughly pulled me out. As we walked down the hallway, he whispered in my ear, "You're not in Kansas anymore, sport."

# CHAPTER 39

**JACKSON ESCORTED ME** back into the front room. Now I noticed a new cage erected in the corner. It wasn't like the others with actual bars. This one looked truly portable. It had a grate instead of bars. I had to crouch to fit through the door. There was a square, about the size of a book, in the door that someone could slide food or something else to me. An actual army cot sat inside the cage. It made me feel like I was at the Four Seasons.

Jackson pushed me in and slammed the door. I turned around to see him locking it. He said, "Back up to the little slot. I'll uncuff you from out here."

It was the first thing he had told me to do that I didn't mind doing. It felt great to have my arms free. I tried to wave them to get my blood flowing, but hit the top of the cage. I went down to my knees and did it. Then flopped onto the cot. After the floor, it felt like a king-size bed with a memory-foam topper.

I almost immediately started to drift off. Then I had

a hitch in my breathing and sprang awake. It was just a quick dream as I drifted off. But my throat still hurt from where the prisoner in the other room tried to choke me. After that experience, the momentary hitch in my breathing terrified me.

Jackson worked at a computer on a proper desk directly across the room from me. His work area and cot next to his desk were clean and orderly. I assumed that was the Marine training in him.

The other two cots were empty, but clearly belonged to someone. The desk closest to my cage had the most files stacked on it. The other desk looked like it was barely used.

Jackson noticed me sitting up and said, "How's the throat?"

I just shrugged.

"These fellas would love to claim they killed an American. I hope you appreciate me looking out for you. You'll be safe up here with us."

"Yeah, I've felt protected since you first kidnapped me."

"What are you getting so self-righteous about? Didn't you come to Afghanistan to hunt me down like a dog? The only thing you can bitch about is being unprepared and underestimating us. I'd say that's an intelligence thing."

"Like tactical intelligence on my enemy or my own mental intelligence?"

He spun all the way in his padded desk chair so he was looking directly at me. "That's a deep question, Mitchum. I could give you a flip answer, but I respect the question enough to think about it." He was quiet for almost a full minute.

I spent the time really exploring the room and Jackson. I noticed we came through the side door. I now realized that if they parked in the carport, no one could see them walk up to the door on the side of the house. This was still the main entry room whether someone walked in through the front door or the side door.

They were trying to keep this place a complete secret. Despite Jackson's assertion that nobody cared, obviously someone did. They didn't want their little holding facility made public.

Jackson said, "Both."

"What? Both what?"

"Your tactical intelligence was suspect and I think your common sense is poor. You're easily goaded into things. I'd never want to work with you."

"You'll get your wish."

I heard a car door slam. Jackson checked a security camera on a bank of monitors. Then the side door opened and a man stepped through the door. He was about Jackson's age. Or in good enough shape that it was hard to tell exactly how old he was. He had short brown hair, cut like he'd been in the military. He wore a dark-blue Wayne State University Warriors T-shirt.

It took me a moment, but I recognized him. I just stared in shock as he walked through the office like he worked at a marketing firm. He looked in my direction, but didn't acknowledge me.

I said out loud, "I remember you."

The man said, "And I remember you, Mr. Mitchum." He looked at Jackson and said, "Do we need to keep this guy alive? Nothing pisses me off more than seeing this turd."

Jackson said, "Easier to keep him alive for now, Dave."

I snapped my fingers. "David Allmand, that's your name. You ran the prison in Marlboro."

Allmand said, "Which is where I'd still be if you hadn't stirred up all kinds of useless shit. Now I'm in Afghanistan. Thank you very much."

# CHAPTER 40

**ALLMAND PULLED THE** rolling chair from his desk right next to my cage. He plopped down in the seat and leaned forward as if he was a priest ready to take my confession. He rested his elbows on his knees then looked up at me.

The only thing I could say was, "Why?"

"I don't view the whole situation with you the same as my friend Mr. Jackson. He thinks it's a game of some kind. You see, we get terribly bored here in Afghanistan. So he bet me a thousand bucks that he could get you to come over here. He risked almost a whole day's salary on this crazy scheme. I would've been satisfied to pop you in the back of the head with a nine-millimeter whenever I got back to the States. But that's me, I'm a nut for efficiency. But now that you're here, you might satisfy some other needs we have."

"So this is just some kind of crazy revenge plot."

The Deep River supervisor shrugged. "I told you not

to screw up our plans in New York. I gave you a chance to just walk away. You didn't listen to me. Why should I explain things to you now?"

There were some shouts from a room in the back of the house. Jackson and the younger man who had driven us earlier jumped from their seats and raced back. Allmand seemed content to keep talking to me. Even though he wasn't telling me much.

Now, instead of just learning Jackson's routine and possible weaknesses, I had someone new to focus on. Clearly, he wasn't rattled easily. I could hear shouts coming from the back of the house, but this guy wasn't bothered by it in the least. He just kept looking at me with those calm brown eyes.

As I was assessing this man, Jackson and his helper carried a moaning prisoner through the main room. His feet dragged along the floor with an arm across Jackson's shoulders. Blood dribbled from the man's nose and split lip.

The man talking to me glanced at them, but made no comment. When I kept staring at them, he said, "They're going to clean him up in the shower in the garage. Everyone gets cleaned up at least once a week."

As Jackson was about to follow the injured man out the door, he said, "He was freaked out because Parwez touched him. I had to smack him just to calm his ass down."

"Parwez is not contagious."

"Everyone is terrified. They don't know he's not contagious. He looks like he died already. It's disgusting."

Allmand said, "I'll check on him in a little bit." He focused back on me.

I said, "Why'd you pick this house, in this neighborhood, to house prisoners?"

"A lot of reasons. Close to the Pakistani border if we want to buy anything to take back. The house is cheap and all the military cares about is if we're warehousing the correct number of prisoners. No one has checked on us at either location in the months that we've been here. It's kinda like our setup in Marlboro if you hadn't screwed it up."

"And it doesn't bother you that a bloody man was just dragged through the room?" I didn't want to let him know how disturbed I was by it. There was nothing right about this whole setup.

Allmand remained placid. "We have a very simple job. We take combatants delivered to us by the military. We hold those combatants until a determination about their fate is made. That determination is made by the US government. We do not capture anyone, we do not interview anyone. We just hold combatants. I am not responsible for how they behave. Our job is to keep them locked up. Looks like a lesson was just delivered."

Allmand's matter-of-fact tone and demeanor were unsettling to me.

I said, "So you guys have a pretty sweet setup here. And you were pissed at me. I still don't see why you went to all the trouble to lure me to Afghanistan. I don't believe a personal bet between you and Jackson justifies the effort."

He nodded his head slowly. "Very sound reasoning on your part. We have something we need to ship back to the US. One thing that's not searched is coffins. We get you on a military flight back to the US and we enter the country with something we can all retire on."

I pointed at a box of statues and cups similar to the one I saw at the last holding facility. "You're raping the country of its heritage and shipping these little statues and shit home with me."

Allmand reached over and picked up one of the statues. A female character in robes. She had big, colorless eyes. Then he slammed it against the edge of my cage and shattered it. "Most of this stuff is worth less than a dollar apiece. Just trinkets the guys like to give out or ship home. No, Mr. Mitchum, we have other plans for you."

That, in no way, made me feel better about my situation.

# CHAPTER 41

**TWENTY MINUTES LATER**, I watched as David Allmand walked down the hallway to the bedroom where the sick man was supposedly scaring other prisoners. I knew that if there was a sick man in a cage next to me, he would be the least of my worries. Now I had to get serious about getting out of here.

The only door ever used was the one on the side of the house that went into the carport. That made sense so the neighbors wouldn't notice who came and went. I hadn't heard much traffic on the street and wondered what would happen if I got outside. There was a window up high next to my cage. But it was too small to crawl through. It was some kind of venting window set about seven feet off the floor.

Jackson joined Allmand in the back room. I watched with interest over the next half hour as one man or the other came out and looked up things on the computer.

Then they'd go back to the other room. I couldn't figure out what they were doing other than looking up symptoms on WebMD.

Their next move surprised me. They brought the man out on a makeshift stretcher. A towel with knots tied in the corners for handholds. Jackson and Allmand carefully set down the man on the floor near Allmand's desk. Jackson rushed and brought him back a glass of water.

The man did look sick. That was an understatement. He was from somewhere in the region, but had lost all the color in his face. His hair was falling out in clumps. Some of it was still on the shoulder of his nice button-down oxford shirt. He was not dressed like any of the other prisoners. With his jeans and button-down, he could pass for someone in the Midwest easily.

Blood started to gush from his nose. Allmand rushed to hand him a paper towel. It was about then I noticed they weren't treating this man like all the other prisoners. I didn't think it was just because of his illness.

The man said in English, "I must go to hospital."

Allmand said, "We're working on it, Parwez."

I saw an opportunity here. Sow a little dissent and reap the benefits later. I said, "What's wrong with him? He looks terrible. He looks like he's going to die." I hid my smirk.

It worked just the way I expected it to. The man looked up at me in a panic, then at Allmand. He wanted to say something, but vomited next to his towel on the floor. He didn't even have the strength to move out of the way.

Allmand glared at me. "Mind your business. Not another word."

"You mean, not another word about how this poor man is going to die if you don't do something right now?"

Jackson had walked back in and stooped down to check their sick prisoner.

I called out from my cage again. "This man needs a doctor. Like right now. You still didn't say what's wrong with him."

Jackson looked up and said, "He ate something that didn't agree with him." Then Jackson looked at Allmand. "What do we do with him? The doctor is going to ask too many questions."

Allmand motioned for Jackson to pick up the makeshift stretcher. They carried the man into the back room, by the sound of it. I was pretty sure the room was empty, but the monitor covering that room was at an angle where I couldn't see. My head snapped up when I heard a single, muffled gunshot.

The other prisoners heard it, too, and started to shout and bang against the cages.

After a while, Allmand and Jackson dragged a heavy garbage bag out to the carport. I knew what was inside the bag. Before the outer door closed, I also heard Jackson say, "What are we going to tell our Pakistani friends?"

Allmand sounded agitated. "We tell them he must've gotten intercepted after he made the delivery. This whole place is the Wild West. We can't be responsible for everyone."

That was the best intelligence I'd received since I'd been locked up. The man they had just murdered was working with them. That's why he didn't get treated like a normal prisoner. Now I had to figure out what it meant.

# CHAPTER 42

**I HAD NOT** made much progress on escaping, even though I spent half the night checking to see how soundly Jackson, Allmand, and their assistant slept. I couldn't figure out how they slept with all the security monitors and various lights flickering. I could look into most of the rooms via the monitors and I now knew there were sixteen prisoners in the house counting me, assuming the room where they murdered Parwez was empty.

I dozed off and woke up the next morning to the sound of someone pounding on the front door. It was fun watching my captors race around trying to get a clear view on the security monitor of who was at the door.

I could tell it was a woman. She was small and her burqa covered her face. She knocked again and called out something. I couldn't hear what she said.

Jackson said, "It's Jamal Hasadi's mother. The one that hired a lawyer."

Allmand said, "How the hell did she figure out we were here?"

"The family has some money. Enough to hire an attorney. Plus, they know the guy we let go after his family paid the ransom. Maybe he told them."

I was starting to see how these guys made so much money. It's not hard when you have no ethics whatsoever.

My captors had a discussion about if they should confront the woman. But Allmand read the situation and was clear on his intentions. "We sit here and keep quiet. We don't add any ammunition to her arguments. We'll be out of here in a few days anyway."

An hour later, I heard Jackson call out, "She's finally left."

Things went back to normal for a while. By *normal*, I mean I sat on my cot and watched the comings and goings of my captors. Then I was startled by a loud crash and breaking glass.

Jackson scrambled over to look at the security camera monitors.

I heard another crash.

Jackson yelled, "The woman is back. And she's got men with her. They're throwing rocks at the windows. Guess they don't realize the windows are all blocked up from the inside." He paused, looked at the security monitors, and said, "Now they're just milling about in the front yard." His call brought Allmand up from the back of the house.

He looked at the monitors, then both he and Jackson stuck pistols in their waistbands and pulled their shirts over them. Allmand said, "We're going to have to move quick."

Jackson said, "We're not nearly ready."

That was followed by another crash outside. It rocked the whole house. Someone threw a heavy rock against the side of the house. It was the most serious message someone from outside had sent us.

My captors raced around the room gathering documents and other things. Allmand shouted, "We're out of time. Grab the box."

Jackson started to pull a long box from under a table at the far end of the room. Allmand moved over to help him. The box was clearly not empty. It looked like a simple pine box, probably the one they intended to use as a coffin for me.

When the box was in the middle of the room, they pried open the lid, then they scrambled to remove a false bottom. It took all of Jackson's strength to lift out a heavy metal case from the bottom of the coffin.

I watched, trying to figure out what was going on.

Then something came right through the drywall that was covering up the front window. Protesters outside had knocked out the window and someone threw a rock about the size of a navel orange through the drywall.

Now they knew how to get inside.

# CHAPTER 43

**I WAS SO** caught up with what might happen to Jackson and Allmand that I didn't consider my own situation. If these people got into the house, they wouldn't make a distinction between me and the jailers. We would all be Americans. They would associate me with these two assholes. It didn't matter if I was in a cage.

When Allmand drew his pistol from his belt line, I started to get worried. There was no telling who he was going to shoot. I didn't think I was one of the targets. I posed no danger to him. But knowing the way he thought, I was worried that he might walk through the rooms and murder all the prisoners.

Jackson spoke up. "You can't fire that here. It'll only draw more people to the house."

I could hear rocks bouncing off the roof. The pace had definitely picked up in the last minute.

Allmand laughed. "Attract more people? Are you insane? There're already fifteen out in front of the house. If you noticed, they've slashed the tires on our car. Joe ran off somewhere, so now it's just the two of us. I say we blast the first couple through the door and hope someone comes to rescue us. I just sent an emergency email to the coordinator at Bagram."

He turned from the door to the hole in the wall where the window should've been. Someone was trying to squeeze through the hole.

Jackson said, "No guns. Trust me. It's for the best."

"What great idea do you have?" He pointed at the man halfway through the hole.

Jackson moved quickly for a big man. He picked up a broom sitting in the corner of the room. He turned and swung like a big league baseball player. The handle of the broom cracked across the head of the man crawling through the hole. He fell unconscious with his arms dropping almost to the floor. He looked like a piece of old fruit caught in some kind of slicer.

Jackson said, "And the hole is plugged for a little while longer."

Both men quickly gathered whatever personal belongings they needed. They snatched up papers, thumb drives, and mementos like photos and some kind of ceremonial shot glass with a lightning bolt on it.

Allmand kneeled by the rough pine coffin. He took the box Jackson had removed from the bottom compartment earlier and carefully inserted it into a backpack that had more insulation and padding.

He slipped the heavy backpack onto his shoulders. It

made his knees buckle. He stabilized himself then felt the pack on his back.

I had to say from my cell, "What the hell is that?"

Allmand smiled. "Our retirement." He yelled for Jackson to follow him as he rushed down the hallway toward the back of the house.

Jackson smashed his computer against the floor. He jumped on the hard drive until it broke loose.

There were more sounds of people trying to get inside.

Jackson rolled up a wad of papers and grabbed a lighter out of his desk. He lit the end of the papers like they were a torch. Then Jackson looked at me. "Sorry, Mitchum. This isn't what I intended. But the only way to clear out evidence is a decent fire."

He stood, holding the burning papers, looking for what needed to be burned.

I tried to keep my voice calm when I said, "You know Allmand is gone. He's left you to take the brunt of everyone's anger." That made Jackson hesitate. That was my goal.

Jackson said, "Allmand is scouting an escape route."

"Really? Because I don't hear your phone ringing with any instructions." He leaned down to light a huge pile of papers in the middle of the floor.

I could already smell smoke as the papers smoldered for a moment. I wasn't going to last long inside a cage and I had no way to get out.

# CHAPTER 44

**THE PAPERS WERE** starting to catch fire. Jackson just left his burning torch next to his desk, hoping it would catch fire as well. A hazy smoke filled the room.

I had nothing to lose now. I leaned back and kicked at the door where it locked on my cage. It barely moved. I picked up the cot and tried to use it as a battering ram. But it had little effect.

The door from the carport burst open. Four men flooded into the room quickly. Two of them barreled into Jackson and knocked him off his feet. Suddenly there were more people pouring into the house.

Now there were four men holding him. One on each arm and leg. Even a powerful man like Jackson could do nothing. He couldn't even reach for the pistol he had stuck in the small of his back.

The smoke was getting thicker. I took the pillowcase off my pillow and wrapped it around my face as a makeshift gas mask. It also hid my face from anyone who strayed too close to my cage.

I had to turn my head when Jackson started to scream. I didn't see what they were doing, but it wasn't anything I needed to witness. I don't care what the guy did to me or my family.

His screams moved from curses to pleading for his life. When I heard someone fooling with the lock on my cage, I turned. An older man had taken the keys from his pocket and was trying them on the lock to my cage. He spoke to me in Pashto. It sounded like he was trying to reassure me. Suddenly the door opened. The man reached in and helped me out. I kept the pillowcase tied around my face. The fire had spread to a desk. The papers were now scattered all around the floor. Each fueling its own little flame.

Most of the intruders had moved to the back rooms to free the prisoners. I had to check Jackson. It only took me a moment to determine he was dead. He had four or five wounds that each would've been fatal on their own.

I glanced around the room quickly. I made sure no one was paying any attention to me. I grabbed the pistol Jackson had stuck into the back of his belt. I slipped it under my shirt.

It was time for me to get out of there. Just as I was about to head for the door, I had to stop and take a closer look at the box that was going to be my casket. I kneeled down next to it and ran my hand across the bottom.

The hidden compartment had been professionally made.

It was also lined with lead. As I was about to stand up, it hit me. I suddenly understood what was in Allmand's backpack.

The sick Pakistani, the hidden compartment, obvious contraband, and the lead lining the hidden compartment told me they were trying to smuggle plutonium. Probably plutonium from Pakistan. They would have plenty of buyers willing to pay big money if they got it out of the country. I shuddered when I thought about what it might ultimately be used for. Anything from a dirty bomb that could be set off in New York to a series of pellets used to irradiate water supplies or something else.

These guys were terrible. The worst. They talked about securing the US and fighting terrorists, but if they could make money, they'd work with them just as easily.

A thick man in western clothing shouted at me. I didn't know what he shouted, but I pointed toward the back of the house. The man marched right up to me and without warning yanked the pillowcase from my face.

He growled something in Pashto. He turned his head to shout at the people in the other room.

I couldn't risk him getting help. I swung as hard as I could and caught him right across the chin with my left fist. It was like hitting a light switch. He was unconscious on his feet. I caught him and gently eased him down to the coffin. He was shorter than me, so he fit easily.

I stamped out the flames closest to the coffin. Most of the other little fires looked like they were just causing smoke. One of the men who had been stuck in a cage in the back room ran through the front room. He laughed with two other men running alongside. They never even looked up to see me.

It was time for me to make my escape. Instead of running, I walked out the door as if I was supposed to be there. I didn't head to the front of the house. That was too obvious. I slipped to the rear.

Now I was on my own in Afghanistan. Great.

# CHAPTER 45

**I KNEW DAVID** Allmand had escaped out the rear of the house. Personally, I didn't care if I ever saw that asshole again. I didn't have any real urge to get even with him. All I wanted to do was make sure no one bothered me or my family again. I was pretty confident that goal had been achieved.

But there's no way I could let someone like him get away with plutonium. There was no telling what he might do with it or who he might sell it to. I surveyed the area and saw a gap in the fence behind the house. Logically, I decided that's where Allmand fled.

The hole led to a long grassy alley. It was just a gap between houses on different streets. I just guessed and turned right and started jogging away from the house. There was no one chasing me. I just hoped to pick up Allmand's track.

Every time there was a break in a fence or between

two houses, I looked out on the streets on either side of
the alley. It felt like more and more people were pouring
into the streets. Rumors of a house holding prisoners in a neighborhood like this would inflame people.
I couldn't blame them. I sort of did the same thing
when I found out there was a prison near my home in
Marlboro.

I noticed many of the people on the street had weapons.
Mostly just sticks or garden tools. Every once in a while
I saw someone with an AK-47. I even saw two different
men carrying rocket-propelled grenade launchers. One of
them had what looked like a homemade RPG launcher. It
looked a little like an old-style bazooka, only smaller and
lighter. It was designed to sit on someone's shoulder and
fire into the line of sight.

I had my head on a swivel and was starting to sweat
from running and the heat. My legs were still shaky from
my captivity. But it sure did feel good to be outside and
moving.

Just as I was about to give up searching in this direction,
I saw someone ahead of me running from cover to cover.
The runner used the fence, and then a bush, then an old
abandoned Cadillac to hide.

I picked up my pace and started running hard in a
straight line toward the figure. My lungs started to burn.
All I could think about was the plutonium and all the
people that might be at risk if Allmand managed to
sell it.

When I was within fifty feet, the man turned and I

could see clearly that it was Allmand. He no longer seemed interested in me, and just wanted to get away. He gave up his idea to run from hiding place to hiding place, and just started to dash away from me. I followed, running as hard as I could.

He stopped fifty feet in front of me. In a smooth motion, he reached behind his back and pulled a pistol. He fired two quick shots at me.

I fell to the ground and tried to use a garbage can as cover. I fired back at him three times. The problem, I knew, was that the gunshots would attract people. Both the curious and the well armed.

Allmand scurried along the fence line then turned left, cutting through someone's yard. I followed only to slow down when I reached the fence. I held up the pistol and cut the corner in increments, trying to avoid being ambushed.

Then I caught a glimpse of Allmand ahead of me. I considered dropping to my knee, stabilizing my hand and trying to hit him even from this distance. Just as the thought crossed my mind, I saw Allmand step out in the road and point his gun at someone.

A blue Peugeot sedan screeched to a halt right in front of him. He moved quickly to the driver's-side door and pulled a woman from the car. He yanked her out by her arm then discarded her on the road. The woman screamed, then sobbed once she hit the asphalt.

I broke into an all-out run. I didn't even change my

trajectory when he fired another round at me. Then I saw the Peugeot pull away. I skidded to a stop in the street. I fired two wild shots at the fleeing vehicle. All I managed to do was knock out the rear window.

Allmand was escaping with the plutonium.

# CHAPTER 46

**I IMMEDIATELY TURNED** and checked on the woman that Allmand had dragged out of the Peugeot. She was dressed in western clothes: a long skirt and long-sleeve shirt. She was in her thirties and still shaken, crying and muttering in Pashto.

I asked her in English if she was okay and she nodded. I helped her to her feet. Then she hugged me tightly. Just an emotional reaction to a traumatic event. I held her for a few seconds, then I turned and saw the car disappearing down the street. Just as I was about to give up hope of catching Allmand, a streak of light cut across the road and struck the Peugeot.

There was a bright light and a moment later the sound of the explosion. Someone had fired a rocket-propelled grenade at the car. The blast lifted it off the street more than five feet and flipped it on its side. The car made a horrible screeching sound as it slid across the rough asphalt and came to rest in a ditch on the side of the road.

I gently released the woman and started jogging toward the car. I knew there was a danger in this, but I needed to secure the plutonium. I had no idea what I would do if I confronted whoever fired that RPG.

As I got closer to the car, another flash popped up in my vision. Another RPG sailed across the street and struck the bottom of the Peugeot, now lying on its side. This time it ignited the gas tank and the explosion was spectacular.

The concussion was enough to knock me off my feet. All I could do was stare as the fireball climbed into the sky. By the time I'd managed to stand up, the entire car was nothing but a giant ball of flames.

A group of four or five men came from the direction the RPG was fired. Each of them was armed and I saw the last man had the launcher across his back. I immediately eased to the side of the road, then ducked into the ditch that the car ultimately slid in a block ahead of me.

I couldn't see anything near the car because of the smoke and flames. The men circled it a couple of times, but multiple small explosions from the vehicle kept pushing them back.

I didn't know what fire did to plutonium, but I realized I couldn't retrieve it right now. I also didn't want these men to see me. I lay in the weeds like some sort of cement lawn sculpture. I didn't move a muscle. I felt like I could hear every noise as random shots were fired in the neighborhood and sirens were starting to blare from different sections of the city. I didn't know if an Afghan police officer would help me. I had no idea what to do other than lay still for a minute and see what happened.

I watched as the men looked around the car some more, then they split up into two groups. Three of them walked away from me, searching the grass and ditch around the car. But two of them started walking toward me.

They hadn't seen me yet. They were focused on the brush and debris right in front of them. Their eyes were looking down. One man carried an AK-47. The other had some sort of old infantry rifle, possibly British. I had Jackson's pistol in my hand. The last thing I wanted to do was shoot anyone. I didn't think these two men approaching me with weapons were gonna give me much choice.

My heart was racing and I could feel the sweat running down my back. My eyes were glued on the two men. The one with the AK-47 could've been a former soldier. He handled the AK-47 professionally, using a hand on the pistol grip as well as the stock. Anywhere he turned, the muzzle of the rifle turned.

I felt something on my leg and almost jumped upright. That would've been a fatal mistake. I turned my head as quickly as I could without disturbing the weeds around me.

It was the woman who'd been dragged from the Peugeot. She motioned me to follow her. She was lying down in the grass just like me. I didn't know if she was trying to hide herself or just didn't want to expose my position. Either way she had more of a plan than me.

I turned and slithered through the weeds like a giant,

bulky snake. We didn't crawl far. She slipped through a break in a chain-link fence, then stood. The men with the rifles never even noticed our escape.

From there I just followed her quick walk down the street. She turned and walked through the front door of a house as if she belonged there.

It turned out she did.

# CHAPTER 47

**I FOLLOWED HER** through the front door and felt a wave of relief when she shut the door behind me and locked the two deadbolts. A man came from another room and embraced the woman. Then two teenagers ran out and hugged her as well.

She spoke to them in Pashto then turned to me and said, "This is my home. You'll be safe here. My name is Jahan."

"I appreciate everything you've done for me, Jahan, but I can't stay here. If they find me, you guys are in terrible danger."

"We're in danger all the time. We've been at war for almost twenty years. The Taliban, Karzai, they've all threatened us at some point. I work for a division of Chase Bank. I know not all Americans are evil."

"Chase. I had no idea they were in Afghanistan."

"My division helps fund infrastructure projects. We hold the money until they need it for payroll and supplies, that way it doesn't end up in politicians' pockets."

Her teenage daughter, who looked a lot like her, with a pretty face and big, soulful eyes, looked out the window and spoke to her mother.

Jahan said, "They're checking each house. It's only a matter of time before they get here."

I said, "That means I've got to go. Right now."

"No, we can hide you."

I shook my head. "It's far too dangerous. They'll burn your house down if they find me." I turned to head for the rear door.

That's when the husband spoke for the first time. He had a deep voice. He said, "No, they'll kill without any hesitation."

"They have to catch me first."

Jahan said, "They got the other man. The one who took my car."

That made me think about the blazing Peugeot. I considered my position. The crowd managed to stop David Allmand while he was in a car. I was only on foot. And I had no idea where to go.

The teenage boy chimed in. He had almost no accent. "Are you some kind of special forces soldier?"

"No. I'm not even a soldier. I got kidnapped and escaped."

Jahan said, "You don't even know where to go?"

"Do you know where the US base is?"

"Fenty? It's about eight kilometers south of us. We can hear their helicopters as they fly over sometimes."

"How often do they fly over?"

"Maybe once or twice a day. It would be a huge risk if you ran out there hoping that one might fly over right now. And that you would be able to get their attention."

The girl looked out the window again and said, "They are three houses away from us now."

I couldn't argue any longer. And I couldn't risk them. I thanked them all again, then darted out the back door. I crouched, then did a low walk away from the house to make sure no one saw where I came from. On the next street, I heard someone shout. Somehow, without turning around, I knew they had seen me and were shouting about me.

I stood up and started to jog. Then I broke into a run. For some reason I was headed back toward the column of smoke that marked where the burning Peugeot had been hit by the missile. It almost felt like a beacon, drawing me near.

# CHAPTER 48

**AFTER A COUPLE** of quick turns, I found myself in a rough, garbage-filled alley with sprigs of grass mixed in with hardy weeds behind a row of houses. Chunks of cement and building debris made a wiry pattern in the ground. It didn't seem like anyone was chasing me. At least no one obvious.

Then I heard a shout and only an instant later a gunshot. The bullet struck the dirt right next to me. I fired a round from my pistol, hoping to scare whoever shot at me. I didn't even see them.

As I ran, I noticed a proper cement wall at the end of the alley. I didn't know what it was protecting or keeping out but there was no way I'd get over it without someone seeing me. I looked to each side, hoping there'd be a hole in the fence or a way to move laterally, where the men pursuing me wouldn't see me.

When I was only about twenty-five feet from the wall, I realized I'd run into a dead end. I had made the worst possible choice while escaping. Now my exit was blocked by armed men and I couldn't fight back effectively.

I turned and saw there were four men in a rough skirmish line walking toward me slowly. One of them raised a rifle. I fired again, then dropped into the weeds.

Instead of a barrage of bullets, there was only silence. I peeked over the weeds and saw the man with the rocket-propelled grenade launcher loading it. That's when I realized he was just practicing how to use the launcher. It would be much more efficient just to shoot me. But this guy was going to use a rocket.

I got up on my knees ready to bolt if the rocket came right toward me.

He fired and a blast of flame came out of the back of the launcher. The rocket carrying the grenade flew at an odd angle. I knew from my experience with RPGs in training that sometimes older, poorly made rockets didn't fly straight. This was a perfect example.

It made a corkscrew-like motion and whizzed past me about fifteen feet to my left. It struck the wall at the end of the alley. The concussion and explosion knocked me back down to the ground. A piece of concrete from the wall nicked my cheek. A half an inch higher and it would've knocked out my left eye. Instead, I just had a trickle of blood running down my face.

More importantly, now there was a gaping hole in the wall. I was able to jump up and bound toward the wall. I dove through the opening just as the men raised their rifles and started to fire. The wall took all of the gunshots.

I could've tried to shoot it out with them from the cover of the wall, but I was down to only two bullets. I needed to get out of here quick. The blast and resulting escape route gave me a burst of adrenaline. It's funny how a rocket will do that to you. I sprang up from the wall and started to run at full speed toward the column of smoke. My plan was to get my bearings from there and decide which direction to run.

There were shouts from the other side of the wall and it sounded like more people were joining the men who shot at me. Briefly, I considered what would happen if I were captured. The idea of being tortured or possibly beheaded did not appeal to me.

Just when I was starting to feel low again, I heard something unusual. At least something I didn't expect. It was a rhythmic thumping—a helicopter. I crouched and looked up in the sky. Immediately, I saw a black blur coming from the south. A US Army Black Hawk, and it looked like it was ready for action. This wasn't just a random flight. They were low and hovering in different spots.

The pilot noticed the crowd and the helicopter roared toward me. It hovered almost above me, facing the crowd that was advancing. Now there were at least ten men and several women. There were even three or four kids. No one was brave enough to fire at the helicopter with a rifle. That was smart.

Then the door gunner on the Black Hawk opened up with 50-caliber. It sent a line of bullets a dozen feet in front of the crowd. The bullets chewed up anything they touched. Asphalt was destroyed, a wooden telephone pole broke in half.

The crowd froze. The helicopter hovered above me, facing them like a mean guard dog. The gunner fired a few more rounds. Suddenly, the crowd started to scatter.

I looked over my shoulder. The first person I saw in the doorway of the helicopter was Vicki Jensen. She was directing the gunner where to shoot. She also tossed me a safety harness and line.

I looked around, wondering if someone would take a potshot at me. The Black Hawk had done its job. Everyone had fled.

# CHAPTER 49

**I DIDN'T SAY** anything on the ride back to Bagram. As soon as I sat down after being pulled into the Black Hawk, Vicki leaned over and said, "Are you okay?" When I nodded, she just reached over and held my hand. She did it for the whole flight and it made me feel better.

Once we were off the Black Hawk and walking toward the main administrative building on the airfield at Bagram, she talked to me.

She said, "I'm so sorry I misread what was going on. I believed Jackson when he said they were just going to ship you home."

"How'd you figure out the truth?"

"Your friend Greg Stout ran into me. He said he heard a rumor about an American prisoner. He didn't make the connection to you. When I asked him if he'd talked to you or knew you'd been shipped home, he said no, and he'd been trying to call you. I figured out the rest and asked my buddies in the air wing to take me for a ride."

We walked together in silence after that. I was a mash-up of emotions, from joy at being rescued to anger that men like that could even operate with the military.

A couple of hours later, I was told to report to Non-Metric Solutions' office. I'd already told my story more than once. I knew there were all kinds of Army investigators in Jalalabad trying to figure out how everything connected.

In the main conference room, my friend DP sat at the table with an Air Force colonel, an Army colonel, and two Army captains. No one seemed happy.

The Army colonel, a stern-looking woman in her mid-forties, said, "Mr. Mitchum, is there anything about your story you wish to change or amend at this time?"

It sounded like they had something they wanted to trip me up on. I just shook my head.

The colonel said, "The house in Jalalabad where you were held was not authorized to hold prisoners. Obviously. There's not much in it now except the empty cages. We don't even know the names of the prisoners that were warehoused there. They were supposed to be held at the facility on this base. Or at Fenty."

I couldn't keep from asking, "What about the pluto-nium?"

One of the Army captains, a nerdy-looking man with

thick, Army-issue glasses said, "The Geiger counters went crazy inside the house. Using that as a baseline reading, we were able to find a box containing radioactive material inside the burned-out vehicle you told us about. We have no idea where it came from, but it's secure now."

The Army colonel said, "We've recovered three bodies from the house. Two looked like they were prisoners who'd been executed with shots to the head. The other man we've identified as Richard Jackson. We have yet to recover the body of David Allmand."

I listened as they each explained the operations going on to complete the investigation. DP was ready to jump in on my behalf several times, but I waved him off.

When they were finished, I said, "What now? Do you need anything else from me?"

For the first time, the Air Force colonel spoke up. He was about fifty with a shaved head and a craggy face. He said, "Mr. Mitchum, the only thing we will require from you is your immediate consent to return to the United States."

"You make it sound like I did something wrong."

"Unless I've misunderstood some of the reports I've read, you traveled all the way to Afghanistan to exact revenge for things Mr. Jackson did to your family. Is that correct?"

"I wouldn't call it 'revenge'..."

The Air Force colonel cut me off. "I don't give a damn what you call it. You used military resources and wasted military personnel time on a personal issue. Therefore, we are sending you home via commercial flight out of Kabul first thing tomorrow."

I said the only thing that would get me out of there quickly: "Thank you."

# CHAPTER 50

**DP HAD TO** fly from Bagram to the Kabul airport with me. No Americans travel by ground in Afghanistan because of the possibility of IEDs or kidnappers. So he and I had almost an entire C-130 cargo plane to ourselves.

I had heard a lot about the international airport in the capital city of Afghanistan. It'd been the scene of a number of horrific bombings. But now, as part of the international coalition, the country of Turkey had taken over security. The Turkish soldiers ran a tight ship and had virtually eliminated violence at the airport.

We proceeded through the different checkpoints to cross from the military side of the airport to the commercial terminal. Each time a Turkish soldier took our papers and inspected them carefully. They also searched the van we were riding in. A mirror under the car, looking for bombs, as well as a bomb-sniffing dog. It was an impressive effort.

DP hadn't said much since our meeting with the military leaders. I knew he wasn't happy with me. I wouldn't be, either. We walked through the main doors of the airport. There were portraits of men in various forms of dress, from traditional Afghan to western business suits. The only one I recognized was Hamid Karzai, the former president. The airport was his namesake.

I told DP I was sorry.

He gave me a little bit of a hangdog look and said, "All you had to do was level with me. We're friends."

"Would you have let me come over if I told you the truth?"

"Of course not. It was a stupid plan. Friends talk friends out of stupid plans."

I smiled and said, "It all worked out."

"Don't use blind luck as a justification for a stupid plan. You could've just as easily been killed."

I shrugged because he made a good point. I embraced him. He hugged me good-bye.

As I walked toward the line for immigration, I asked DP to say good-bye to Vicki for me. "I didn't get a chance to do it myself since she disappeared as soon as we got back."

DP shook his head. "Because she didn't want to lie. The military has chosen to just skip over the entire incident. You might want to do the same."

The airport was small by US standards. Most men were dressed in traditional robes with headdresses. There were very few people in western clothes. It made me stick out.

I pulled out the phone I'd bought on Bagram Air Base. There was still time left on it. DP had been nice enough to find it in the truck I'd been driving the day Jackson detained me. The first person I called was Alicia. I didn't know if she'd care.

Now I knew for certain that I cared about her. She meant the world to me. I felt like a moron that I had to fly halfway around the world to figure that out. I got no answer so I left a simple message. "I'm safe and coming home."

It was pretty close to the message I left on my mom's answering machine. Only with her I added, "Everything worked out." I was confident that if Jackson had someone watching my mom, they had already bugged out.

The first leg of my flight was to Dubai. I was stunned at the differences in airports. Dubai was clean, well organized, and air-conditioned. They even had showers in the bathrooms. I ate an honest-to-God burger at a chain restaurant then took a shower. I felt like a new man when I found my seat on the giant Boeing 757.

I looked at all the movie selections and picked a few for the sixteen-hour flight. Then I dozed off. Something jolted me awake later and I realized it was the plane touching down at Kennedy. I guess I was more exhausted than I realized.

At the airport, I splurged on a rental car. When I threw my duffel bag in the backseat, I decided to dig through it for my personal iPhone. I hadn't even pulled out of the parking spot when I looked down at the screen and saw there were forty-two messages.

The first message was from Alicia, as were most of the others. Her message said, "I couldn't reach you on the phone you called me from. Are you safe? Where are you? I can't wait till you get home and I can see you again."

I had to sit in the car, grinning like a hockey player with all of his teeth. Then I dialed her number from my phone. My heart soared when I heard her breathless answer. "Mitchum, please tell me you're back in the US."

My biggest fears were of bad cell service.

# CHAPTER 51

**AFTER A TERRIFIC** reunion with Alicia, my mom, and brother, life quickly settled into a comfortable routine. I had to come to terms with the fact that my paper delivery service was all but dead. I enrolled in several business classes at Dutchess Community College on the other side of the Hudson. I also started a class with a private company on basic investigations. It would all work toward my official license as a private investigator one day.

Three days after I got home, I sat quietly with Bart Simpson, watching our favorite show: *Rick and Morty*. I was especially happy to be sitting in a room with no fear of missiles falling on me.

I'd had a couple of nightmares and worried about my captivity consuming me. I couldn't remember the last time I focused on my feelings so much.

Yesterday, I got a call from Cheryl Kravitz, the Department of Homeland Security agent who gave me the idea to travel to Afghanistan in the first place. I appreciated her following up with me. I thought she was happy she didn't have to write up any warrants. She could never admit she was glad Jackson was dead, but I thought she felt about the way I did. And I knew I could use the other information she gave me.

The federal government didn't have the same interest in Rick Jackson and David Allmand as I did. The flip side of that was, no one was going to bother me about what had happened in Afghanistan. Aside from the military being a little bit pissed off, and DP being annoyed, it looked like I'd skate on any other potential charges.

I'd admit to feeling anxious as I sat with my dog, then Bart's ears popped up. He lifted his head from my lap. I checked the app on my phone that controlled my surveillance cameras in the back and by the front door. The cameras had been a real bargain at Costco. A quick scan showed nothing out of the ordinary.

Then Bart Simpson let out a low growl. I rubbed the dog's back and said, "It's okay, boy. I'd know if someone was trying to get inside."

That's when I heard a male voice say, "I don't think you would."

No matter what my state of mind, that surprised me. Maybe "startled" is a better word. My head jerked up and I stared toward the entryway. The house was pretty dark except for the TV. The man had to step forward before I could clearly see him.

David Allmand stepped into the living room where the light caught his face. He had a decent-size flesh-colored bandage on his forehead and his neck.

He also had a grin on his face that wasn't good news for me.

# CHAPTER 52

**ALLMAND STOOD TALL** with his hands in the pockets of a dark-blue windbreaker. He wore a Wayne State baseball cap low on his head. He didn't look nervous or concerned in any way. I'm sure it was just another way to unnerve me. And it worked.

No matter what I was expecting, seeing Allmand relatively unharmed in my entryway was a shock. And I suddenly felt a wave of fear, maybe it was a flashback or maybe it was genuine, in-the-moment fear. It didn't matter.

I took a shot at some unnerving myself. I swallowed my fear and gave him a big smile. After I was sure he was confused, I even let out a little laugh. Somehow it gave me some confidence.

Allmand frowned and said, "You don't seem to be that surprised to see me."

I kept stroking Bart Simpson calmly. I wanted him to stop growling. Then I said, "Frankly, I didn't expect you to show up so quickly." I kept my smile in place. Even though that was Jackson's line when I first saw him in Afghanistan, I thought I'd reuse it now.

Allmand kept his cool. "Really? You were expecting me? How is that?"

I slowly stood up from the couch. I carefully set Bart Simpson on the hardwood floor. He turned and scampered toward his bed in the corner of the room. At least he was good company.

To hide my fear, I took my time turning back toward Allmand. Finally, I said, "I'll answer your question if you answer mine."

Allmand said, "What's your question?"

"I'm curious how you survived the blast in Jalalabad."

He stepped a little farther into the living room. "I bailed out into a ditch just as the first rocket hit the car. I was fifty yards away by the time the second rocket destroyed it. The savages that shot the rockets only looked for me right around the car. When you ran, they all chased you. I waited to retrieve the plutonium, but the Army beat me to it." Now he gave me a glare and said, "Now answer my question. Why aren't you surprised to see me?"

I said, "The Department of Homeland Security agent who arrested you last time? She called me to tell me their computers picked up that you entered the country through Kennedy. I figured you'd make it here eventually."

Allmand let out a laugh. "You knew I was coming and I still caught you alone and unprepared. Typical."

"Who said I was alone? Or, unprepared, for that matter."

Just then, my friend Hassan, from the convenience store in Newburgh, and his two brothers, appeared at Allmand's sides.

Allmand jerked his right hand out of his pocket. He held a semiautomatic pistol. He fired one wild round toward me. Before I could react, the gun was pointed at me. The sound of the shot felt like a bomb in my house. I figured my time had finally run out.

That's when I saw the hole in the arm of my couch. My nice leather couch. The one I'd bought on discount but still could barely afford. The bullet had ripped the leather, then shattered the armrest, which tore the leather even more.

My fear shifted more to anger. Sure, I was pissed that the only nice piece of furniture I owned was ruined. But my experience in Afghanistan caught up to me. Even as Hassan's two beefy brothers subdued the frantic Allmand, I moved to deliver my licks.

Just before I launched a kick that I intended to split his testicles, I stopped myself. I froze, staring at this man who had caused me so much pain. Kicking him felt like torture, and I wasn't going to stoop to his level.

I let Hassan's brothers manhandle Allmand for just a moment, then said, "This is Hassan. Recognize him?"

Allmand growled, "Just another one of your Muslim buddies."

"That's true, he's a friend of mine. One you and Jackson held illegally at the prison up in the mine shaft." I could see the color drain out of his face. He was starting to understand what was happening.

He struggled for a second and said, "You guys are insane."

"Is that for us to use as our defense if we get caught?"

Allmand struggled, trying to break free.

I said, "You held these men for seven months up in that hidden hellhole. They have a few things they'd like to discuss with you."

"You can't do this. I'm an American citizen."

Khalil mumbled, "So are we."

I had to throw in another of Jackson's favorite lines in Afghanistan: "Don't worry, no one here asks any questions."

# ABOUT THE AUTHORS

**James Patterson** is the world's bestselling author and most trusted storyteller. He has created many enduring fictional characters and series, including Alex Cross, the Women's Murder Club, Michael Bennett, Maximum Ride, Middle School, and I Funny. Among his notable literary collaborations are The *President Is Missing*, with President Bill Clinton, and the Max Einstein series, produced in partnership with the Albert Einstein Estate. Patterson's writing career is characterized by a single mission: to prove that there is no such thing as a person who "doesn't like to read," only people who haven't found the right book. He's given over three million books to schoolkids and the military, donated more than seventy million dollars to support education, and endowed over five thousand college scholarships for teachers. The National Book Foundation recently presented Patterson with the Literarian Award for Outstanding Service to the American Literary Community, and he is also the recipient of an Edgar Award and six Emmy Awards. He lives in Florida with his family.

**James O. Born** is an award-winning crime and science-fiction novelist as well as a career law-enforcement agent. A native Floridian, he still lives in the Sunshine State.

# JAMES
# PATTERSON
*RECOMMENDS*

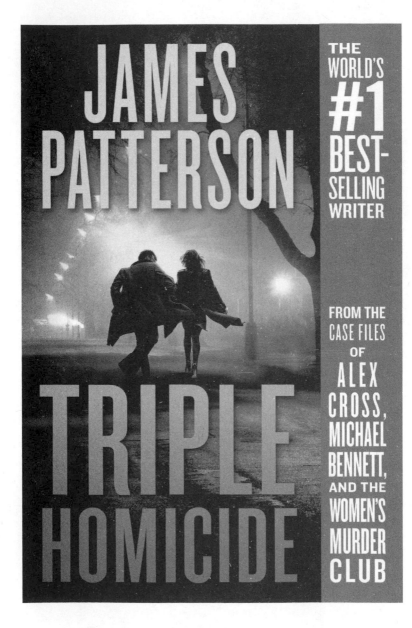

# TRIPLE HOMICIDE

I couldn't resist the opportunity to bring my greatest detectives together in three shocking thrillers. Alex Cross
receives an anonymous call with a threat to set off deadly
bombs in Washington, D.C., and has to discover whether
it's a cruel hoax, or the real deal. But will he find the truth
too late? And then, in possibly my most twisted Women's
Murder Club mystery yet, Detective Lindsey Boxer inves-
tigates a dead lover and a wounded millionaire who was
left for dead. Finally, I make things personal for Michael
Bennett as someone attacks the Thanksgiving Day Parade
directly in front of him and his family. Can he solve the
mystery of the "holiday terror"?

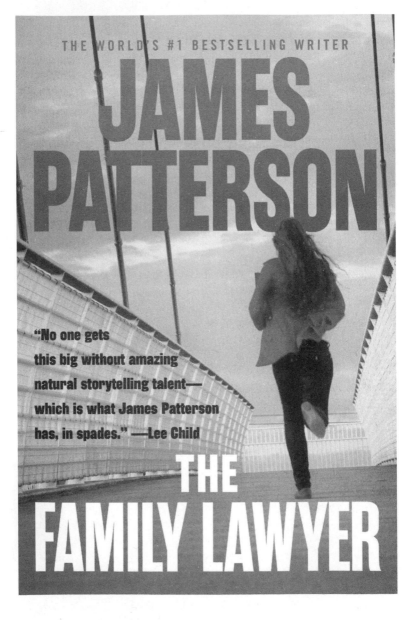

THE WORLD'S #1 BESTSELLING WRITER

# JAMES PATTERSON

"No one gets
this big without amazing
natural storytelling talent—
which is what James Patterson
has, in spades." —Lee Child

# THE FAMILY LAWYER

# THE FAMILY LAWYER

*The Family Lawyer* combines three of my most pulse-pounding novels all in one book. There's Matthew Hovanes, who's living a parent's worst nightmare when his daughter is accused of bullying another girl into suicide. I test all of his attorney experience as he tries to clear his daughter's name and reveal the truth. Then there's Cheryl Mabern, who is one of my most brilliant detectives working for the NYPD. But does that brilliance help her when there's a calculating killer committing random murders? And finally, Dani Lawrence struggles with deciding whether to aid in an investigation that could put away her sister for the murder of her cheating husband. Or she can obstruct it by any means necessary.

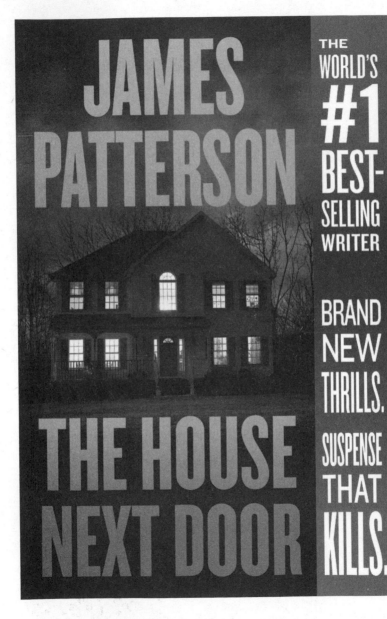

# THE HOUSE NEXT DOOR

There's something absolutely bone chilling about a danger that's right in front of you, and that concept fascinates me. Everyone always thinks there's safety in numbers, but it isn't always true, and those closest to you can sometimes be the most terrifying. In *The House Next Door,* Laura Sherman's neighbor seems like he's too good to be true; maybe he is. And then in *The Killer's Wife,* Detective Mc-Grath is searching for six girls who have gone missing but finds himself dangerously close to his suspect's wife. Way too close. And finally, I venture out there in *We Are Not Alone.* Robert Barnett has found a message that will change the world: that there are others out there. And they're watching us.

For a complete list of books by

# JAMES PATTERSON

VISIT
## JamesPatterson.com

 Follow James Patterson on Facebook
**@JamesPatterson**

 Follow James Patterson on Twitter
**@JP_Books**

Follow James Patterson on Instagram
**@jamespattersonbooks**